Coming Soon From
Lady Leo Publishing

Can A Sistah Get Some Love?
An Anthology with stories by Tinisha Nicole Johnson, Nathasha
Brooks-Harris, Zana Kane, and Gail McFarland
(Love Storm)
(Paperback)
Available February 12, 2010
$6.99

Death At The Double Inkwell
Shonell Bacon
(CatEye)
(Paperback)
Available June 15,2010
$6.99

Dominique stood and walk away. She didn't want to hear another word he had to say.

"Please, Dominique," Victor pleaded, placing a hand to his chest. "Hear me out." She turned back to face him. Her heartbeat slamming against her chest wall. He looked and sounded so sincere. She wanted to listen, and for one moment she almost relented, but she held back. "No," Dominique said, her voice barely above a whisper.

Victor dropped his head and spread his arms apart. "Do you believe in fate?"

Dominique shook her head no.

"I do. I believe fate has given us a second chance. I plan to do everything within my power to make you see that. Even if it takes me the rest of my life."

7 Days

SAMMIE WARD

CATEYE MYSTERY/SUSPENSE

An imprint of Lady Leo Publishing

Lady Leo Publishing
P.O. Box 14283
Silver Spring, MD 20911

This is a work of fiction. All characters, places and events are from the author's imagination and should not be confused with fact. Any resemblance to person's living or dead, events or places is purely coincidental.

ISBN: 13 DIGIT:978-09841076-4-3
ISBN: 10 DIGIT:0-9841076-4-9
Manufactured in the United States of America

Second Edition
Visit us at www.ladyleopublishing.org

To my mother Georgia Tims, thank you for all of the love and spiritual support. To my sisters, Betty Fowler, Lisa Jenkins, Shirley Fowler-Tillman, and Barbara Ezenekwe. DeMarcus, Dominick, and Eugina, you are the best. I love you.

To all my brothers and sisters in uniform, I salute you.

Chapter One

DAY ONE - FRIDAY

*L*ieutenant Colonel Victor Sexton had to go through with it. He realized it the moment he was handed the message from Rosetta Upton, the wife of his former Delta Force Commander and now senator. He was certain she was calling to make sure he'd keep the blind date that night with her niece. A mixture of dread and anticipation bounced through him.

Victor stuffed the message in his army fatigues front pocket. His thoughts scattered as he strode through the highly polished hallway of CID. Long, smooth, and confident strides carried him to the office of Captain Jose Benitez. The room was empty. Since it was Friday and payday, Victor had dismissed a majority of the staff, a privilege he rarely allowed, but they had done exceptionally well on their last training exercise; therefore, they'd earned the day off. He was tough on his personnel, but the brand of military discipline and training he enforced could save lives — theirs and his.

Shifting his briefcase to his left hand, Victor pulled out the manila folder containing a copy of his discharge orders from underneath his right arm and placed it in the box on the desk marked IN. Next week he would begin his life as Victor Sexton, civilian, not commander of the Criminal Investigation Division, which conducted criminal investigation ranging from deaths to fraud on and off the military post.

"Attention!" Sergeant Juarez bellowed.

"At ease," Victor responded. "I hope you have a quiet night."

"So do we, sir," Private First Class Bone replied.

"Colonel Sexton." Turning, Victor headed towards Sergeant James who met him before he left the building. "Sir, I'm glad I caught you," he said. "I need your signature on some promotion orders."

Victor nodded at the highly efficient soldier. "How many do we have?"

"Five, sir."

"I'm happy to sign the orders. I like it when we pin more rank on our men and women. It helps keep morale up. Anyone from your section?"

"Sergeant Vivian Givens, sir. She made staff sergeant."

"Outstanding," Victor said.

Victor quickly signed each document and returned the folder to Sergeant James.

"Thank you, sir. Enjoy your weekend."

"You do the same."

Victor exited through the barracks doors and made his way to his black Pathfinder, throwing the briefcase onto the passenger seat. He turned the key in the ignition and pulled out into the late afternoon traffic.

To keep his mind occupied, he turned on the radio. Najee's smooth saxophone playing accompanied him. It was hard to believe that he let himself be persuaded into a blind date. *What was I thinking?* He should have just said thanks, but no thanks. It's not as if it was part of his military obligation, but Rosetta talked him into it. It was too late to back out without looking unsympathetic.

Rosetta's niece had arrived two months earlier from Frankfurt, Germany. If he believed the senator's wife had been the type to set him up, he would never have agreed to the blind date. Instead, he believed she was helping her niece be acclimated to the area.

Rosetta informed Victor she would make reservations at Cadence at eight under her name. Victor would meet his date there. Though Victor's family owned and operated the club, he wasn't so sure he wanted to meet his date there.

Indecision was a characteristic people who knew Victor would never associate with him. His outstanding military career demonstrated this. Commissioned in1987 through the Army ROTC program with a Bachelors Degree in International Affairs and a Master Degree in Business Management from Howard University in Washington, DC, he was a third-generation soldier. Neither his father nor grandfather came close to matching his outstanding military career. The walls in his office and home were covered with awards and plaques. His uniform held ribbons for service.

Victor took pride in putting his life on the line for what his country stood for —freedom and democracy. As for his accolades and the danger and risks he took, the way Victor saw it, he was simply doing the job he was sworn in to do sixteen years ago. Before he was the commander of CID, he served fourteen years as a member of Special Operations, one of the most elite units in the world. He had represented the United States in numerous campaigns: Grenada, Haiti, Somalia, Bosnia, Afghanistan, and the Persian Gulf where he was wounded. He was awarded a Purple Heart, his second for bravery during combat.

Victor eased his truck in and out of the traffic forty-five minutes before parking in front of his split-level house and surrounding acreage. Victor had moved to Gaithersburg, Maryland two years after transferring from Fort Bragg, North Carolina. He'd passed the house with a 'For Sale' sign in the yard after visiting Major Raymond Hall, a former team member who currently works at the Pentagon. Victor had stopped and copied down the Realtor's telephone number.

A couple days later the agent set up an appointment to show him the house; two months later, Victor closed.

Victor got out of the truck and headed toward the front door. Shifting the briefcase to his left hand, he put the key in the lock and unlocked the door. When the door opened, he bent down to scoop up the mail. He entered the foyer then the living room.

Decorated in tan, the room possessed enough space to include the European wall unit and bar he had purchased on an assignment in Germany three years before. Standing six foot three, Victor needed space to move freely without bumping into furniture.

He maneuvered around the La-Z-Boy chair and dropped the keys and mail on the coffee table in front of the sofa. He tossed his briefcase on one of the cushions and looked at the telephone a few feet away sitting on the end table. It rang. Victor walked over to the phone. *Maybe it was Rosetta calling to tell me she'd found someone else to take her niece out.*

"Hello."

"It's about time," the woman's voice said on the other end.

 No such luck. It was his sister, Tonya Sims.

"Hello to you, too, sis." Victor sat down on the sofa.

A soft chuckle came through the receiver. "Looking forward to your date?"

"I'd rather be in actual combat."

"Stephen, I told you he'd try to wimp out," Tonya yelled to her husband.

"I am not wimping out," Victor said adamantly. He began unlacing his Forced Entry Tactical Boots while he held the phone to his ear with his shoulder. He removed the boots, placing them next to the sofa. "I'm just not sure, that's all."

Victor tried to come up with an image to match the description Rosetta had given him. Beautiful face; medium body frame; long, flowing hair; outgoing personality; and intelligent. She laid it on so thick that within seconds he visualized the opposite. Dog like features, horn-rimmed glasses, thick body, clothing buttoned from head to toe, and unsmiling.

He shuddered. That's all he needed to spend the evening with, an ice princess.

"I'm sure she feels the same way about going out with you. I mean, I can see how you would be apprehensive, but I'm sure it's going to be fine."

Victor closed his eyes and leaned his head back against the sofa. "I thought you would understand my predicament. She could be psycho or something."

Tonya laughed. "I don't believe the senator and his wife would set you up with someone with mental problems."

Victor became silent.

Tonya interrupted his thoughts. "Is it her emotional or physical state that you're worried about?"

"Both." Victor laughed.

"Men," Tonya said, grunting before joining Victor in laughter. "It's always the looks."

"I know you're not talking, Ms. Stephen-Is-So-Fine," Victor said in his best Tonya imitation. When she first laid eyes on her husband, Tonya had gone on for hours about how handsome she thought Stephen was.

Victor had no problem reminding her about that as they both laughed again.

"Okay, okay. So looks are a little important. Who knows? She may look like Halle Berry."

He chuckled. "I should be so lucky. If she looks like Halle Berry, I don't think she would be going on a blind date."

"You need to get back out there, Victor," Tonya said in a serious tone. "I know how you felt about Felicia, but you have to get past that."

Victor spoke to Tonya for a few more minutes, promising to tell her about the date. He knew his sister was right about one thing — he had to get on with his life. He'd been distrusting of women since Felicia Connors, his ex-fiancée, called off their wedding two years ago and knew this blind date could not turn into something serious.

He should have known better. In his line of work chances for a serious relationship, let alone marriage, was practically nonexistent. He was traveling to remote locations, sometimes at the last minute, and deployed for an unspecific time, which left him little opportunity for a social life. Felicia decided she didn't like the uncertainty or the danger of his job. The excitement of being with a man in uniform soon wore off, reality set in, and the engagement ended. Even though Victor had seen it happen he believed their relationship was different and could stand the test of time. He was wrong.

Victor headed to the kitchen. He opened the refrigerator door and grabbed a bottle of water. The liquid vanished in seconds. He headed into his bedroom. After turning the TV to CNN news, he went into his adjoining bathroom and lifted the water lever in the tub. Stripping off his uniform, he stepped into the warm, inviting downpour of the shower. He closed his eyes, enjoying the invigorating feel of the water on his physique. Rosetta never told him the name of his blind date. It didn't matter. After tonight he'd never call her again.

ʘ ʅ

At five o'clock Friday afternoon, Captain Dominique Frazier floored the gas pedal in her Altima and zoomed across the Connecticut Avenue intersection. New to the Washington, DC area, she had been out purchasing items to decorate her apartment.

She had gotten up earlier that morning to make a day of it. It was the first time in the two months she had transferred from Germany that her life had slowed down enough for her to get settled. As an officer in the Army Nurses Corp, her days were filled with long hours in the emergency room at Walter Reed Army Medical Center. It was the first time she had nothing scheduled, and she intended to take advantage of the free time.

Although Dominique was dog-tired, she had forced herself to get out of bed. She had managed to unpack some of her household goods, which had arrived from Europe but still had several boxes to go through. She let out a small sigh. She hated moving, but it came along with her career choice.

Dominique looked through the windshield. It had been raining for the past two days. Some people complained about the absence of the sun, damp days and nights, but from where she transferred, no sunshine was the daily forecast.

She took a couple of days off to finish unpacking, view a couple of movie DVD's she had purchased several weeks ago still buried in a box somewhere, visit Aunt Rosetta and Uncle Harold on Sunday for dinner, and attend Lieutenant Robbin Greene, her friend/ coworker, 32nd birthday party.

Dominique stopped for the traffic light then glanced along M Street aligned with shops, bars, restaurants, and nightclubs. The light changed and she pulled off. Her aunt and uncle were pleased she transferred to the area, but her uncle, Harold Upton, retired as a

Brigadier General, and now served as senator of Virginia, was disappointed that she chose to live in D.C. instead of Virginia. Aunt Rosetta and Uncle Harold were the only family she'd ever known. They had raised her since the age of two when her own parents died in a motor vehicle accident. Everyone was surprised when Dominique joined the military. Despite her Master's degree in Nursing from the University of North Carolina at Chapel Hill and a sufficient trust fund left by her parents, Dominique believed the army was the obvious choice. She considered herself a military brat. She traveled and lived in numerous locations: Europe, Texas, Georgia, Japan, and North Carolina, to name a few. Uncle Harold, a former special operations commander, commanded troops in several campaigns and had a great influence on her. She was proud of his military and civilian career and hoped to achieve half of his accomplishments.

Dominique was anticipating decorating her apartment as she pulled in front of her building forty minutes later. Adjusting her bags in hand, she opened the door and stepped in the entryway just in time to hear the antique Grandfather clock chime the hour — six o'clock. She placed the bags on the sofa and noticed the red light flashing on the answering machine. Wondering who phoned, she opened the top drawer of the end table and retrieved a notepad and pen as she listened to the messages. There were two. One from a long distance representative trying to get her to switch carriers. *How did they find me so soon?* The one that caught her attention was from Aunt Rosetta.

Aunt Rosetta had called Dominique a week earlier and informed her that she was giving Dominique's phone number to a fine commanding officer whom she and Uncle Harold looked at as a son. She thought they would make a cute couple. Dominique could just imagine why her aunt and uncle would like him. He was a former special operations officer like Uncle Harold.

Dominique listened as Aunt Rosetta voice filled the air.

"Hi, sweetie. I've arranged a blind date for you at eight o'clock at Cadence Supper Club. The reservation is in my name. I really think you're going to like this young man. He's like the son your uncle and I never had. Call me tomorrow and let me know how things go. Love you."

Dominique took a deep breath and tapped her pen. Her aunt was meddling in her life again. She wondered how her date felt about Aunt Rosetta's interference. Dominique was sure he was used to being in control, but not of this situation. He was only taking her out because her aunt had asked him to. It appeared Dominique's aunt assumed she would be lonely at her new assignment.

Dominique wanted to make Aunt Rosetta happy, but wanted her

to stop interfering once and for all in her love life. Aunt Rosetta and Uncle Harold Upton had been married more than thirty years, and Aunt Rosetta felt it was her job to match up all the single family members. Dominique agreed that she wanted a man in her life, but she didn't need a mercy date, especially one from an unwanted arrangement.

Dominique stood, staring at the telephone. She actually felt sorry for her date. It wasn't his fault he was in this situation. She knew how persuasive her aunt could be. Her head tilted to one side. "Why not?" Dominique said to herself. "It's only one date." She punched in Aunt Rosetta's number and listened as the answering machine clicked on.

No one's home, Dominique thought and shook her head. *I can't believe she set me up on a blind date.* She left a message.

"Aunt Rosetta, I got the message and will meet..." Dominique realized she didn't know the name of her date, "...my blind date tonight at Cadence."

Dominique hung up and walked into her bedroom. She slipped out of her black, low heel pumps and glanced at her watch. She had two hours. She unbuttoned her green army jacket, shirt, and her matching slacks. She hung the uniform on a padded hanger and wondered if she had lost her mind accepting the blind date. She briefly thought about calling back to cancel. No one would blame her if she did. It was a blind date, and for all she knew he could be psycho. She pushed the thought away. There was another way to handle it.

Dominique sauntered over to the nightstand, picked up the phone, and pushed the numbers to Lieutenant Robbin Greene. Although married to Lieutenant Thomas Echols, Robbin chose to keep her last name, claiming it was a hassle to go through the paperwork to legally change it. Dominique hoped she did not have plans and could accompany her to the club. If her blind date didn't turn out to be a wacko, then Robbin could make a hasty exit.

"Hello."

"Hello, Robbin." Dominique's voice came across the line.

Although Dominique was an Army Captain and Robbin was a Second Lieutenant, they became fast friends after only two months of working together at the Medical Center. "Dominique, how are you?"

"I'm fine. You?"

"Things could be better."

"Maybe I have the answer."

"Oh?"

"Do you have plans for this evening?"

"I don't have any plans," Robbin vented. "Lover boy got started early watching sports. He's parked in front of the TV."

Dominique was aware of the strained marriage between Thomas and Robbin. Robbin had confided to her that she believed Thomas was involved with another woman, but she didn't have proof. "How would you like to go out with me tonight?"

"Where are we going?"

"Cadence."

Robbin was celebrating her birthday at the upscale and classy establishment tomorrow night. Dominique was invited. She'd never been there, but her other girlfriend/hairstylist, Rowena Harris, recommended the club, boasting the clientele was impressive among the African-American community.

"What do you say?" Dominique pressed.

Instead of answering Dominique's question, Robbin replied, "Maybe some fresh air is just what I need."

"Meet me at my apartment at seven-thirty. I'll fill you in on what's going on."

"What do you mean, fill me in?" Robbin asked.

"I'll tell you once you get here," Dominique said. "See you around seven-thirty."

Chapter Two

*D*ominique replaced the phone in the cradle. She finished undressing and slipped on a cream-colored silk Victoria's Secret robe with matching sandals. Entering the bathroom, she turned the oval glass knob on the tub and water flowed from the faucet. Twenty minutes later, with her skin wrinkled from sitting in the water, she dried herself and then moisturized her body with Marc Jacobs Body Lotion. She stood in her closet and agonized over what to wear. She wanted to select the perfect outfit. She'd heard from other service members who frequented Cadence that it was known for its music, excellent food, and diverse clientele. Cadence drew people between the ages of thirty to sixty. It was more of a social and dining club for professionals who wanted to mingle with other professionals. It was a place where new friendships were formed and contacts made.

Dominique held a blue pantsuit to her chin as she slowly turned in front of the mirror.

"Too boring," she said, tossing the garment onto her canopy bed. Since she agreed to the date, she wanted to select the perfect outfit. A moment later, she settled on a cappuccino colored, off the shoulder top with raglan sleeves and a bandless waist skirt with stitched down pleats.

The doorbell rang at thirty-five minutes after seven. Dominique put on her two inch cappuccino colored, sling back sandals and pressed the button for the intercom.

"Robbin?"

"It's me," Robbin's excited voice said through the speaker.

Dominique buzzed Robbin in from downstairs. She left her apartment door open and headed to the bedroom. Exhaling, she performed one final appraisal in the floor-length mirror. She smiled, pleased with the image.

Robbin found Dominique in the bedroom, primping in front of the mirror. "Nice outfit," Robbin complimented.

"Thank you. You look nice. I like that brown on you."

Robbin stepped in the bedroom. She sashayed to the mirror in her brown wraparound miniskirt. The outfit was completed with matching four inch heel pumps, which showed off her long, shapely legs. "So what's going on that you couldn't tell me over the phone?"

Dominique turned around, looking at herself from behind in the mirror. She knew once she told Robbin the news, Robbin would think she had lost her mind.

"I'm going on a blind date tonight."

Robbin looked at Dominique as if she'd grown two heads. "Blind date? You can't be serious." Her lower lip trembled as she attempted to come up with another comment. "Why?"

"I'm serious. I want you to come along with me to check him out."

"Check him out?" Robbin placed her hands on her hips. "I don't believe you."

"Believe it. When it doesn't work out, my Aunt Rosetta can stop trying to fix me up with every available man in the Army."

Robbin raised a perfectly arched eyebrow. "Have you talked to her about this?"

"Of course. You don't know my Aunt Rosetta. It's like talking to a brick wall. I'm through talking. I intend to prove blind dates don't work." Dominique went to the closet to retrieve her black, short jacket.

"How long has it been since you've been on a date?"

Robbin's question caught Dominique off guard, and she stopped in mid-motion.

"It's been a while," she answered, putting on the jacket.

"What's a while?"

"Why all the questions?"

"Don't you want a man in your life?"

"Of course I do."

Robbin smiled wickedly. "The way I see it, the Army is a smorgasbord of men waiting for you to make your selection. You can have him any way you want him." Robbin counted on each finger. "Short, tall, younger, older, light, dark."

"I get the picture." Dominique knew Robbin and Aunt Rosetta didn't understand why she felt the way she did about dating men in the military. "It doesn't matter. As long as I'm in the military, I'll remain single."

Robbin frowned. "As long as you're in the military, you're going to remain single?"

"Yes. I definitely won't date a man in Special Operations."

"Hmm. Special Operations. Sounds like my type of man. Intriguing, dangerous, and tough."

"Whatever." Dominique grabbed her clutch purse off the bed. "Can we get this night over with?"

Robbin playfully bowed at Dominique and with a wave of the hand stated, "Lead the way. I still say he sounds intriguing."

ೞ ೲ

When Victor arrived at the club, it was in full swing. That was no surprise to him. Many of the patrons had fast become regulars.

"Hello, Colonel," said the bartender, Israel Hunnicutt. "What's going on in CID?"

Victor settled himself on the tall, padded barstool. "Same thing, just a different day." He took a handful of peanuts from the bowl then popped some into his mouth.

"Then how about the usual?"

Victor nodded and Hunnicutt placed a scotch and water before him. Before he was a bartender, Hunnicutt served twenty-one years in the Army, retiring as a sergeant major. He moonlighted as a bartender several nights a week for enjoyment. Since Victor first met Hunnicutt more than a year ago he'd liked him.

"Is my brother in his office?" Victor asked, lifting the glass to his lips. The drink felt good going down the back of his throat. The warm sensation helped calm his jittery nerves.

"No. He's somewhere out in the club. He's training a new employee."

"When you see him, tell him I'm in the office."

"I'll be sure to relay the message." He raised his right hand and gave Victor a military salute.

Victor returned the salute and headed toward the office.

The hostess, Kim Moffett, clothed in black slacks, red vest, and a white blouse, came into view. "Hello, Colonel," she greeted. "Are you ready to be seated?" She flashed him a warm smile. "Your party hasn't arrived yet."

Victor's brows rose a moment. He let out a small sigh and then glanced at his watch. His date had fifteen minutes. "No. I'll wait until she arrives to be seated. I'll be in Mr. Sexton's office. If she arrives before I return, escort her to the table and make sure she's taken care of."

"Yes, sir," Kim responded.

"Thank you, Kim." Victor turned and continued toward the office.

Victor went inside the office, making himself at home. He settled behind the large oak desk. Their parents would be pleased at how successful his younger brother, 35-year-old Gerald Sexton, had made Cadence.

Gerald never served in the armed forces, preferring to pursue a college education, graduating from Howard University with a major in Business Management and a minor in Music.

Upon Gerald's graduation their father, William Sexton, offered him co-ownership of Cadence. When William passed away four years ago, Gerald became a full owner. William Sexton, a retired Army First Sergeant, had opened Cadence two years after leaving the service. It had been a dream of both parents to open a supper club. The club opened, but their mother died of breast cancer a year later. Under the leadership of William, Cadence became very prominent in the area. Many top performers had graced its stage: Sade, Brian McKnight, Will Downing, and Branford Marsalis, to name a few. Not to mention a cuisine to die for. Since their father's death, Gerald had managed to run Cadence with the same grace and style.

Victor looked at the family photos in elaborate frames arranged on the desk. Photos of their sister, Tonya; her husband, Stephen; and their two children, Roderick who was five and Kiara, three; Gerald dressed in cap and gown; and Victor in his military uniform. A photo of their parents, William and Elizabeth Sexton, had been blown up and hung on the wall along with Gerald's diploma from Howard University. African-American paintings of Alice Kent Stoddard's *Young Man in the Blue Suit* and *Bus Stop Hyacinth Manning* added to the ambience.

Victor stared at his photo, sitting alone. He was thirty-three then and ready to start his own family. He wanted a wife. Thought he had found her once. What if his blind date...

No way. He didn't even want to think about his date being the future Mrs. Victor Sexton. Gerald's appearance interrupted his thoughts.

"You plan to hide in here all night?" Gerald asked, smiling from ear-to-ear. "Tonya told me about your date tonight." He walked over to the wall safe, putting in cash and receipts.

Victor nodded. "I'm meeting her tonight at eight."

"Great. I'm dying to see what she looks like," Gerald said, trying to smother a laugh.

"Me and you both."

"What made you decide to go out on a blind date? It's not like you're obligated to the senator's wife."

"I don't know. One moment Rosetta was talking about how beautiful her niece is, how talented she is, how we would make an attractive couple, and the next thing I know, I was agreeing to meet her."

Gerald laughed. "Wait a minute. I gave the same description for the eligible ladies I tried to hook you up with and you weren't interested."

Victor joined in his brother's laughter. "I've seen some of those women you tried to set me up with. No thank you."

"What are you saying?" Gerald took a seat in the chair across from the desk. "I have ugly lady friends? Besides, you don't know what your date looks like."

Victor became quiet. Gerald was right. Ever since his breakup with Felicia, Gerald and Tonya had been trying to fix him up with every single woman they knew. They didn't have to worry, Washington, DC, unlike the military community, had more women then men. Victor could have had a date with a different woman every night if he wanted. He didn't have to be ambushed into one.

"Eight o'clock, huh." Gerald glanced at his watch. "You still have a few minutes."

"Don't remind me."

"Don't look at it like that. She may turn out to be the woman of your dreams."

Victor sat up straight in his chair and chuckled. "Yeah, right."

രു ഔ

At 7:45, Dominique pulled her Altima in front of the club. She glanced out the window and saw a well-dressed couple get out of a Lexus, heading for the entrance to Cadence Supper Club.

Dominique self-consciously ran her hand over her skirt and hoped the outfit wasn't too revealing. Too late, she could do nothing about it. *I can't believe I'm going through with this,* she thought.

"Look at the people," Robbin said enthusiastically. "I wonder who's here. I hope we see someone famous."

A valet stood waiting for the keys. A moment later the young man sped away.

"This is it," Robbin announced. "Last chance to change your mind."

Dominique forced a tight smile. "Let's go inside."

They stepped inside a set of massive mahogany doors affixed with brass fixtures and found themselves engrossed in a beautiful spacious foyer, with soft beige furniture. Dominique's coworkers had been right. She didn't know if she was taken aback with the clientele or the scenery.

"Good evening and welcome to Cadence." A woman greeted them with a friendly smile. "My name is Kim."

"Good evening," Dominique spoke. "I believe you have a reservation for me for eight o'clock. It should be under Rosetta Upton."

"Yes, we have your table ready for you." Kim threw Robbin a curious look. Following Kim's gaze, Dominique offered an explanation. "This is my friend Robbin Greene. She's going to join me for a quick drink. I hope it's okay."

"It's fine." Kim beckoned for a waitress who came and escorted them to a table where they had an unobstructed view of the stage.

"I'm Mya, and I'll be your waitress for this evening. The colonel will be right with you. He has instructed us to take care of you until he arrives. While you wait, can I offer you a drink on the house?" Mya handed them each a menu.

Dominique arched an eyebrow and looked at Robbin. She was impressed. She wondered what clout her blind date had for her to get preferential treatment. "Thank you. That's very kind of you." She ordered a cosmopolitan. Robbin ordered an apple martini.

"I'll be back with your drinks."

The sultry lyrics of Anita Baker's "Rapture" filtered through Cadence's built-in speakers.

"This is nice," Robbin said, moving her body to the music. "No matter what he looks like, the man has good taste. The evening is starting out fine."

"You just remember you agreed to stay with me until he checks out."

"I know. I know. I promise I won't leave until we check out Mr. Special Operations."

At Dominique's uneasy expression, Robbin said, "You don't have to go through with the date. We can get up and walk out. All you have to do is say the word."

"I've told you, I'm staying."

"Good."

Dominique shot her a look.

Robbin shrugged. "What did I say?"

The waitress placed their drinks on the table.

"I heard they have live bands here on the weekends," Robbin offered. It was obvious she was attempting to lighten the mood. "Maybe I can talk Thomas into bringing me back to check it out." She took a sip of her drink and popped her fingers to the beat of "Can't Stop," by After 7.

Dominique continued scanning the interior of the club. The golden recessed lights glistened against gold-toned fixtures, floor-to-ceiling stained-glass windows, and green leafy plants near a man-made waterfall. There were large pillars erect like military soldiers standing at attention. Customers seemed to be enjoying themselves, laughing, talking, or sitting at tables with dim shaded lamps. She couldn't help but wonder if her date was watching her at that very moment.

∞

"Colonel, your guest is here," Kim offered, poking her head in the office. She grinned like a Cheshire cat.

Victor and Gerald traded curious glances.

Kim sauntered farther into the office. "She brought a friend with her," she offered.

Gerald chuckled.

She was cautious, Victor thought. *Nothing wrong with that.*

"What does she look like?" Gerald questioned before Victor had time to cross examine Kim. With his connections Victor could have downloaded a picture of her from the military locator if he had gotten her name.

"Come see for yourself." Kim still had the smile pasted on her face. It made Victor a little nervous. He couldn't determine whether he would be pleased or disappointed.

Victor stepped out into the club. He zeroed in on the table. His gaze fixed on two women engrossed in conversation, heads bobbing up and down in synchronized motion. Then he sharpened his gaze, recognizing the familiar face.

It can't be. What were the odds of Dominique Frazier being his blind date? He looked around, glancing at Kim to make sure she'd given him the proper table. She was seating a couple. He gestured with his finger in the direction of the table. Kim nodded at him and grinned.

He allowed himself to think about how long it had been since he'd seen Dominique. It was three years ago when they met in Frankfurt, Germany. Victor was on temporary duty, teaching a class on terrorism, and Dominique was assigned to a nearby hospital unit.

Victor remembered an intense curriculum during the day and the passionate nights they shared. He felt his body tremor when he remembered how Dominique felt hot, naked, and needy underneath him. Most of all, he remembered lovemaking that left them both fulfilled.

"Are you satisfied?" Gerald asked, walking up behind Victor.

Victor glanced over at Gerald and saw Gerald looking at him curiously. "Very." Victor glanced back in the direction of the two women and saw Mya removing empty glasses from their table. Victor took a deep breath to control the soft groan threatening to escape him.

Gerald followed the direction of Victor's gaze. "Wow!" His eyes widened. "I should have the senator's wife set me up on a date. Which one is yours? Don't tell me, I guess it's the one with the nice assets."

Victor shot a look at Gerald. He'd forgotten how crude his brother could be sometimes. Gerald shrugged. "What did I say? You like women who are heavy on top."

A smile ruffled Victor's mouth. "True. It's just that I know one of the women."

"What?" Gerald glanced back in the direction of Dominique and Robbin.

Victor tugged on the end of his jacket sleeve. He'd never discussed the two weeks he'd spent with Dominique. What they had shared was private and personal. He had been engaged to Felicia, but Dominique was never too far from his mind.

"I met her while teaching a class in Germany," Victor said proudly, hoping that would quiet Gerald, letting him know he wasn't the only male Sexton with game.

"You mean that beautiful woman is in the military?"

"Last time we met," Victor answered.

"What about the other lady?"

"We've never met."

"Why don't we go over and say hello?"

Victor noticed the challenge in Gerald's eyes. Victor returned his look with one of his own. "Give me a second."

The smile at the corner of Gerald's lips widened. "Don't tell me the big, bad army man is scared."

"I'm not afraid of anyone, and to prove it I'm going to march over there and say hello." Victor strolled with purpose toward the table.

As he headed toward them, again he thought about what he and Dominique shared. It was a period in his life he'd never forgotten. How could he? Their time spent together was passionate, sensuous, and mind-blowing. As he neared the table, he hoped Dominique was willing to pick up where they left off.

ominique felt her heart drop into her stomach the moment Victor Sexton came into view. The sights and sounds in the club faded as her gaze held Victor and another man heading in her direction. Dominique's thighs clenched, her heart rate skipped a beat, and her breath caught in her chest. It reminded her of the first time she laid eyes on Victor almost three years ago in Frankfurt, Germany. She had wanted to get to know the handsome man up close and personal. Their two weeks were the most fulfilling she'd ever had. What they shared was unforgettable, perfect, and then it ended when he left without a word. To see Victor was definitely a strange turn of events, one Dominique would have to deal with discreetly and carefully.

"Who are you staring at?" Curious, Robbin glanced over Dominique's shoulder and noticed the men moving in their direction. "Maybe one is your date."

Dominique never took her eyes off Victor. She inhaled slowly and answered, "There's no way that could be."

"They're headed in this direction," Robbin pointed out.

Dominique looked up to see her former lover and his companion had stopped at their table.

"Hello, ladies." Victor was speaking to both of them, but his eyes never left Dominique's.

Dominique heard the familiar voice — strong, husky, like a favorite love ballad, and every cell in her body responded. No man had caused her to feel that way before or after Victor. She stood to her feet. "What are you doing here?"

She watched Victor's lips curve into a slow, sensual smile, and she remembered the first time they kissed. It was one kiss that drained her thoughts, feeling, and emotions. It felt as if their tongues were reacting to bury emotions they were expressing for each other. She remembered his taste, his intensity, and the interior of his mouth, hot and inviting. Later, she would benefit from the expertise of his knowing how to please a woman in several other ways.

"I'm meeting my date here."

"I'm not her," Dominique muttered hastily, trying to convince herself that she didn't care.

"It's with Senator Upton's niece," Victor said matter-of-factly.

Dominique's eye's widened in surprise when realization set in.

"You're my date if you're related to the senator." Victor's smile widened, causing a warm sensation to move through Dominique's body. "I know you told me you were raised by an aunt and uncle, but I had no idea it was the Uptons. It's a small world."

"Not small enough," Dominique mumbled.

Robbin cleared her throat, reminding Dominique and Victor they were not the only ones present.

Dominique looked over at her friend. "I'm sorry, Robbin. I'd like you to meet Victor Sexton. Victor, I would like you to meet Robbin Greene."

Victor made eye contact with Robbin, extended his hand to her, and gave her a warm smile. He could feel Dominique's eyes on him.

Robbin returned Victor's smile as she accepted his strong handshake. "It's a pleasure to meet you, Victor."

Glancing at Gerald, Victor said, "I would like to introduce my brother, Gerald Sexton, owner of Cadence. Gerald, this is Dominique Frazier and Robbin Greene."

Gerald stepped closer, shaking both Dominique and Robbin's hands. "It's a pleasure to meet two beautiful ladies."

Victor could still feel Dominique's eyes boring into him. He turned to face her; his brown eyes fastened and held hers.

"Have a seat, gentlemen," Robbin requested. She threw Dominique a sly wink and grinned.

"No. I don't want to intrude," Gerald said. "I just wanted to come by and say hello. I have to check on things in the club. Dominique, Robbin, nice meeting you both." He gave both women a brief nod.

"Nice meeting you, Gerald," Dominique said.

Robbin nodded. "Dominique, I'll be at the bar if you need me."

Dominique's breath caught in her chest. There was no way she was going to be left alone with this man. How could her blind date possibly be the one person she never wanted to see again? *Aunt Rosetta, you've really done it this time. I'm never going to forgive you for this,* Dominique thought.

The smile on Victor's face faded when he turned back to meet Dominique's icy glare. "I can explain."

Ignoring his efforts, Dominique grabbed her clutch purse off the table and hurried off behind Robbin.

Victor took off after her. "Just listen a minute." When she kept walking, all he could do was drop his head in defeat. "Damn," Victor mouthed.

"What happened, man?" Gerald asked, appearing out of nowhere.

"What happened?" Victor repeated. He knew if he ever ran into Dominique, she would be upset. He spent almost two beautiful weeks with her, and then had to leave Europe without a chance to say goodbye.

"I thought you said you knew her," Gerald said, waiting for Victor to answer. When he didn't, Gerald added, "You do have a way with women."

"Hey, let it go, Gerald," Victor finally answered. "We just have some unfinished business to work out."

"What business?"

"I…" Victor began to explain.

Gerald's eyes widened with interest. "Well?"

"Never mind." Irritated, Victor scanned the room and growled. "Where's Mya?"

"Chill, man. She's probably at another station. She'll pass through in a second."

"I need a drink now." Victor stomped off toward the bar.

ର ଛ

"So are you going to see Victor again?" Robbin asked as they rode a few minutes in silence.

"No, I'm not," Dominique said, looking straight ahead at the road.

"Why not?"

Dominique narrowed her eyes. "I don't want to."

"Sure you don't," Robbin replied, her smile widening. "You almost passed out when you saw him. What are the odds that Victor would be your blind date?"

"Yeah. What are the odds?" Dominique said, showing her irritation.

Robbin's eyebrows lifted. "I left to let you and Victor get reacquainted."

"There was no need for that." Dominique glanced over at Robbin.

"You won't tell me what happened between you two?"

Dominique shrugged.

"Come on Dominique. There was still chemistry there, strong chemistry."

"Let it go." Dominique would have loved to tell Robbin that she was exaggerating, that she felt nothing, but seeing Victor drudged up old emotions that she wasn't ready to face, let alone talk about.

19

"From the way he was looking at you, he wanted to pick up where y'all left off."

"I already told you, I'm not dating a man in the military." *Especially Victor Sexton,* she thought.

"Oh, come on. You're not dating a civilian man either. Military or not, Victor Sexton is fine. If I wasn't married, I would definitely go for him," Robbin said and grew silent. "I could fix him up with Rowena. I'm sure she'd appreciate a fine Alpha man like him."

"Go ahead," Dominique said.

Robbin laughed. Dominique's comment did not put her off. "Oh, stop faking. You don't want me to do that, and you know it."

"I'm not faking. Fix him up with another woman. You have my blessing. Let someone else have him."

Dominique knew Robbin would want to know what happened between her and Victor, but she didn't want to discuss him. "How's the preparation for the birthday party coming along?" Dominique changed the subject.

Robbin shook her head and chuckled. "Everything is taken care of."

"I believe you will like the gift I got you."

"If you want to remain in denial about your feelings—"

"I thought you got the hint. I don't want to hear another word about Victor."

"Victor Sexton's last name does have *sex* in it," Robbin continued, teasing.

Dominique turned and gave her friend a no-you-didn't look. "I am through with you."

"Not another word," Robbin teased.

"Good," Dominique said.

A few minutes later, Dominique pulled in front of Robbin's building. Robbin exited the vehicle, then leaned back in. "S-E-X. You know you haven't had any lately." She flashed a devilish grin then scurried up the sidewalk.

"Damn, is it that obvious?" Dominique said to herself.

೫ ೮೦

Robbin walked inside the apartment. The place was quiet except for the soft humming of the air conditioner. "Thomas," she called and strode toward the bedroom. There was no sign of him.

On the King size bed, several of his outfits were thrown about. He must have dressed in a hurry after she left. Angry, she walked over to the vanity table, throwing her purse on the glass-top, sending the lipstick containers and perfume bottles crashing to the floor. Not bothering to remove her clothing or shoes, she crawled into bed and cried.

಩ ಬಿ

The first thing Dominique did when she arrived home was undress and then she went into the bathroom and turned on the water in the tub. Fifteen minutes later she dried herself off and smoothed lotion over every part of her body. She went into her bedroom. Going into the high chest, she grabbed a nightgown and pulled it over her head. She snatched her brush off the dresser and brushed her hair into a ponytail.

Deciding to read, Dominique crawled into bed and picked up an *Essence* magazine. She got comfortable. Dominique turned the pages slowly but didn't remember reading. She did not comprehend. On the drive home, Robbin tried to engage her in a conversation about Victor, but she didn't want to talk about him. She placed the magazine across her chest as she lay with the pillows propped against the headboard. Then the memories she tried not to think about caught and held her prisoner. She closed her eyes, letting her mind drift back to the day she'd met Victor. It was six months into her tour at Frankfurt.

Dominique had seen him several times from a distance. He was always in civilian attire. She'd figured him for a military spouse.

One day he'd literally fallen in step with her. Dominique had been on her way to the military hospital cafeteria for breakfast. She'd just finished her night shift in the intensive care unit and was sporting regular clothing. She'd yawned and he took the opportunity to initiate a conversation.

"Just getting off work? Or on your way to work?"

The genuine concern in his eyes had made it difficult for her not to respond.

"Getting off work."

"I see. Where do you work?"

Dominique had looked into the darkest, most beautiful brown eyes she'd ever seen. She'd nervously cleared her throat. "I'm a nurse on the intensive care unit."

"Military or civilian?"

"Civilian," she'd said coyly. Women had been serving in the armed forces for many years and in many capacities. Many men were not comfortable with her career choice. Most she'd met felt she was too headstrong, independent, and trying to fit into a man's world, a misconception about women in the military. To be safe she'd decided not to reveal her career choice until she felt comfortable.

"Hey, I'm sorry about being so forward. I've seen you around." He'd smiled, displaying straight, white teeth. "I wanted to say hello, but you were in a hurry. What's your name?"

"It's Dominique Frazier," she'd said.

"Mine is Victor Sexton. Look, I'm going to be late for a meeting. Can I have your number?"

"I don't give out my number, but you can give me yours." Victor had given her a smile that warmed her through and through. "Okay. Have it your way, pretty lady."

Dominique had smiled at the compliment.

"I'll give you my cell phone number." Victor reached in his back pocket, pulled out his wallet, took out a piece of paper, and wrote his number on it. "Don't just take my number and add it to your black book. If I don't hear from you by tomorrow, I'm coming up to ICU to find out why." Victor grinned, boldly taking Dominique's hand in his. "Hope to hear from you."

Dominique made the phone call, and they'd spent the next couple of days getting to know each other. Victor had told her he was from Washington, DC, and was a major in the army. He'd come from a military family. His father had retired, and he planned to retire as well. He was in Frankfurt, Germany for two weeks to teach a military class on terrorism.

She in turn had told him that she was a second lieutenant in the Army Nurses Corp. Frankfurt was her first duty station. She was raised a military brat. Her parents were killed in a motor vehicle accident and her aunt and uncle had adopted her.

Victor had been attractive three years ago, but something more had been added during the almost three years they had been separated—intensity, a tumultuous attraction that was at the same time compelling and a little frightening. *He showed up for the blind date. Obviously, he's still single,* Dominique thought. Why should it matter? The tryst was what it was. Nothing about it was serious. They were just two soldiers who happened to meet in Europe and had a good time. Most relationships in the military didn't last. Dominique's aunt and uncle's marriage was successful, but theirs was the minority. Her mind was aware of that; too bad her heart wasn't.

She'd refused to allow herself to get involved in a serious relationship. With Victor it was different. He was the only man who made her think about settling down, and then he disappeared and broke her heart.

Dominique thought about the day she'd gone to Victor's Officer's Quarters to be told he'd checked out that morning. Three days early. Without a word. During their time together he'd told her he was falling in love with her. He was going to miss her. *Miss her.* He couldn't even tell her he was leaving.

Aunt Rosetta mentioned that Victor was a Special Operations Officer. He'd never informed her he was in an elite unit. *Maybe he was called away on an assignment,* Dominique thought, but she knew that was no excuse. She deserved to know he was leaving.

After tossing in bed for hours, Dominique dropped off to sleep and dreamed about Victor. She couldn't help but recall how she felt when he'd been on top of her, looking in her eyes, gently, passionately stroking her body and running his fingers through her hair. He'd whispered words of intimacy in her ear that made her feel like she was a woman. At the same time he was taking her mind and body on a perfect rhythmic ride. The dream was so erotic that she woke up in the middle of the night hot, achy, and knotted in her sheets.

 C3 80

"Thomas, we need to talk." Robbin leaped to her feet from the sofa when he finally came through the door at 3:00 a.m. She was more sure than ever that there was another woman. It was time for him to admit it.

"I don't want to hear it," Thomas said, coolly. He nonchalantly strolled past her and headed for the bedroom.

Robbin followed him. She was incensed. She wasn't sure what infuriated her more, the fact that he strolled in and out as he pleased as if nothing was wrong or that he wouldn't admit their marriage was in trouble. He was not going to tune her out. Not this time. "Stop shutting me out, Thomas. Talk to me." She was on the defensive. "You can start with where you've been."

Thomas looked up at Robbin through narrowed eyes. "Don't start this, Robbin. I told you I don't want to hear it."

"I'm not starting anything. I just want to talk."

"No, you don't. You want to argue. I'm not going to argue with you."

Robbin folded her arms across her chest and gazed at Thomas for a long time. "I just want to know what is going on between us. Tell me what's happening."

"What do you want to know, Robbin? What?"

She wondered where the Thomas was she first met three years ago at Fort Riley, Kansas. He was kind, loving, and sincere. It seemed like that Thomas walked out one day and was replaced with a clone.

"Where have you been?" she repeated.

23

"I was out!" he barked.

"I know that!" Robbin snapped back. She couldn't believe her ears. Where was his lack of commitment coming from? "Who were you out with?"

"The fellas." Thomas eyes skidded away quickly.

Robbin's head bobbed up and down. "The fellas," she repeated, annoyed. He was lying and she knew it. He couldn't even look her in the eyes. "Is there..." A knot swelled in her throat. She didn't want to know the answer to her question, but had to ask. "Is there someone else, Thomas?"

Thomas stopped in mid-motion. Robbin saw him square his shoulders. This time his gaze locked with hers. "What makes you think there's another woman?"

"Your habits, Thomas. Staying out late at night. I enter the room you hang up the phone. We don't spend time together. We haven't made love in months. Shall I go on?" It had been months since he'd touched her. When they first met, Thomas would rush home from work, they would make love, and then afterward lay in each other's arm. They would talk for hours about their plans for the future. Now everything was disappearing before her very eyes.

"That doesn't mean there is another woman," Thomas replied.

As he began to turn away, Robbin patted him in the chest with her finger. "You would tell me if there was someone else," she pleaded.

"Robbin, there's nothing to tell."

"But if there were, you would tell me?" Robbin's eyes misted. "Thomas," she began, when he held up his hand stopping her.

"There is no one else." He pulled her into his arms and planted a kiss lightly on her forehead. "I'm going to take a shower."

Robbin watched him enter the bathroom. There was someone else, she could feel it. Her mother taught her to trust her instincts. Her instincts were screaming *another woman.*

Chapter Four

DAY TWO - SATURDAY

The next morning, Victor completed the necessary ten minute body stretch and warm-up. He was clothed in a black and gray army sweat suit. Maybe a good five or ten mile excursion around the local school track was what he needed. His brain and body kept him tossing all night in his king-sized bed.

He set the timer on his Army Seal chrome watch and then begin a slow trot before extending into a full jog.

He couldn't believe it was her, the one woman who'd made him break his own rules — never get emotionally involved. Dominique wasn't like the other women. She had a mind of her own. He liked that. She was the most intriguing, compelling woman he'd ever laid eyes on. It wasn't just that she was beautiful, there was something else about Dominique that put him under a spell. She was captivating, intelligent, vibrant, alive, and definitely sexy.

Victor picked up the pace, remembering how Dominique had given herself freely to him. He missed her, missed the way he looked at her, missed the sweet open response of her body during lovemaking. It wasn't until he was on the other side of the world that he realized how much she had meant to him.

He smiled as he remembered her outfit. The skirt revealed every curve of her long, gorgeous legs — the beautiful extremities that wrapped around him. Her attire in Germany ranged from military during the day to nothing at night. Of course he preferred the latter.

Victor completed the first lap with ease, thinking he desperately wanted to see Dominique again. This time there wasn't any military mission pulling them apart. He had a hunch she was still attracted to him. She was angry, and she had a right to be considering the way things ended with them. Lord, how he wanted her back. First, he had to get her to speak to him again. It wasn't going to be easy, but it was a mission he was ready to take on.

Ê€

It was five minutes to eight when Dominique found a parking space at Cadence. Walking toward the entrance, she looked at the Marquee. The show tonight was headlined by the local duo, Phase II.

Gift in hand, she stepped through the double door of the club and saw Gerald greeting the people. He saw her and his face parted in a wide smile.

"Good evening, Dominique. Welcome back to Cadence," he said.

Dominique returned the greeting. "Hello, Gerald."

"Give me a hug." Moving closer, Gerald pulled Dominique in his arms and planted a light kiss to her cheek.

Dominique took a step back and looked up at the shorter, younger Sexton. Though Gerald was more handsome than his brother, Victor was just as attractive, more her type of man — taller and heavier built.

Gerald released her hands. "Are you here to see my brother?"

Dominique raised the gift-wrapped box. "No. I'm here for Robbin's birthday party." She had to smile. Victor wasn't the reason she was at the club, but she had to admit she hoped to see him.

"The Greene birthday party. Let me get someone to show you to the room." Gerald signaled to the host, Cordell Reeves. He approached them with a friendly smile on his face. Gerald leaned over to whispered instructions to him.

"Enjoy the evening, Dominique," Gerald said. "I will stop in later to see how things are going."

"I will see you later," Dominique replied.

"Follow me please," Cordell said.

As Dominique trailed the host, her gaze roamed the room. Soft conversations flowed from tables and booths, mixed with the mellow sound of "Two Occasions," by The Deele. The host escorted her to a private room labeled the Fountain Room.

Dominique glanced around the room decorated with balloons, a 'Happy Birthday' banner hanging from the ceiling, and music playing full blast. There were a number of guests, including Rowena Harris the owner of Rowena's Place; Charlene Flanders, the Medical Clerk; Dr. Judith Rice; and Paul Bartholomew, a Physician Assistant. She recognized the other guests from other units of the hospital. She spotted Robbin at the DJ station and waved to her.

"Happy birthday, Robbin," Dominique squealed when Robbin greeted her. "It's a nice turnout." Dominique's eyes scanned the room, waving at Latosha Hunter, another employee from the emergency room.

"Yes, it is." Robbin gave her a hug. "It's about time you got here."

Dominique scowled when she stepped back and saw the pasted smile on Robbin's face. "What's wrong?"

"Nothing. I'm all right."

"No, you're not. Tell me what's bothering you," Dominique whispered and led Robbin by the elbow away from the other guests. Robbin told her about the argument between her and Thomas.

"It's my birthday. Do you know I didn't get a card from him?" Robbin said calmly as she tried to keep her voice from trembling. "Not even a card. Where is he now? He hasn't even shown up."

Dominique could tell she was upset and trying to hold on to her anger. "Maybe he will show up later," Dominique explained, trying to reassure Robbin. "It's still early. The party has just begun."

"Yeah." Robbin folded her arms across her chest and looked down.

"Hey, we will have none of that." Dominique unfolded Robbin's arms. "Until he arrives, we're going to have a good time, and make sure you have the best 32nd birthday party ever." Dominique turned and led her host toward the table and gaped at the variety of dishes.

"Ham, potato salad, greens, cornbread, yams, green beans, and macaroni & cheese. What kind of birthday meal is this?" Dominique questioned. "Whatever happened to cake, ice cream, chips, and cookies?" Dominique put her arm around Robbin's shoulder and gave her a hug.

Robbin added Dominique's gift with the others. " The club catered the food. There's a chocolate cake. I baked it myself," she added proudly.

Dominique filled a cup with punch. "There goes my diet," she mumbled. Several hours later, the party began to wound down and the invited guests made their way toward the main floor of the club.

Dominique wondered where Victor was. Gerald made an appearance as promised, even danced with Robbin. She was tempted to ask Gerald where Victor was and then decided against it.

After cleaning up, Dominique and Robbin followed the guests to the front of the club. They managed to find a spot with an unobstructed view of the stage. A few minutes later, Gerald appeared.

"My next guests need no introduction. They have topped the music charts for the past three years, giving us hit after hit. They're here with us tonight. Cadence, put your hands together for Maryland's own Phase II," he announced and pointed as the two men appeared.

The applause and cheers filled the club in anticipation of their performance. Dominique looked over and saw a small smile on Robbin's face.

Phase II performed their upbeat singles then slowed the tempo. Dominique was so caught up in the show that she didn't see Victor until his voice over her right shoulder asked, "Are you enjoying yourself?"

Her heartbeat sped up when he walked around and stood right in front of her.

"Hi," Dominique whispered.

"Hello."

"Phase II is one of my favorite groups," Dominique replied, making conversation.

"Mine too." Victor's gaze skidded to Robbin. "Hello Robbin. Happy birthday. Good to see you."

Robbin nodded. "Good to see you, Victor."

"How old are you? Twenty-one?" Victor teased.

The remark brought a smile to Robbin's face. "Dominique, I knew there was something I loved about this man. He knows the right thing to say to a woman. He's a keeper."

"Keep telling Dominique that," Victor said, smiling.

Dominique blushed and looked over to find Victor staring at her. Victor extended a large hand to Dominique. "May I have this dance?"

"Sure," Dominique said.

Robbin nodded in agreement.

Dominique extended her hand to Victor, who led her through the crowd. He pulled her into his arms and they began circling the floor to the slow beat of the song. Dominique leaned her head in his chest, smelling the fragrance of his cologne. She clasped her hand around his neck. They moved in perfect rhythm. His hands traveled the hollow of her back. She locked herself into his embrace, matching the movement of his hips. He gently lifted her chin up forcing her to look into his face.

"Still angry at me, Dominique?"

"What do you think?"

"Yes," he said softly. "I can't blame you."

The song ended before she had a chance to respond. He politely escorted her to a table up front.

Dominique glanced around, finally spotting Robbin on the dance floor. There was still no sign of Thomas.

"May I join you?" he asked, seeking her consent.

"Sure."

Dominique watched as his long fingers pulled out the chair next to her.

"Dominique, will you have dinner with me?"

Dominique knew he would want to see her and ask her out if they ran into each other again. She wasn't sure how she felt about Victor. *It was only dinner,* she thought. She hadn't been out with a man in ages and they were not strangers. As long as she remained in control of the situation there could be no harm done. *But why take chances?*

Victor suddenly moved closer, leaning across the table, taking her hand in his. His gaze examined every square inch of her face, lingering on the soft lips he'd sampled so many times. He remembered the feel of her tongue interacting with his. He felt an erotic shiver ripple through him.

"Well?" he prompted.

Dominique didn't answer.

"You're going to tell me no, aren't you?"

"Victor, I don't think that's a good idea."

"It's only dinner," he added quickly. "I promise to be on my best behavior."

Sure you will, she thought. Dominique had learned from her past involvement with Victor and had no intentions of falling for him again.

"One date. If I'm not on my best behavior, you never have to go out with me again."

Dominique heard the plea in his voice; she knew it was hard for a man like Victor to ask her for a date. He could never fathom how badly she wanted to say yes.

"The answer is no."

Victor hid his disappointment and forced a tight smile. "Thanks for the dance."

Dominique watched him disappear through the crowd. She felt as if Victor walked out of her life a second time.

DAY THREE – SUNDAY

Around 1:30 a.m., Dominique and Robbin stepped out into the warm night air and gazed up at the clear sky. Thomas never showed. They sauntered slowly off toward their vehicles in silence.

"I hope nothing happened to Thomas," Dominique finally said as Robbin opened her car door. She was parked a few feet away.

"If not, when I finish with him, he's going to wish it had." Robbin's voice was firm, as she climbed into her car and turned the key in the ignition.

Robbin stepped on the gas pedal and sped through the yellow caution light. The street was busy with cars leaving the club going to their destinations. As her vehicle crossed the intersection, she spotted Thomas' white BMW in the far right hand lane, traveling in the opposite direction. He made a turn at the light. *Where was he headed this time of night?* she thought as she pulled into the abandoned Safeway parking lot, making a U-turn.

Adrenaline pumped through her body when she caught up with his vehicle. She paced her driving speed to ensure she wouldn't get stuck at a light while the BMW drove down the street. She was sure she was undetected. Thomas made no attempt to stop. At a closer glance she made out a silhouette of a passenger but couldn't determine whether it was a woman or man.

CR ED

At 2:00 a.m. Sunday morning, he stood across the street waiting for her to come home. For the past week he'd kept his movements under the cover of darkness. It didn't bother him. He was used to it. His military instincts were on target and would allow him to choose the correct moment.

All he had to do was wait for her to show. He took a gulp of water from a bottle then quickly finished the rest of it before tossing the empty container into a trash can. If it wasn't for this assignment and covertly meeting his contact at the motel he'd checked into for the week, he'd still be washing dishes at some dead-end odd job. He once believed that the military took care of their own, that the government could be trusted, but that was an error in judgment that had cost him his career.

He stepped farther back in the cloak of darkness when the Military Police vehicle circled the block. They were on time. They always circled around 2:00 a.m. That didn't deter him from his mission. For it to be successful, he had to finish before the Military Police circle again at 2:25 a.m.

Three minutes later, a white BMW pulled in front of the Officer's Quarters. A moment later, a tall, slender built gentleman stepped out of the vehicle. He went around the car and opened the passenger side door and extended his hand to a medium height, dark haired woman. They walked toward the building. Although her guest wasn't part of the plan, he would not deter from it. The orders were specific. It had to be done and completed tonight. Besides, two victims weren't tough for him. He glanced at his watch. He'd give them a few minutes to get inside and then he would make his move.

CR ED

Robbin guided her car into the Army base and pulled in front of the Officer's Quarters. She drove by slowly, taking a careful glance as

30

Thomas exited the car. She watched Thomas in the rearview mirror as he got out of the car, walked around, and opened the passenger door. She blinked to make sure her eyes were not deceiving her. The passenger was a woman. She recognized her as Lieutenant Tamara Hill, an Army nurse who worked with her in the hospital emergency room. She sat a moment, her fingers drumming a staccato on the steering wheel to curve her anger. A sourness settled in the pit of her stomach.

❧ ❧

The sound of the car door woke Esther Cunningham, the resident manager. She'd fallen asleep on the sofa in front of the television set.

"Who is that this time of night?" Mrs. Cunningham muttered as she padded over to the window and slightly parted the curtains. She knew all the officers in the building by name and face.

Mrs. Cunningham watched as Lieutenant Hill and her male friend walked up the sidewalk. She glanced at the digital clock on the VCR; it was 2:04 a.m.

❧ ❧

He heard the sound of another car door and stepped back into the shadows. Peeping cautiously around the building, he watched as a young, African-American woman strolled down the sidewalk. She mumbled something then stopped in mid-stride and turned suddenly in the other direction. The movement caught him off guard and she zeroed in on him standing beside the building. He quickly moved back into the shadows. He wondered if she saw him. He saw her stretch her neck trying to get a better glimpse.

She must've decided she imagined the figure. She shook her head from side-to-side, then hurried and got back inside her vehicle. He watched as she drove off and he made a note of her license plate number. Lucky for him she parked underneath the light.

❧ ❧

Silence enveloped them as Thomas escorted Tamara to her quarters. They spent a beautiful, romantic evening in Baltimore, Maryland, followed by a boat ride along the harbor. He hoped her silence didn't mean she was having second thoughts about their relationship. Tamara knew he was married and worked with his wife at the hospital.

31

Tamara was growing impatient and wanted Thomas to tell Robbin their marriage was over, or she would tell Robbin about the affair. Thomas loved his wife and had no intention of telling Robbin about Tamara.

An irritated Tamara pulled the key from her purse, unlocked the door, and walked inside the quarters. Thomas followed her in, closing the door behind him. His hand automatically reached for the lamp on the end table, like he'd done so many times before.

Tamara dropped the keys on the coffee table.

Pulling her into his arms, Thomas thrust his tongue in her warm mouth with a kiss that curled his own toes. "I meant what I said on the boat. I'm going to tell her it's over."

"When?"

"Sssh." He put a finger to her mouth. "Don't worry your pretty little head about her."

 "I'm ready for us to begin our life together."

"I know. Just be patient." He pressed his lips to hers again. "I better get going. It's late. I know I'm going to hear it about missing her birthday party." He picked up the box of chocolate covered cherries he'd given her earlier. Removing the top, he popped a piece of chocolate into his mouth. "Sweet, just like you."

Tamara blushed at the compliment.

"Lock the door behind me." He gave her a final hug and a quick kiss then turned and walked out the door.

For a moment she stood there in the doorway, then finally went back inside the quarters. She settled down on the sofa, feeling more depressed then she had ever in her life. Was it possible they would be together? It wasn't as if he and Robbin were happy, not like the man in her previous relationship. He was powerful, connected, much older, and very married. She wasn't about to make that mistake again.

Tamara picked up the latest copy of *Times* magazine from the coffee table. She frowned as she looked at the man on the cover — Senator Harold Upton. A man for the people, he based his campaign on family morals and values and was now seeking reelection.

What would his constituents think if they found out the truth about the senator's past?

A light tapping at her door interrupted her thoughts. Maybe Thomas decided to spend the night. Even though it was against army regulation to have an overnight guest, he'd spent some nights with her, leaving early in the morning hours.

Tamara raised herself off the sofa and went in anticipation to the door. She opened it, but no one was there. She stepped into the hallway and looked up and down the corridor. The building was eerily quiet.

Tamara shivered and rubbed both arms to heed off the chill. She retreated back inside her quarters to get ready for bed. She glanced over at the magazine and shivered again.

She headed into her bedroom and turned on the television, then headed into the adjoining bathroom and turned on the shower. She re-entered the bedroom and began to undress. As she pulled the dress over her head, she found herself watching a repeat of the news segment. *"The race for the Senatorial seat is heating up as Republican candidate Robert Baines is closing in on George Guliano,"* the female news reporter was saying. *"A fifteen point deficit separates the two men. Just who will run against Virginia's popular Senator Harold Upton?"*

Senator Harold Upton was one name Tamara didn't want to hear. She finished undressing then preceded toward the bathroom. She heard the bedroom door open behind her. She jumped and then turned around sharply.

The black stocking was around her neck so quick, it took her completely by surprise. She began to struggle for her life, but it was useless. The killer was an expert at what he did.

$\mathcal{D}$ominique drove around the parking lot twice before she found a parking space at Giant's Supermarket, a needed stop before heading to her aunt and uncle's house. They were expecting her for their weekly Sunday dinner.

Ten minutes later, a smiling Rosetta opened the door. "Sorry, I'm late," Dominique said, entering the modern kitchen.

Dominique barely had time to set the plastic bag containing celery, a loaf of white bread, and can of pet milk on the kitchen counter when she was enveloped in big, warm arms.

"How are you doing, sweetheart?" Rosetta said, smiling.

"Hello Princess," Harold, appearing from one of the back rooms, came over and patted Dominique on the back. He was casually dressed in a white polo shirt, blue jeans, and open toe brown sandals.

Rosetta let her go and Dominique hugged Harold. Harold served 30 years in the Army. At 54-years-old, the man was still athletically built and kept his body in shape. He was still as fit as he'd been during his years on active duty, running at least five miles, three days a week and working out daily. His hair was still completely black, while Rosetta possessed a few unnoticeable strands of gray in her hair.

"Uncle Harold, how are you?"

"I'm outstanding," he answered in military jargon. "How's Walter Reed emergency room treating my favorite nurse?" Harold went to the refrigerator and retrieved a bottled water that was always in stock. "Rosetta and I drove pass the hospital the other day."

"Thought about stopping to see if you were available for lunch," Rosetta explained, wiping her hands on her apron labeled *Officer's Wives Club*. "But your uncle was running late for a meeting."

"It's been a busy week in the ER," Dominique said, feeling embarrassed about the inevitable conversation she would have with her aunt. "Call ahead next time. I'll get someone to cover for me and we can have lunch together."

"Will do," Harold answered. "I'll be in the library." Her uncle approached her and said, "You and your aunt can talk freely without the man around."

Dominique turned towards her aunt. She inhaled sharply, taking in the aroma of onions and bell pepper. "The meatloaf smells delicious." Her uncle's departure cleared the atmosphere to discuss Victor Sexton.

"I fixed your favorites: potato salad, meat loaf, candies yams, green beans, cornbread, macaroni and cheese, and for dessert, banana pudding," Rosetta beamed proudly.

"Aunt Rosetta, I can't believe you still cook. You have servants to do that."

Dominique peeped at the counter aligned with food. She thought about when fellow officer's, their spouses, and siblings in her uncle's unit would meet at her aunt and uncles home for dinner. The adults would discuss world events, military missions they were involved in, and of course politics. The weekly gathering continued while the spouses were on training exercises or deployments. Aunt Rosetta was a guardian angel to many of the spouses entering the military. She was always available to offer encouragement, support, and comfort when needed.

"I like to cook. This is for a small private gathering," Aunt Rosetta said.

"Then why all the food?"

"Force of habit."

Aunt Rosetta wiped her hands again on her apron. "Now tell me, how did it go with Colonel Sexton? Isn't he a dreamboat?"

"He is that." Upon Victor's appearance Dominique recalled how her heart fell in her stomach and a pool of liquid settled between her thighs. "It didn't go to well. We didn't hit it off, so we went our separate ways. End of story." Dominique glanced at her aunt who stood in the middle of the kitchen, surprised by her comment.

"You're kidding?" Rosetta said, sounding disappointed. "I was sure the two of you would hit it off. The two of you make a handsome couple. You have so much in common."

"We didn't, Aunt Rosetta." Dominique needed to answer, plain and simple, so her aunt wouldn't question her. She didn't want her to uncover that there was a history between her and Victor. The last discussion Dominique wanted to have was how they could work the situation out. As far as she was concerned, it was irreconcilable.

"What was wrong with him?"

That's it. There's nothing wrong with him, Dominique thought.

Rosetta walked over to the silverware drawer, opened it, and grabbed utensils. "He's perfect for you. Victor's a good man. You're a good woman. After Felicia called the engagement off, he's been alone. Far too long as far as I'm concerned. He needs a good woman in his life," she said staunchly. "I believe that woman is you."

Dominique's body stiffened upon hearing the revelation. *Victor was engaged?*

"He was engaged?" came Dominique's reply. She had to phrase it as not to let her aunt know she was interested. "Did you ever meet her?"

"Never met her. Got a wedding invitation from him when he was at Ft. Bragg inviting us to the ceremony. Then a week before the wedding he phoned and said it was off. He didn't give an explanation. We didn't ask. If you ask me, she's not very bright, letting a good man like him go."

"Maybe she had her reasons."

"Don't be sassy, young lady. All I'm saying is whatever it was, it could have been worked out. Men like him are hard to find. When you run across them, you snatch them up. If you don't, another woman will."

"You know him that well?"

Rosetta glanced at Dominique over her shoulder. "Well enough," she assured her. "He's getting ready to retire and is part-owner in Cadence Supper Club." She held up a large finger. "In other words, he's a good catch."

Victor was retiring. There goes her theory about becoming involved with a military man. He was the reason she refused to date another soldier. That stipulation no longer applied. It also explained how he was able to offer her preferential treatment at the club. However, it didn't explain why he ended their relationship abruptly without a word. *Was it because he had to get back to his fiancée?* she wondered.

"Aunt Rosetta, I know you mean well," Dominique found herself saying. "I'm not saying Victor Sexton is not a good man, I'm just saying he's not the man for me."

Rosetta stopped in mid-motion and gave Dominique a motherly glance. "How do you know? You never gave the man a chance."

Dominique crossed her legs to heed off the warm feeling settling between her thighs. She knew him. Knew him well. Victor Sexton was very well endowed. She remembered the first night they were intimate. She'd carefully undressed him, removing each article of clothing. When she removed his shorts, she got an eye full. She swallowed. A soft moan threatened to escape her lips when she remembered how he'd pleased her, over and over.

Dominique returned her gaze to her aunt's face and saw that she had been watching her. "Did you say something?"

Rosetta eyes watched Dominique in a way that displayed concern. "I asked if you're all right?"

Dominique frowned. "I'm fine." The doorbell chime interrupted them. "I'll get it," she answered and walked to the door, graceful to be released from her aunt's watchful eye.

Dominique opened the front door and came face to face with Victor Sexton. She almost fell over as she looked at the man standing in the doorway. What a coincidence. Did she think him up?

"What are you doing here?" The question left her lips as she looked him up and down. Sensual awareness she'd been feeling a moment ago rushed throughout her body. During their time together he'd worn form fitting, short sleeve shirts, showing off strong arms and broad chest. This man could style a pair of jeans. Long legs and firm, tight bottom covered in denim was a sight to behold. Today was no exception. He looked absolutely stunning in a white, short sleeve shirt with blue jean walking shorts, and a pair of sandals. The casual outfit was accessorized with a gold bracelet on his left wrist and a cross around his neck. Shades concealed his brown eyes. The brother had the nerve to smell good. Victor knew Fahrenheit cologne on him turned her on. She'd complimented him on the scent numerous times while nuzzling on his neck, often leading to intimate liaisons. What an ambush.

Dominique sucked in a deep breath as she continued staring at Victor. *Proceed with caution, girlfriend.* A Captain in the United States Army, she could handle the situation. First thing she had to do was stop ogling him. Act normal, like his fine self had no effects on her. Her eyes gave his body one last go over.

Dominique returned her gaze to his face and noticed he had been watching her, watching him. She'd lost this battle. She cleared her throat. "You didn't answer my question. What are you doing here?"

"Hello, to you too, Dominique," Victor spoke, as he stepped farther into the room. He removed his shades.

"Hello, Colonel Sexton." Rosetta's excited voice greeted her guest. "Glad you could make it. I cooked enough food. I know how much you can eat."

Victor's face split into a wide grin. "Thanks for inviting me. You know I never turn down a home cooked meal."

Rosetta patted him on the back. "You're always welcome. We haven't seen much of you lately. CID keeping you busy?"

"Busy enough."

Dominique shook her head. Her aunt never gives up.

"Can I help with anything?" Dominique asked.

"Don't be silly. Everything is ready. Just have to place it on the table. You two go on in the living room. Victor, I'll let the senator know you've arrived."

"Thank you, Rosetta."

Dominique waited until Rosetta vanished from the room, then she lit into Victor. "Why are you here?" she asked through clench teeth.

"Your aunt invited me."

"You could have said no. I thought I made myself clear last night."

"Look," he whispered back. "I've known your aunt and uncle for several years. We're good friends. Just because you and I—"

"Don't put you and me together, Victor," Dominique said, cutting him off. She sauntered over to the love seat and plopped down.

Dominique was tough. But Victor was tougher. Nothing worth having comes easy. Dominique Frazier was worth having.

"We were together," Victor stated, taking a chair across from Dominique.

"It was a mistake!" Dominique snapped.

Victor's heart dropped. He couldn't believe Dominique said their relationship was a mistake. He knew she was lying. He could see the mixture of fear and longing in her eyes when she looked at him. She was afraid of him, emotionally, not physically. "You don't mean that. What we experienced was special, and you know it."

"So special you left in the middle of the night," Dominique said in a sharp voice.

"Dominique, let me—"

She refused to let him complete the explanation. "Without a word," Dominique added with extra emphasis.

"Can I?" Victor whispered huskily, knowing he'd made a mistake leaving the way he did. At the time he could not help it.

"If that's your definition of special, I would hate to think what you would have done if I was stupid enough to believe it was more than what it really was."

"What are you saying? That—" he tried to inject again.

"It's a good thing," she continued.

Victor rolled his head to one side when Dominique continued the verbal assault, not letting him get a word in.

She pointed a perfectly manicured finger at him, "I found out what kind of man you are. You're an officer, but you're definitely no gentleman." Dominique peeped over her shoulder to ensure her aunt and uncle did not overhear. "Listen to me, Victor, it is over between us. Finished. Over. O-V-E-R." She spelled the word out to get her point across. She attempted to rise from the sofa but he kneeled in front of her and reached out, taking her hand in his, refusing to let her leave.

"It will never be over between us." Victor's gaze was intent and challenging. "You see, I'm retiring in less than a week, which means I'm going to be here." He bought the back of her hand up to his lips in a smooth move. He wanted her to know the time they spent in Europe was more than a fling.

That wasn't enough for him. Victor deliberately, seductively took Dominique's ring finger, placed it in his mouth, and wrapped his warm tongue around it, reminding her of the special type of intimacy they'd shared three years ago.

Dominique almost jumped out of her skin. The suckling of his lips on her finger set her body aflame. Her kitten cooed from the impact of the sensual simulation. The effort to resist him slipped away and she automatically let him take the next finger, tasting and feeding on it.

He looked up at her and saw reluctant passion in her eyes. He'd made good on his words that it wasn't over between them and he made sure she was aware. No matter what obstacle she placed between them, he intended to tear them down.

Dominique instantly removed her hand. "Stop it, Victor." She had no intention to pick up where they'd left off.

"Why?" Victor asked huskily, knowing she didn't mean it. He reached out and grabbing her hand again. "I still care about you."

She withdrew her hand again. "I told you it's over."

He stood to his feet and looked down at her rebellious, yet desire glare in her eyes. "I meant what I said. I'm here to stay. So get used to seeing me." Victor reached down and traced his finger along the curve of her cheekbone. "There's nothing to take me away this time."

"It doesn't matter, Victor." She turned her head to the side, blinking back tears. "You hurt me. I trusted you."

"I know you trusted me," he said softly. "I handled the situation badly. I know that."

"Yes, you did!" Dominique snapped.

"Dominique, you owe me the right to explain why I left."

Her eyes widened in disbelief. The man had a lot of nerves. She owed him? "I don't owe you anything."

He threw his hand up in a surrendering gesture. "You're right. You don't owe me anything."

Dominique stood and walk away. She didn't want to hear another word he had to say.

"Please, Dominique," Victor pleaded, placing a hand to his chest. "Hear me out." She turned back to face him. Her heartbeat slamming against her chest wall. He looked and sounded so sincere. She wanted to listen, and for one moment she almost relented, but she held back. "No," Dominique said, her voice barely above a whisper.

Victor dropped his head and spread his arms apart. "Do you believe in fate?"

Dominique shook her head no.

"I do. I believe fate has given us a second chance. I plan to do everything within my power to make you see that. Even if it takes me the rest of my life."

Victor sidestepped Dominique and walked out the room without giving her a chance to reply.

ڣ ۀ

After dinner, Victor followed Senator Upton into his elegant library. Once inside, Victor closed the door behind him.

"What's going on between you and Dominique?" the senator asked, getting straight to the point. He crossed the oriental rug to the carved armoire. Keeping his back to Victor, he poured himself a scotch, neat. "Don't tell me nothing. I have a nose for this type of thing."

Victor carefully sat in the large, cushy chair. "There really is nothing going on. We just didn't hit it off."

"Bull," the senator said with a nod. "I asked you not to tell me nothing," He turned and then grinned like a Cheshire cat. "I know Dominique. I raised her. I know you. I commanded you," he said with ease. "There's something going on between you two. Whatever it is, I hope you work it out. You're the kind of man she needs in her life. I know she is headstrong and stubborn. Lord knows she is my sister, Vanessa's, child. I guess it runs in the family."

Victor smiled at the senator.

Harold pointed the glass of scotch toward Victor.

Victor nodded his head no.

"Have you given any more thought to my offer to come work for me after your retirement?"

"No, I haven't," Victor answered honestly.

The senator moved from the armoire. He propped his hip on the corner of his desk. Senator Upton was seeking reelection and offered Victor the opportunity to become his aide.

The Senator was well liked and powerful and one of the most admired on Capitol Hill. Just the way he wanted it. As far as Victor was concern, he'd chosen his second career correctly. Victor admired and respected Harold, but he never had the desire to be in the political arena. His political interest only went as far as being a soldier. Now that that part of his life was closing, he just wanted to retire quietly and work alongside his brother, Gerald, at the club.

The senator's eyes never left Victor's face. The men were stationed together in the Persian Gulf and several years later in Haiti. Victor had served well as his Special Operation Commander. He was damn good at what he did. The other team members respected him. Never questioned his commands, knowing he did what was best for his men to carry out the missions safely. Victor was the kind of man the Senator wanted on his staff. Someone he could trust, get the job done behind the scenes, makes the deals, and deal with the power makers with ease. "You can't be serious about retiring and becoming part-owner in a night club?"

"I'm serious, Senator. That's exactly what I plan to do, sir. Four days and counting. I don't plan to be anyone's glorified gofer."

"Gofers don't have dinner with Senators or the Presidents," the senator stated. "With all due respect, sir. I have to pass."

"What kind of life is running a club to a man with your background? You can write your ticket in politics and everything that comes along with it. Money, power, and connections. I can do that for you. First as my aide, then on your own. You could be Mayor, Congressman, even Senator." The senator took a sip of Scotch. "The sky is the limit."

Victor leaned back in the chair and crossed one leg over the other. "Senator, politics has always been your dream," he said, watching the senator's expression intently. He was a man used to getting what he wanted. "You accomplished what you set out to do. I have done more than my share for this country. I'm proud of that. Now, I just want to leave the military for a quiet and simple life."

Senator Upton nodded. "I know you have. That's why I wish you would reconsider. This country needs more men like you in office. Men with firsthand experience, who knows what it is like to put their life on the line. Men who can decide policies based on experience, not just instinct and textbook. Not like the majority of these ivy league graduates running this country who haven't been to war."

Victor smiled again. "My job was to carry out the missions, not question the reason behind it. You're in office and will be reelected. You're the voice for people like me."

The senator sighed. "I'm not going to give up on you." He stood to his feet, went around the desk, and sat in the chair. "Are you still attending my fundraiser for my reelection campaign? It's Friday night."

"I wouldn't miss it for the world, sir."

Regardless how Victor felt about the political scene, he couldn't get out of this one. He'd given his word to attend. Not that he had any other commitment. Dominique made it clear she didn't want to have anything to do with him.

"Dominique will be there," the senator said with a grin.

Victor nodded. "I figured she would be."

"I believe you like her," he said jokingly.

Victor had to laugh.

"If I can't have you as my aide, I would love to have you as my nephew." He tilted his head to one side and grinned.

"Sir, it's not that simple. We—" Suddenly, Victor's cellular phone ranged. "It's Captain Benitez," he said, recognizing the number. "The only time he calls me on my day off is when it's an emergency. Excuse me a moment, Senator."

"Of course," the senator said. "This conversation is far from over."

"Yes, sir."

The senator left the library to give Victor privacy.

Victor flipped open the sleek black phone. Benitez was the executive officer at CID. The two worked together one year since Benitez's transfer from Ft. Hood, Texas. They liked and respected each other as men and officers. "What's going on Benitez?"

There was a pause on the other line. "We have a murder, sir. On post and in the Officer's Quarters," he explained with a Spanish accent.

"I'm on my way."

s Victor drove along Interstate 395 toward Washington, DC, his thoughts were not on the crime at hand but on Dominique Frazier. Even though Dominique made it clear it was over between them, he wasn't satisfied with her declaration. For all practical reasons he should respect her wishes and move on. But he wasn't a practical man.

Suddenly, he was looking forward to the fundraiser Friday night. The pretense and game playing that was part of this social event would be tolerable with Dominique's presence.

Before he could dwell on the upcoming party, he was at the main gate of the army base and all thoughts of Dominique were pushed to the back of his mind. As he proceeded toward the address given to him, he passed the 26 Victorian style homes that lined the streets of the army post known as Generals Row. The first home was built more than 75 years ago. Officers from Brigadier too full General reside in the houses along the row. Many of the Army's great leaders have resided in the quarters. General of the Army, Douglas MacArthur, George C. Marshal, Dwight D. Eisenhower, Omar Bradley, and the present post commander, Brigadier General Andrew Goss.

A few minutes later, Victor parked his truck on the street in front of the Base Officer's Quarters. The white building was old but well maintained, surrounded by a well-manicured lawn. A uniformed military police officer rendered a hand salute and then led him along the brick sidewalk aligned with flowers. The officer led Victor past other officers who were keeping curious onlookers at bay and into the quarters of the victim.

"Here we are, sir," the officer said.

Military Police and CID officers were already working together collecting and methodically searching for evidence. Benitez saw Victor and headed in his direction.

"Sorry to disturb you Colonel on your day off, but I figured you would want to know about this one. The victim's name is Lieutenant Tamara Hill. The building manager, Mrs. Esther Cunningham, that's her over there," he tilted his head toward the elderly woman sitting at the dining room table, "found the body. The Coroner is in with the body now."

Victor looked around the small living quarters with plain, simple, brown furniture. The room contained a couple of chairs, a small sofa, and coffee table. A wall unit shelved an entertainment center. The TV, VCR, and DVD player sat untouched, but books and papers were thrown on the floor. It appeared as if the killer was looking for something. Cream-colored walls provided the backdrop for numerous paintings. Despite ordinary pieces, the victim was able to create a warm, homelike, and comfortable ambience.

Victor noticed a box of chocolates on the coffee table. He reached in his pocket for his handkerchief, flipped it out, and removed the top. It was half empty. He hoped Forensics could lift usable fingerprints.

Victor handed the handkerchief-covered box to Benitez. "Make sure Forensics dust it for prints. See if they come up with something."

"Yes, sir," Benitez replied, then turned to one of the officers with instruction to take care of the box of chocolates. "I informed the manager that you would want to ask her some questions." Benitez led Victor over to an extension of the living room used as the dining room area.

Mrs. Cunningham attempted to come to her feet as Victor approached. He motioned for her to remain seated. Benitez made the introduction.

After all three were seated, Victor said, "I know you've been through a lot, Mrs. Cunningham, so I'll keep it brief. Can you tell me what happened?"

Mrs. Cunningham took a couple of deep breaths to compose herself. "It's such a tragedy. I've never seen anything like that before." She dropped her head, her eyes fastened on her hands clasped together in her lap. "She was a lovely girl. Friendly." She paused to draw another breath. " Tamara and her mother talked on the phone every Sunday and when she couldn't get in touch with her, Tamara's mother asked if I would check on her. She said she felt something was wrong." Her voice choked. "A mother always knows when something is wrong."

"Take your time, Mrs. Cunningham," Victor said gently, knowing this was hard on the woman. He opened a small, green tablet to take notes.

Mrs. Cunningham visibly shaken, continued. "I guess it was a mother's intuition. A mother knows when something is not right."

"Yes ma'am," Victor replied.

"I came over to check on her. When Tamara didn't answer the

door. I used my passkey to let myself in. I went into the bedroom and found her in the bed."

"Did you hear anything? Notice or see anything suspicious?"

Mrs. Cunningham shook her head. "No. I saw her come in last night with her male friend. She was fine. Everything was quiet."

"Male friend?" Victor repeated.

"Both came in last night around 2:00 a.m. It was 2:04 exactly. I looked at the clock on the VCR," she said proudly.

"Do you know her friend's name?" Victor asked.

"No."

"Can you describe him?"

Mrs. Cunningham frowned. "Well," she began. "I'm not good at giving description."

"Is he taller than me?" Victor coached. "Shorter?"

"Definitely shorter." Mrs. Cunningham turned and looked at Benitez who stands at around 5'10". "He's a little taller than this gentleman. Slim built. Around 165-170 pounds. He's African-American. About thirty. Drives a white BMW."

"White BMW?" Benitez inquired.

"I'm sorry," she apologized. "I can't tell you the year of the car."

Victor asked a few more questions. He found out Lieutenant Tamara Hill had transferred to the post over two years ago. She was a quiet, respectful tenant. Mrs. Cunningham didn't know if she had any enemies.

Victor took a card from his wallet and handed it to Mrs. Cunningham. "If you think of anything, anything at all, don't hesitate to call me or Captain Benitez."

Mrs. Cunningham left the quarters without a backward glance.

"Let's go take a look," Victor said with a sigh.

"It's not a pretty picture," Benitez said as they headed toward the bedroom. Benitez didn't exaggerate. The contents of Lieutenant Hill's black purse were dumped on the floor next to the bed. The victim laid on her back, nude, her eyes open and staring. Her mouth was opened in a silent scream.

"What a shame," Benitez said. "She was a beautiful woman." He picked up the photo of her on the floor with a gloved hand. He showed the picture to Victor of an attractive, fair skinned, light eyed woman with a medium figure. It was clear from the imprint and the black nylon stocking around her neck that she'd been strangled.

Victor leaned forward slightly and examined the corpse. The lips and fingernails were pale. The body was cold, and parts of it were hard. He turned to Benitez. "What time did the coroner place the time of death?"

Benitez opened his notebook. "The Coroner placed the time of death between two and six this morning."

"Any signs of forced entry?"

Benitez shook his head. "No. I'm willing to bet Lieutenant Hill knew her killer."

Victor nodded. "I'd say you were right."

ぼ &

Senator Harold Upton stared out the window of the library. No matter what directions he chose, he could only see the beam of light that illuminated the spacious background of the old Colonial split-level house that he and Rosetta purchased after his retirement. He looked up at the twinkling of the stars. Life was funny, he thought. It had a way of bringing transgressions back to you. Transgressions you tried to forget. Maybe he should have discussed the situation with Victor. He could trust him. Bradford Farrell, his administrative assistant says no one would understand, and if anyone found out it would hurt his chances for reelection. Don't worry, Bradford had said. He would handle the situation.

He might as well go to bed. There was nothing he could do about it tonight. Just let Bradford do his job. The Senator pushed himself out of the chair, left the library, and walked up the circular staircase. Quietly, he opened the bedroom door and slipped inside. Rosetta had been asleep for hours, and he didn't want to wake her.

"Thinking about your discussion with Victor?" Rosetta asked, pushing herself up on one elbow.

"I thought you were asleep." Harold turned toward the bed. He leaned over and pressed the button on the bedside lamp. "What makes you think I'm thinking about Colonel Sexton?"

"Because I know you." She chuckled, sitting up straight in bed. "I know how much you were looking forward to working with him again."

Harold chuckled. The simple act released the tension that had swelled up inside him. He loved this woman for thirty-six years and didn't want to lose that. They'd met when he attended a cookout thrown by her father, Colonel Rogers. From that day forward she'd been his inspiration. His life. His love. She respected and trusted him.

"I could never fool you," Harold said, removing his white shirt.

Rosetta pushed the covers aside and got out of bed. She wore a silk, off-white, clinging gown that showed off her body. At fifty-two, she was still desirable to him; big-boned, not fat but bosomy, and firm. She was never able to give him children, but he didn't love her any less. Raising Dominique together after the death of his younger sister, Vanessa, filled the void in their lives. He felt like he was raising their own child.

"No, you can't." She tenderly pressed her lips to his.

"I'm not beaten, yet," he said, wanting her. He pulled her close and smelled the scent of the perfume she always wore. Conflicting activities sometimes kept them apart that when they were together the times were special. He thought she would have disapproved when he decided to run for Senator. After all, she had gone through numerous deployments, followed him from post to post, and country to country. He'd promised to settle down when he retired. But he should have known, she'd been supportive, traveling and campaigning beside him. Harold held her body tighter, feeling his own arousal. He turned her face to his and found her mouth.

"Senator, what would your constituents think of your actions?" Rosetta asked in a low, sexy voice, breathing against his ear.

"I'm sure they would think Senators need love too," Harold said, easing her down onto the bed.

"They're right," Rosetta crooned.

DAY FOUR - MONDAY

"Attention!" Private Atkins bellowed and stood at attention upon Victor's arrival the next morning at CID. Benitez accompanied him. They'd spent the early part of the morning at the Coroner's office and then stopped at the Personnel Division.

"At ease," Victor commanded. "Good morning, Private Atkins," he spoke, stopping at the Charge of Quarters' desk.

"Good morning, sir."

"Any messages?"

"Yes, sir." Private Atkins handed Victor several messages. One from the Post Commander, Brigadier General Andrew Goss, Major Stockton from the Public Affairs Office, and Lester Hill, father of the victim. No doubt he wanted to know what happened to his daughter.

Although Victor didn't have biological children of his own, he considered his niece, nephew, and soldiers under his command his own. He understood what Lester Hill was going through and sympathized with the family. The loss is deep. Lester wanted answers. So did Victor. Who would commit such a crime? Why? Questions Victor didn't have the answers to at the moment.

"Why would anyone want to kill Lieutenant Hill?" Victor glanced at the photos Benitez had handed him moments ago. He tossed the photographs on his desk and leaned back in the chair. He sighed and ran his hand down his face. "What do we know?"

"Just what the report confirmed for us." Benitez handed Victor a large manila folder. "Lieutenant Hill was strangled. No sign of forced entry. Nothing appeared to have been taken. Time of death was between two and six in the morning. We're waiting to see if Forensics can identify any usable fingerprints and the Coroner's report."

Victor nodded and took the report as Benitez reached for Lieutenant Hill's military personnel records.

"Let's see. Name. Tamara Hill," Benitez read. "Black female, 30 years old, five-six, one hundred and twenty-five pounds. Born in St. Louis, Missouri. Graduated with a Bachelor of Science degree in Nursing from Morgan State University in Baltimore, Maryland. Joined the army six years ago. Never married. One child. A son, four-years old. It says here, the son lives with Lieutenant Hill's mother, the grandmother in Baltimore, Maryland."

Victor shook his head. "Jesus."

"That's it," Benitez said. "I'm going back over to the crime scene to take another look. Maybe we missed something. I'll check in later."

"Keep me posted."

"Yes, sir," Benitez said. He rose from the chair and started toward the door, then paused. "We will find whoever did this."

"I know we will," Victor answered. "I have three days to do it."

Benitez left the office. A moment later, he stuck his head back inside the door. "Heads up. General Goss is on his way in."

Victor stood to his feet in anticipation of the General's arrival. He sighed again and ran his hand along the back of his neck. "It's too early in the morning," he groaned.

Brigadier General Andrew Goss waltzed in the office, accompanied by his two aides, Lieutenant Charles Lux and a female civilian, Dakota March. He stood only a little over 5'8", but his mean temper made up for his height. He could easily pass for a Ross Perot look-alike.

He must have come directly from his morning run because he was still dressed in his black and gray running suit. Victor had watched him deal with numerous cases on and off post: robberies, drugs, burglaries, even arson. However, he'd never shown up at his office unannounced and with a tight face.

"You mind telling me why you haven't returned my phone call?" General Goss asked with that Southern drawl of his. "I have upset parents wanting to know what happened to their daughter. I had the media first thing this morning ringing my phone off the hook. I don't know what to tell them because the Commander of CID," his voice rose an octave, "won't return my phone calls. For your sake, Colonel, I hope that means you have something to tell me."

Victor took General Goss through what he and Benitez found at the crime scene and what the witness, Mrs. Esther Cunningham, had shared with them.

"It's not very much," his assistant, Lieutenant Dix, chimed in.

"It's a start," Victor answered with a non-committed glance. He then refocused his attention back to General Goss. "It's only been a couple of hours, sir. We haven't had time to follow up on what we have. We're waiting for results from Forensics and the Coroner. I assure you, sir, when I have something you will be the first to know."

General Goss seemed to be satisfied with the reply. Victor could have sworn he noticed his shoulders sagged just a little. "Make sure that you do. I don't have to tell you how this murder has affected this small military community."

"No, sir, you don't."

"The sooner the killer is caught and behind bars, the better it will be for everyone. Therefore, I want you to follow this investigation wherever it leads."

Victor nodded.

"Another thing," General Goss continued with his list of instructions. "I don't want anyone talking to the press without talking to me first. Understand? We want to be careful about leaks to the press. We don't want a panic on our hands."

The others filed out of the room, but General Goss stayed behind. "I know this is a difficult time for you, with you retiring in a few days."

"You don't have to worry, General. I know I'm working on borrowed time, but I owe it to her family to find out who murdered Lieutenant Hill."

General Goss nodded. "You forgot someone."

"Who?" Victor asked curiously.

"Me. It happened on my post. Whatever you have to do, do it quickly," he ordered, then walked out the door.

After General's Goss visit, Victor turned his attention back to the homicide report. His thoughts switched to Dominique. Both women were close in age, nurses, and female officers. He pushed the thought aside. He didn't want to think how it could have been her. He picked up the personnel record again and read down the computer-generated sheet until he found her work section. She was assigned to Bravo Company, Walter Reed Army Medical Center.

Chapter Seven

*R*obbin went to the ladies locker room. She studied her appearance in the mirror. Her eyes were red from lack of sleep. Turning on the faucet, she splashed some cold water on her face. Everything was going to work out.

She glanced at her watch. It was 7:30 a.m. Tamara still hadn't shown for work. As soon as she arrived, Robbin was going to have a word with her. The moment Thomas came home, she'd gone ballistic, yelling, screaming, and demanding Thomas end the affair. He insisted nothing was going on between them and he only gave her a ride home.

Despite the way things were between them, Robbin was determined to remain in the marriage. It could be salvaged once Tamara was out of the way. She would remind her that adultery is conduct unbecoming of an officer and is a crime under military law. If that didn't work, she would go straight to Dominique and report the relationship. Yes, things were going to work out fine.

Robbin washed and dried her hands, walked out of the ladies room, and headed back to the registration area. She picked up the next chart to be triaged with satisfaction as she waited for Lieutenant Hill to show up.

෪ ෨

Dominique began Monday morning listening to reports from the eleven to seven shift. Checking the staff's accountability, she'd discovered that Lieutenant Tamara Hill had not shown up or phoned her status. It was unlike her not to report for work.

Despite the hustle and bustle of the emergency room and recounting of the medication, Dominique couldn't keep her mind off Victor. No matter how she denied it to herself, she missed him after he was called to CID. The atmosphere wasn't the same after his departure. All he'd said was there was an emergency on post and he had to leave. Jealous, she stood by and watched him kiss Rosetta on the cheek and shake Harold's hand. When he said goodbye to Dominique, he'd simply nodded his head and left.

Dominique swallowed hard. After the way she'd treated him, she couldn't blame him if he never spoke to her again. Victor had tried to apologize but she refused to let him get a word in. *You could have at least let him explain,* she thought. *Stupid!* She was supposed to be angry, but she couldn't deny how her heart beat faster when he kissed her fingers. When he revealed he still cared about her, Dominique's body felt warm all over. There was no doubt about that. *Fate.* Victor said he believed in it; that he believed they were given a second chance. She wasn't so sure about that.

Dominique relocked the Narcotic Box and stepped into the emergency room. Doctors, nurses, medics, and technicians were attending to active duty, retirees, and their dependents.

"What happened?" Dominique asked a young man in the waiting room. His companion, another male, was assisting him. The injured man stared at her. She noted the rigid set to his strong jaw line. He was in pain. He attempted to put pressure on his foot and then winced in discomfort.

His frown deepened. "I was running in physical training formation this morning. I misjudged the height of the sidewalk and landed incorrectly. I think it's a sprain. I don't believe it's broken. I can move my toes." He looked at her. Vertical lines appearing in his blue eyes.

The other gentleman helped him to a brown, oval shaped chair. "I had to talk him in to coming here to have his ankle looked at."

Dominique signaled to a passing medic. "Take his military identification card, sign him in, and then let's get one of the doctors to put in an order for Radiology," she commanded in a soft tone. The soldier pushed himself to a standing position, and with his uninjured foot, hopped over to the registration desk.

Dominique's gaze swept around the area and landed on a young Hispanic woman sitting alone with a little girl who looked around 2-years-old. The mother attempted to comfort the toddler, placing her on her right shoulder, rocking to and fro, and speaking soothing words in Spanish. The child let out a wail of a scream.

Dominique turned and walked over to the registration area, an expression of concern on her face. She wasn't fluent in Spanish and knew no one on her immediate staff that could translate. If the patient did not speak English, she'd have to place a call to the staff duty office and ask for a translator.

"Robbin, has anyone attempted to take information on the mother with the toddler sitting out in the waiting room?"

"We attempted to interview her, but no one can speak Spanish. I phoned the staff duty office. They are sending someone."

"How long ago was that?"

"About fifteen minutes ago."

Dominique sighed. "That's a long time." She looked out in the waiting area to see that the mother was now pacing back and forth trying to calm the child. "Did they say how long it's going to be?"

"No. Just that they were sending someone."

"I'll phone them again," Dominique muttered and headed towards her office.

"Good luck. You know how slow they can be."

Dominique had only been in charge of the emergency room a short time, but she ran an efficient department. Patients waiting for an extended period of time was unsatisfactory. No patient should have to wait longer than forty-five minutes before being treated.

Robbin looked up to see Victor walking through the emergency room door. Dominique didn't divulge what happened between them. She hoped he was coming to see Dominique. All Robbin knew was that it was only seven-thirty in the morning and Victor was looking good enough to eat. The way she saw it, whatever transpired between them, Dominique would be foolish not to want to work it out.

"Good morning, Lieutenant Greene," Victor spoke, walking up to the registration desk.

Robbin grinned. "Good morning to you, Colonel Sexton. It's good to see you again."

"Same here."

"Come to see Captain Frazier?"

Victor managed a smile at the mention of her name. He was looking forward to seeing her again. He just wished the visit were under a different circumstance. He flashed his badge. "Yes. Is she busy?"

Robbins' smile vanished. "No more than usual." She strolled from around the desk. "She's in her office," she said as she gave Victor directions to Dominique's office.

ʘ ≋ᣙ

"Why didn't I pay attention in Spanish class?" Dominique said to herself as she flipped through her personal Rolodex for the number to the staff duty office.

Suddenly, out of the corner of her eye, she caught a flash of movement in the doorway. "Has the Spanish interpreter arrived?" she asked, turning in the direction of the movement. "It's about time…" The rest of the sentence died in her throat at the sight of the man standing in the doorway.

"Victor? I mean Colonel Sexton," Dominique corrected, remembering they were in a military setting. He was the last person she'd expected to see, but pleased just the same. "I'm always asking you this question, but what are you doing here?"

"I'm here on business," Victor said dryly. "So if you got a few minutes, I need to talk to you." He whipped out his badge, moved from the doorway, and walked farther into the office.

Victor was here to see her, but it was business. Not personal. Her eyes narrowed at the expression on his face as he moved with a slow pace. Upon closer examination, she noticed he looked fatigued. She guessed he didn't get much sleep last night. "Sure, I can spare a few minutes." She motioned to the chair across from her.

"Have a seat."

"Thank you," Victor said, dropping in the chair across from Dominique's desk. He crossed one lone leg over the other. "I'm here about one of your soldiers."

Dominique frowned and sat up straighter. "Which one?"

"Lieutenant Tamara Hill."

Dominique's eyes widened as she sat motionlessly. "What about her?" she said softly. "She didn't show up for work this morning."

"She was found murdered Sunday morning," Victor said, without hesitation. He believed it was the best way to deliver this type of news — straight forward.

Dominique felt like a hole had opened and swallowed her whole. That must have been the phone call he received at her uncle's home. She'd just worked with Lieutenant Hill on Friday. She was so full of life. It was hard to believe that she wasn't going to see her again. She took a deep breath to compose herself then asked, "How?"

"She was strangled."

In response to his answer, Dominique's hand touched her neck. "Oh my God." Just the thought of someone choking the life out of Lieutenant Hill sent a shudder through her.

"We don't have a suspect, yet," he continued. "That's why I'm here. I need to take statements from you and your staff. It may help shed some light on the case."

Dominique cleared her throat. "Of course, anything me or my staff can do to help."

"For starters, can you tell me why anyone would want to kill Lieutenant Hill?"

Dominique blinked. "No. I didn't know her very well. I liked her though. She got along with everyone as far as I know. Very devoted to her job as a nurse. A good officer."

"Any close friends? Boyfriend?" he asked coolly. He was trying his best to be as professional as he could. Maybe Dominique overheard her mention the name of the man that Mrs. Cunningham saw her with.

"She didn't have any close friends as far as I knew. She was friendly enough, but she never allowed anyone to get too close." Dominique dropped her head a moment to collect her thoughts.

"Are you okay?" Victor wanted to take Dominique in his arms and assure her everything would be all right. He would find the person responsible for this horrible crime. For a moment, he almost did. But he held back. It wasn't military regulation.

"Take your time. I know this is hard on you. It's not easy losing one of your soldiers."

The sound of his husky voice sent a warm shiver through Dominique's body. She shifted uncomfortably in her chair. She was feeling guilty. This was neither the time nor place to feel sexual attraction toward Victor. "I'm sorry I'm not able to help you more," she mumbled. "We were not that close."

"You have helped more than you realize." He was watching her intently.

He realized this was the first time he'd seen her in military clothing. She sported a white lab coat over the green uniform. Her hair was twisted in a French braid that sat atop her head. Small stub earrings were attached to her ears. Dominique possessed a natural beauty enhanced by a light application of makeup. Civilian or military attire, she always looked beautiful. "This is the first time I've seen you in uniform," Victor said softly, as if speaking to himself.

"I know." Heat rushed to Dominique's face as she tried not to be affected by his words of remembrance. "I always changed my clothing before we would meet."

Victor cleared his throat again. "I remember."

The ringing of the cellular phone interrupted them and caused Dominique to jump.

Victor groaned. "My cellular phone." He reached inside the front pocket on his uniform and pulled out a black, flat phone. "Excuse me a moment," he said in an exasperated tone.

"Sure," she replied, trying not to listen to his conversation. To busy herself Dominique placed another phone call to the staff duty office. They again told Dominique the interpreter was tied up with another family and would be there shortly. After she hung up she heard Victor tell someone to meet him at the hospital emergency room.

☙ ❧

"We know she was seeing someone. Did she ever mention his name?" Victor wanted to know.

Dominique didn't want to appear nosy, but she wanted to know what was going on. The door to her office was open. Inside, Robbin and another employee, Charlene Flanders were in discussion with Victor and another agent who was introduced as Captain Benitez. Uniformed Officers were questioning other staff members.

Dominique stood outside her office. She could hear Charlene between sobs saying how tragic it was and she hoped they catch the killer soon. Apparently, she had been the last person to speak with Lieutenant Hill on Friday.

"Lieutenant Hill just said they were going on a boat ride Saturday night around the Baltimore Harbor," Charlene said in a broken voice. "She seemed to be in a good mood, looking forward to the date."

Dominique looked into the office and saw Victor was sitting at her desk, taking notes as he spoke with the blonde haired woman. Benitez was standing behind him. Almost on instinct, Victor looked up and saw her.

Robbin spoke, drawing his attention back to the matter at hand. "Tamara kept to herself the majority of the time. She didn't discuss her personal life."

Charlene agreed with Robbin and Victor nodded as he wrote. "How did you know about her plans for Saturday night?" He glanced at Charlene.

"I overheard a phone call she made."

Victor nodded then turned to Robbin.

"What about you, Lieutenant Greene? When did you last see Lieutenant Hill?" Robbin frowned. She seemed a bit rattled by Victor's question. "Friday. I left around 3:45. Lieutenant Hill was still here. She was at her locker in the ladies' room. She was getting ready to leave."

"Did you get along with her?"

"Ah. I guess," Robbin replied.

"So you wouldn't know anything about the man she's been seeing?"

"No," Robbin answered quickly, shrugging her shoulders, "I wouldn't."

Victor fired a few more questions to Charlene and Robbin then dismissed them. The other staff members went through the same routine. No one knew anything.

"No one seems to know anything about the man Lieutenant Hill was seeing," Victor said to Benitez after the last employee left the office.

"Maybe she had a reason for being so careful," Benitez said calmly.

Victor nodded. "Maybe she did. Either she was very private or he was very married."

"Exactly."

"Check on the officers in the women's locker room," Victor instructed.

"Yes, sir," Benitez said, carrying out the orders.

After Benitez departure, Dominique hurried into the office. Victor came from around the desk. "We're almost done in the women's locker room."

"I overheard. You think the man may be married?" Dominique asked.

"Maybe," Victor replied.

"Colonel," Benitez said, sticking his head in the door. "They're finished."

"I have to go. I'll talk to you later. Okay?"

"Okay," Dominique said. Victor gave her arm a light squeeze and walked out the office.

A few minutes later, Robbin came into the office and took a seat across from Dominique.

"Can you believe that?" Not waiting for Dominique to answer Robbin continued. "Lieutenant Hill murdered. Strangled. I still can't believe it."

"I know it's hard to believe," Dominique said. A chill slithered through her.

Victor had no leads and the killer was still on the lose.

CB EO

"Colonel, we got something." Benitez breezed through the doorway back at CID. "Found this in Lieutenant Hill's locker. It may be something."

Victor sat up straight. "What is it?"

"A picture," Benitez explained. "It could be our mystery man."

"Hope so." Victor reached for the picture with a white handkerchief. The picture was Lieutenant Hill in an intimate embrace, cheek to cheek with an African-American man. She was smiling. He flipped it over and read aloud. "Tamara and Thomas Echols. It's dated June 04. Last month. Someone was thinking about marriage."

"Seem like it," Benitez said.

Victor handed the photo back to Benitez. "Let's show the photo to Mrs. Cunningham to see if we get a positive identification. Also, let's get an address on Thomas Echols."

"I'm on it, sir."

Victor followed Benitez out into the main room of CID. "Anything back on the prints?"

Benitez swirled back around to face him. "Not yet, sir." He motioned to Sergeant Santo Juarez to accompany him to Mrs. Cunningham's.

"What's taking so long?" Victor looked around the room and spotted Private First Bone chatting with Agent Tillman. "Bone, get Forensics and find out what's going on with the prints on the Hill case! I needed them yesterday."

"Right away, sir," Bone replied, punching in the phone number.

"Thank you." Victor headed back into his office, slamming the door behind him.

ΩΩ

Dominique was on her way out of her office when the phone rung. Her first intention was not to answer. She was running late for a staff meeting. But instincts got the best of her.

"Hello?" she spoke into the receiver.

"Dominique?"

"Victor?"

"I guess you weren't expecting to hear from me so soon."

"No, I wasn't, but I'm glad you called." He heard Dominique say. Somehow Victor felt she was sincere.

"We may have a break in the case," Victor said. "Found a picture of Lieutenant Hill and a man that may be our mystery man."

Dominique maneuvered the phone to her other ear. "That's good news, Victor."

"My staff is checking it out," he replied. "We should know something shortly."

"You may have the killer?"

"Maybe," he said, then added, "Just wanted you to know. Look, I'm about to plan for dinner. Would you care to join me?"

Dominique realized this may be cause for celebration, but she didn't trust herself to be alone with him. "Victor, why do you insist on asking me out? I've already told you that there can be nothing between us."

She heard him take a deep sigh. "Dominique, why can't it just be two friends having dinner together." Victor paused. "I want to unwind a little with good food and good company."

A pause pounded in Dominique's ears. As much as she denied it, she really did want to see him.

"Dominique," Victor prompted. "You still there?"

Dominique knew she would be making a huge mistake if she became involved with Victor again. When she was around him, all caution flew to the wind. But she wanted to know about the Hill case. Who was the mystery man? "When and where would you like to meet?"

Victor glanced at his watch. It was 1:55 p.m. "How about we meet at Cadence? Seven o'clock? I'll call ahead and reserve a table."

"Okay. I'll see you then," Dominique said.

"See you then."

Click.

Victor closed his eyes briefly, wishing like hell it was a regular date.

Chapter Eight

*V*ictor maneuvered his truck on Kilo Street. He was on his way to see Lieutenant Thomas Echols of the 10th Signal Brigade. After showing the picture to Mrs. Cunningham, she confirmed Lieutenant Thomas Echols was the man coming to see Lieutenant Hill the past couple of months and escorted her home the night she was murdered.

The 10th Signal Brigade was the first brown building on the right side of the street. Soldiers running physical training and singing a rhythmic cadence can be heard in the background. Victor got out of the vehicle and with a confident stroll headed along the brick sidewalk. Three soldiers — two females and one male — were exiting the building. Upon his approach they rendered a sharp salute. "Good afternoon, sir."

He returned the greeting with a snap salute of his own. "Good afternoon."

Victor entered the building and found himself inside the company's headquarters. The tan walls were adorned with military photos of the unit history. Next to those were photos of the Commander-in-Chief, George W. Bush, and Secretary of Defense, Donald Runsfeld.

As he approached the counter, he spotted a blonde female soldier. Her back was to him, facing a computer screen as she typed on a keyboard. "Excuse me, soldier."

The woman turned around and blinked in surprise. Her face broke into a smile at the handsome Victor Sexton. "May I help you, sir?"

Victor reached inside his army fatigue pocket and presented his CID badge. "My name is Lieutenant Colonel Sexton. I'm from CID. I need to speak with your Company Commander. Is he/she in?"

The woman looked him up and down in surprise then said, "One moment, sir." Victor watched her knock on the door of an office a few yards away, then disappeared inside.

"You can go right in, sir," she said as she stepped back outside the office.

"Thank you," Victor said, attempting to read the name on her nametag. "Specialist Gold."

She replied, "You're welcomed, Colonel Sexton."

"Colonel Sexton, come in, come in. I'm Major Willett." The officer introduced himself, zooming from around the desk. Major Theodore Willett could have passed for a college student with his boyish looks. He was athletic looking with a hair cut close to his head. Despite his youthful appearance, Victor knew you didn't get to become a company commander at his age being timid. "What can I do for you?"

"Nice to meet you, Major. I don't want to take up too much of your time. I just want to inform you that CID is interested in questioning one of your officers."

"One of my officers." Major Willett mused. He motioned to the black leather chair across from his desk and then sat in the chair behind the desk.

Victor dropped down in the seat. "Yes. A Lieutenant Thomas Echols. I need to question him about a murder here on post. In the Officer's Quarters."

Major Willett looked at Victor in disbelief. "A murder? Is he a suspect?"

"I didn't say that."

Major Willett nodded his head up and down and said, "I see," then cast Victor a curious glance. He had a feeling the colonel wasn't being straight with him, but there was nothing he could do about it. He picked up the phone and punched in a series of numbers. "Specialist Gold, can you let Lieutenant Echols know I need to see him in my office." Major Willett replaced the phone back in the cradle. "CID just believes he might have known the victim?"

"I'm just following up on a lead," Victor answered as he regarded the man who sat across from him. Major Willet was concerned. He understood. One of his officers could be involved in a terrible situation.

Moments later, the door opened and a tall, slender, African-American male walked in. He looked curiously from Major Willett to Victor sitting across from him. "You wanted to see me, Major?"

"Yes, come on in, Lieutenant Echols. This is Colonel Sexton. He's from CID. He needs to ask you a couple of questions."

Lieutenant Echols face was blank.

Victor stood to his feet and extended a hand. "Lieutenant Echols."

"Colonel Sexton," Lieutenant Echols handshake was firm but a little sweaty. He managed a tight, force smile. "Nice to meet you, sir."

"Same here. I just wish it was under different circumstances."

"Sir?" Lieutenant Echols answered bewildered.

"Can we speak in private?" Victor suggested.

"In my office," Lieutenant Echols offered.

Major Willett looked disappointed. He was hoping to sit in on the meeting to find out why CID wanted to speak with one of his best Signal officers.

"This way, sir." Lieutenant Echols walked out of the office with Victor close behind.

Specialist Gold looked up from her computer screen as they approached. Her smile slipped at the look on the officer's face. She dropped her eyes to her keyboard and resumed typing the document she was working on.

૏ ૐ

"Lieutenant Hill is dead?" Lieutenant Echols repeated. He leaned back in his chair and absorb the news, then clasped his hands together. "When? What happened?"

"Early Sunday morning. Sometime between two and six in the morning. She was strangled."

Lieutenant Echols shook his head from side to side. "I don't believe it. She was such a nice person."

"How well did you know Lieutenant Hill?" Victor asked.

"Not well, sir. I ran into her a couple of times when I visited my wife at the hospital. Lieutenant Greene."

"Lieutenant Robbin Greene?"

"Yes, sir. We've been married two years. She works as a nurse in the emergency room."

Victor felt the stakes in this case just rose a little higher. "I've met your wife. The difference in last names threw me off."

"Yes, sir. My wife is a very independent woman. When we married, Robbin was adamant about keeping her last name."

Victor watched Lieutenant Thomas Echols leaned back in the chair, crossed his arms over his chest. He quickly looked away when their eyes met. It was obvious that the Lieutenant was nervous.

"Relax, Lieutenant Echols. You seem nervous," Victor said.

"It's not that, sir. I'm just wondering what CID wants to talk to me about. I barely knew Lieutenant Hill."

"Only acquaintances?" Victor asked.

"Yes, sir."

"We have a witness that has identified you coming to see Lieutenant Hill for the past several months, and we found this in Lieutenant Hill's locker." Victor reached in his pocket and threw the photo of them together on the table.

Lieutenant Echols eyes widened and Victor noticed a twitch at Lieutenant Echols' lower jaw line. He didn't bother to pick up the picture.

"How do you explain that photo?" Victor asked. "According to what's written on the back, you were more than just acquaintances."

Lieutenant Echols knew he'd been caught in a lie. "That's not against the law."

"Adultery is in the military. You know that. But we're talking about murder."

"What?" Lieutenant Echols was furious. "I didn't kill her. I wasn't even there that night."

Victor sat calmly as he watched Lieutenant Echols closely. A small bead of sweat appeared on his forehead. "You weren't there?" Victor repeated. "The Resident Manager said you were."

"The Resident Manager is mistaken. I wasn't there," Lieutenant Echols sputtered.

Victor stared at him again. "So where were you Sunday morning between the hours of 2:00 and 6:00 a.m.?"

Lieutenant Echols frowned. "I was home."

"Home? Any witnesses?"

"My wife?"

"Your wife?"

"Yes, sir."

"Saturday… Wasn't that your wife's birthday? She threw a birthday party at Cadence's Supper Club."

Lieutenant Echols sat upright. Victor's revelation caught him off guard. "Yes, sir. How did you—"

Victor cut him off. "You wasn't at your wife's party."

Lieutenant Echol's blinked. "We had a argument. I didn't attend," he stumbled out. "When you're married, you have disagreements. You know how it is."

"Of course," Victor replied. "What did you argue about? Lieutenant Hill?"

Lieutenant Echols gave Victor a long stare. "That's personal, sir."

Victor didn't miss a beat. "For the moment. I have one more question. What kind of car do you drive?"

Lieutenant Echols rolled his head to one side. "1996 White BMW," he finally answered.

Victor came to his feet, never taking his eyes off Lieutenant Echols. "That's all I have for now. I'll be in touch."

ଔ ଚ

Pacing back and forth in his hotel room, the killer was basking in the success of his mission. Thinking about it sent a rush throughout his veins like hot flowing lava. His body wound up tight as a coil spring.

Learning to kill had been his reason for joining the army. The elite group — Special Operations — had taught him to be good at it. He was fascinated with death. It didn't bother him to kill and he wasn't afraid to die. He relished the look that comes into the victim eyes when they knew they were about to die, and there was nothing they could do about it. It made him feel powerful, invincible. Nothing compared to having flesh between his strong hands. He pulled the stocking tighter as she fell to her knees. She clawed at his hands, then silence. No one was better at killing than he was. No one. The mission was just like old times. It was so easy. She never knew what hit her. He smirked. He stopped pacing when the headline on the news program caught his attention. He walked over and turned the volume up on the television. *"A female army officer was found dead in her quarters on the army post,"* the newscaster was saying. He was famous. A hero, that's what he was. The adrenaline quickly vanished and was replaced with a boiling anger when he saw the face of Victor Sexton, his former team leader and the man responsible for ruining his military career.

"Major," he said aloud. The subtitled read he was a Lieutenant Colonel. "Well, well, look whose been promoted and now commander of CID."

"We don't have a motive or a suspect at this time," Victor was saying. *"But I assure you we're using every available means to bring the person responsible to justice."*

"That's what you think, Colonel," the killer said to the television. "It was you that taught me everything that I know. But I'm better and smarter. To prove it, just wait until you see what I do next."

ଔ ଚ

"What did you tell them?" Thomas asked Robbin. He'd come home from work frightened out of his mind after Victor questioned him about Lieutenant Hill's murder.

"I didn't tell them anything," Robbin said over her right shoulder as she placed dishes in the automatic dishwasher.

Thomas ran a hand over his face in anguish. "Then how do you explain Colonel Sexton from CID coming to the unit and asking me questions about the murder." His voice rose.

"I don't know!" Robbin screamed back.

Thomas looked at Robbin and scowled. His long, lean legs closed the small gap between them. "He said he knew you."

Robbin didn't like the dark expression she saw in his eyes. She took a careful step back. Thomas has never struck her before, but she believed that was about to change. The kitchen was a small room; compared to Thomas' large frame, it shrunk even more. If she had to make a run for it she wouldn't make it. There was only one way out; that was past Thomas.

"I've met him twice." Robbin raised her chin high as a sign as defiant. "The night when Dominique asked me to go with her to Cadence and again at my birthday party. He's co-owner of the club."

"So, Captain Frazier knows him too?" His eyes stretched in frustration.

"Yes."

Thomas threw his hands up in aggravation. "I know you have discussed our marriage with Captain Frazier. Always running that mouth of yours. Telling her all of our business." He walked into the living room, taking a seat on the sofa. He glanced over at Robbin. "Did you ever tell her you believed I was having an affair?"

Robbin nervously picked up the dishtowel from the kitchen counter. She nodded in response. "Dominique is my friend," she explained. "I needed someone to talk too. I tried talking to you, but you shut me out."

Ignoring Robbin's remark, Thomas came to his feet again and barked, "I bet you also told her that you followed me to Lieutenant Hill's quarters on the night she was killed!"

"Of course not," Robbin answered hastily.

"Colonel Sexton said the resident manager saw me when I walked her to her quarters." Thomas was pacing the living room floor. He made a fist, thrusting it in the palm of his hand. "I just wanted to make sure Lieutenant Hill make it to her quarters' safe. I can tell from the Colonels' questions that he thinks I had something to do with her murder." He failed to tell Robbin about the photo of him and Lieutenant Hill together.

Robbin watched as Thomas walked off his agitation. She didn't believe for a minute that he and Lieutenant Hill just happened to meet the night she was killed. Robbin saw them together. There was a special brand of intimacy between them that night. She had mixed emotions. Love, anger, and sympathy. At the moment she didn't know which was overriding the other.

"If you weren't having an affair with Lieutenant Hill, you wouldn't be in this mess."

Thomas stopped pacing and cut Robbin a look. "I've told you a thousand times that nothing was going on between me and Lieutenant Hill."

"And I have told you that I'm not stupid. I can see right through your lie," Robbin shouted. "If I can see through it, you think Victor didn't see through it?"

"What are you saying?" Thomas threw back at her. "You think I'm lying?"

"Yes. I do," Robbin said in a firm tone. She walked over and stood in front of Thomas. "Admit it, Thomas. You were having an affair with Lieutenant Hill."

Thomas' eyes locked with Robbins. Silence enveloped the room for what seemed like eternity.

Robbin was the first to speak. "Thomas, if we're going to get through this. You have to tell me the truth. We have to be able to trust each other." She reached out taking his hand in hers for reassurance. "You can tell me the truth."

Thomas tilted his head sideways, looking Robbin straight in the face. He frowned and released her hand. "You think I killed her."

Robbin's jaw dropped. "No. No," she mumbled. "I don't think you killed her."

"Yes, you do. I can see it on your face." Thomas was backing away from Robbin.

Robbin attempted to grab his hand. Thomas pulled away. "I want to believe you," she finally admitted. "Victor said Lieutenant Hill was killed between 2 and 4 a.m. You were there at that time. I saw you go into her building. I didn't see you leave."

Thomas' eyes clouded with anger. "I don't believe this. My own wife. Is that what you told Colonel Sexton this morning?" He reached out, grabbed her right arm, and twist.

Robbin felt the pain as it crawled up her arm. "Thomas?" She winced as he applied pressure. "Stop it. You're hurting me."

"Is that what you told the Colonel?" he asked through clenched teeth.

"No. I swear I didn't tell him anything." Thomas must have believed Robbin and released her arm. She quickly took refuge in the kitchen.

Thomas just stared in her direction for a moment. Then like a man defeated he turned and slowly walked over and slumped down on the sofa. He leaned forward and put his head in his hand. Robbin could hear the agony in his voice. "I didn't kill her. We were having an affair," he finally admitted, "but she was alive when I left."

୨୧

Dominique hurried through the door of her apartment. Once inside, she plopped down on the sofa and picked up the remote control. *"The body of a female officer…"*

"Just in time," she said as the army photo of the victim appeared in the right side of the screen. *"…was found dead in her Officer's Quarters yesterday morning on the army post. Lieutenant Tamara Hill, from St. Louis, Missouri, was a nurse assigned to Walter Reed Army Medical Center. Lieutenant Colonel Victor Sexton, the commander of the Criminal Investigation Division, says at the moment they have no motives for the murder and no suspects, but assures the person responsible will be brought to justice."*

The newscaster quickly moved to another story. Dominique sank back onto the sofa. "That's it," she said annoyed, pointing the remote at the TV to turn it off. The newscaster didn't mention Lieutenant Hill was strangled. She guessed Victor didn't want to release that information to the public.

Dominique rose from the sofa and trekked off to the bedroom. She removed her shirt, followed by her pumps. Wearing only slacks and bra, she went into the bathroom.

Looking into the mirror, she jumped back in alarm when she saw the reflection staring back at her. "You look horrible," she said aloud.

Turning on the sink faucet, she splashed some cold water on her face, then rummaged around underneath the sink for her *Anew* revitalizing cream which she applied an ample amount around her eyes. She turned on the water in the tub and added one capful of Raspberry Foam Bath. Along the tub ledge she placed three scented Orchard berry candles and lit them. She removed the rest of her clothing and then wrapped her hair in a towel.

A few minutes later, she slipped down between the bubbles, letting the steamy water slowly ease the stress and tension of today's events away from her limbs and mind. She eased her head back, remembering the sobs and shock of the employees when Victor informed them of Lieutenant Hill's murder. The rest of the shift was oblivious to her, but she was proud of the manner in which the staff managed to deliver excellent medical care under the circumstances. She'd stuck around after the shift in case the staff had questions. She also placed a phone call to the Chaplain Services, asking that they send a representative to give grief counseling.

Dominique's mind then went to Victor. She wondered what he was doing at the moment. What was he thinking? She was sure he'd like to solve the murder. He had only three days left to find the killer.

03 80

Dominique spotted Victor sitting at a table and her mouth went dry at the sight of him. She wondered again why she agreed to have dinner with him.

She approached the table and Victor stood to his feet. He came around the table, taking her in his embrace. She felt warm all over as their bodies meshed together.

"Good to see you, Dominique. I'm glad you could make it on such short notice."

"Hello Victor," she said, her heart rate beating a mile-a-minute. She didn't know what to say or do to ease the sexual tension still between them. *This isn't a good idea,* she thought. If Victor was affected by the embrace, he didn't show it. He pulled her chair out and then sat himself. "Thank you."

"My pleasure."

Dominique looked up at Victor. His expression was unreadable. Their eyes met, hers quickly skidded away. This was going to be difficult. Difficult because she should never have agreed to have dinner with the man who broke her heart three years ago. Difficult because every time she looked at him, she was forced to confront her own feelings for him.

Since he'd come back into her life, she'd been reliving memories. They stayed with her, never leaving. The romantic dinners, walks along the river, she remembered how he ran his fingers through her hair after lovemaking. She shook her head, refusing to think about them.

Dominique didn't want to think about how she fell in love with Victor. She just wanted information about the case. That was the only reason she found herself having dinner with a man who had damaged her emotionally.

Dominique glanced up to find Victor studying her. Just like before, her heartbeat kicked into fifth gear and she felt a wave of heat wash over her. But she had to put the past behind her. She had no future with Victor.

She prayed her voice wouldn't give away her inner turmoil when she spoke. "You mentioned you have a break in the case."

He grinned. "Do you mind if we order first, then talk?" He wanted to put the discussion off a little longer. Dominique and Robbin were close, and he wasn't sure how she would react to Lieutenant Echols being the number one suspect.

"Not at all," she said, avoiding direct eye contact with him. "I'm famished."

Victor signaled for the waiter, Cordell. A few minutes later, he was giving their orders to the waiter. "I'll have a scotch and soda. Dominique will have a cosmopolitan. We will both have the special."

Dominique glanced up at him surprised he remembered her favorite drink. Victor smiled at her response.

Cordell nodded, removed their menus, and walked away.

"That is your favorite drink, isn't it?" Victor asked.

"Yes it is," Dominique replied.

"It's been a long day." Victor's eyes caught hers so that she was unable to look away. He could always get lost in her beautiful, brown eyes. "Your being here has made me feel better," he said smoothly.

Again, she didn't know how to respond. Her mind was blank. The way he was looking at her made her shiver. Dominique cleared her throat. "Victor, I—"

"Dominique," Victor said, cutting her off. "I know how you feel about me," he said. His voice was low and husky.

"You do?" she thought. *"You know I'm still I'm love with you?"*

"But I can't help how I feel," he continued. "So, I guess we're at an impasse."

She nodded. "I guess we are."

His response was a lopsided grin.

Cordell brought dinner and for a few minutes they ate in a comfortable, compatible silence.

Dominique finally interrupted the silence between them. "Is the mystery man married?"

Victor looked up at her. He still wasn't ready to divulge the information to her, but Dominique was determined to know what he'd found out. "Yes, he is."

Dominique shoveled a fork of salad in her mouth. "You're close to making an arrest?" She was dying to know who the suspect was, but wasn't sure how much Victor would or could share with her.

Victor dabbed his napkin at the edge of his mouth. "Very close. We're awaiting results from Forensics and the Coroner's office."

"Good. Whoever did this deserve to be put away for life?"

"I'm looking forward to telling Mr. and Mrs. Hill that we made an arrest in this case. It won't bring their daughter back, but it will give them some closure, knowing the person responsible has been caught."

"I know they will appreciate that."

"When you investigate cases, you never know where the investigation leads."

Dominique didn't know where Victor was going with the statement. She shrugged. "I guess it happens all the time."

Victor took a sip of his drink. "For instance, the man we suspect of killing Lieutenant Hill is Lieutenant Thomas Echols."

The moment he mentioned Lieutenant Echols, Dominique's hand stopped in mid-motion.

"Thomas is a suspect?"

"A witness, the resident manager," he quickly added, "identified him as the man Lieutenant Hill has been seeing for the past several months. He was there on the night she was murdered."

Dominique scowled. "She's sure it's Lieutenant Echols?"

"Positive," Victor replied. "Identified him from the photo that Lieutenant Hill had of the two of them together."

Dominique nodded as she absorbed the information. Lieutenant Echols was seeing Lieutenant Hill. Robbin mentioned at her birthday party that they'd argued earlier in the day and that she'd suspected him of being unfaithful.

Dominique wondered if she should tell Victor of Robbin's suspicion. Would he have to question Robbin? The entire dilemma was surreal. A woman was dead. The case had to be solved. Dominique told Victor earlier that she would do anything to help.

"Dominique?"

She heard her name and looked up to see Victor studying her.

"I know this may be difficult for you. Robbin is a friend, an employee."

"Lieutenant Hill was also an employee. At a time like this, I can't afford to be bias. A soldier, a woman is dead. You have to do your job, no matter where it leads. I understand that, Victor."

"I'm glad you understand."

"I appreciate you letting me know about Thomas. You didn't have too." Dominique swallowed the lump lodged in her throat. Still not sure whether she should tell Victor what she knew about Thomas and Robbin's relationship. "Victor?" she began.

"Yes," he answered.

Dominique took a deep breath, and then said, "What I'm about to tell you may confirm your suspicions about Thomas."

Victor studied her expression. What she was about to divulge to him must not be easy for her to say. "What is it?"

"Robbin suspected Thomas of being unfaithful," she said, feeling as if she had to tread softly. She repeated to Victor what Robbin had told her about Thomas's change of behavior and his coming in all hours of the night.

Victor listened, nodding his head as he followed the story.

"She told me the night of the birthday party that they had argued earlier in the day about him coming home at three in the morning."

Before he could answer, the waiter interrupted them. "Would you care for anything else Colonel? How about dessert?"

"None for me, Cordell, thank you." Victor glanced over at Dominique. "Would you like anything else, Dominique?"

"No, I'm fine."

Cordell removed their plates from the table.

"Lieutenant Echols admits he argued with Robbin," Victor said once Cordell left. "However, he refused to say what they argued about. Now I know why. But he did say that's the reason he didn't attend the party. He also said Robbin can vouch he was home between two and six that morning."

"Robbin and I left here around 1:00 a.m. She was angry with him for not attending. He may have been home, but I don't know. I didn't see or speak to Robbin again until this morning."

"I doubt he was home. Remember, the resident manager places him at Lieutenant Hill at two. She saw him go into her quarters. She didn't see him leave."

"That doesn't mean he killed her," Dominique argued.

"The Coroner placed Lieutenant Hill's death between two and six, which means he's our number one suspect."

"Thomas killed Lieutenant Hill. It can't be true."

"It may be."

She threw him an unbelievable look. "Why would he kill her? It doesn't make sense."

He returned her look. "One reason could be that Lieutenant Hill threatened to tell Robbin about their relationship. Adultery is a crime under military law. That is if Robbin didn't already know about the affair."

Dominique's mouth dropped. "Robbin didn't know. She would have told me."

"Are you sure?" Victor questioned.

Dominique leaned forward in the chair. "Yes, I'm sure. She told me about her suspicions. I'm sure she would have told me if she knew he was having an affair with Lieutenant Hill."

"When I questioned Robbin about Lieutenant Hill's mystery man, she was hesitant in answering. I got the feeling she knew something."

"I don't believe she knew anything," Dominique defending Robbin.

Victor took a deep breath. "There's only one way to find out," he said, coming to his feet. "Let's go pay the Echol's a little visit."

ominique and Victor sat on the sofa and watched a nervous Robbin pace back and forth. "I've told you that Thomas was here with me."

"Robbin." Victor stood. "The resident manager swears Lieutenant Echols escorted Lieutenant Hill around 2:00 a.m. He can't be at two places at once. Which means one of you is lying."

Robbin stopped in a misstep then turned to face Victor. "Are you saying I'm lying?"

"Are you?" Victor threw back at her.

Instead of answering, Robbin said, "I don't know who the resident manager think she saw. Thomas was here. I will swear to that."

"I see," Victor replied. He gave Robbin a hard look then glanced at Dominique.

"Look," Robbin said. "When I came home from Cadence, Thomas was here. We argued about him not coming to my party."

"Why didn't he come to the party?" Victor fired the question at her.

Robbin squared her shoulder in an attempt to calm her nerves. The question made her uneasy. "That's none of your business," she finally said.

"Robbin?" Dominique said surprised at her response.

Victor pointed a finger at Dominique, letting her know he had everything under control. "I'll accept that answer for now. Let's move on. Did you know your husband was having an affair with Lieutenant Hill?"

A moment of silenced followed the question. Robbin's lower lip quivered. She glanced at Dominique as if asking for help. "That's a lie," Robbin fired back.

Victor reached inside his jacket pocket and handed Robbin the photo of her husband and Lieutenant Hill.

Robbin looked at the photo as her hands trembled. Victor could tell she was struggling to keep her composure. "Tamara and Thomas Echols," she read aloud.

"I'm sorry you had to find out this way," Dominique said, putting an arm around Robbin's shoulder to comfort her.

Robbin handed the photo back to Victor. "It doesn't mean he killed her."

As Victor prepared to speak, he was interrupted by the sound of keys turning in the lock. Thomas came through the door. "Robbin, I spoke with…" his voice trailed off when he saw Victor and Dominique standing in his living room. "What are you doing here?"

"Lieutenant Echols," Victor said, greeting him coolly.

The young officer continued to stare at Victor for a moment. "I already answered your questions." His voice was cold.

"We came to see Robbin," Dominique said, trying to calm the situation.

Thomas looked over at his wife, then back to Victor.

Dominique's eyes narrowed as she noticed the situation brewing between the two men. It was obvious that Thomas was still upset over being questioned by Victor. "I had a few more questions to ask your wife," Victor said calmly.

"My wife and I both answered your questions this morning. We have nothing else to say."

Victor didn't blink an eye.

Thomas' voice hardened. "What you are doing is harassing us."

"What I'm doing is trying to solve a murder."

"Then go and find the person responsible and leave us alone," Robbin interjected.

Victor gave Thomas a tight smile. "If you're not involved in Lieutenant Hill's murder, then you have nothing to worry about."

Thomas' face clouded with anger. Without answering, he walked over and stood next to Robbin. "Please leave."

Dominique turned and looked at Victor and then her glance fell on Robbin.

"Robbin, I want you to know that I'm here for you. If you need anything—"

"She won't call you," Thomas spoke for his wife. "Now get out!"

Dominique's eyes misted as she looked at her friend, looking for help. Robbin's response was to cross her arm over her chest and look off.

଼ଓ ଃ୭

"I'm sorry, Dominique," Victor said as he hustled her down the sidewalk to his truck.

"Thomas is her husband, and I understand her standing by him,"

Dominique said as they walked around to the passenger side. Victor held the door open for her. She left her car at Cadence. Victor insisted they take his truck and pick up her car later.

"At the rate they're going, both will wound up in jail," Victor said then came around and slipped behind the wheel.

"I believe she knew Thomas was seeing Lieutenant Hill. If he hadn't shown up, I believe she would have admitted it. She was interested in what proof you had."

Instead of starting the engine, Victor turned toward her. "I know. I'm more convinced than ever that Echols is our killer. Robbin is covering for him."

Dominique looked at Victor for a moment than sighed. "I can't wrap my mind around this, Victor."

"It's always hard to understand."

"Why would he kill her? Committing adultery is one thing. Murder is another."

"The possibility of losing his military career may have backed him into a corner. Bad situations make people do desperate things. We all have said or did things we didn't mean to," Victor said.

She looked over at him. "People should think before they react."

"Sometimes it's just not that easy. You just react, not thinking about the consequence until it's to late."

Dominique shifted uncomfortably.

"Are you referring to yourself?" she asked. She had a felling he was.

"Yes, I am." He glanced sideways at Dominique then turned to face her, looking directly in her eyes. "I'm sorry about what happened in Germany. I received a phone call in the middle of the night. I had to leave."

"Victor—" she tried to interject.

He held up a finger to stop her. "Let me finish. I never meant to hurt you."

Dominique's eyes studied his, trying to gauge his sincerity. From what she knew of Victor he was a man not afraid to admit when he was wrong. He didn't give her a chance to respond.

"I'll take you back to the club to pick up your car." He started the engine. "Then I'll follow you home. It's going to be another long night for me."

"You don't have to follow me home."

"Yes, I do. It will make me feel better."

From the tone in his voice, Dominique knew that arguing with him was useless.

After Victor took Dominique back to Cadence to pick up her car, he followed her home. To be honest she didn't mind. She felt safe with him there.

Victor escorted her to the front door. She reached inside her purse for the key. Victor took it from Dominique, unlocked the door, then handed the key back to her.

He said quietly, "I'll call you tomorrow."

"You look like you can use some sleep."

"I am pretty tired. I'll be all right." He turned to leave.

"What's going to happen to Thomas?" Dominique asked, stalling. She didn't want Victor to leave.

He turned back to look at the woman who stood before him. He didn't want to leave either. Talking about the murder case was the last thing on his mind at the moment. Dominique was more beautiful and alluring then he remembered. He tried not to think about what they once shared, but it was no use. Every time he looked at Dominique, Victor was more determined to renew what they once shared.

"Don't worry about Lieutenant Echols," Victor said in a low, husky tone. He stepped inside Dominique's apartment and closed the door behind him.

"I'm not," Dominique murmured, turning to face him. "I'm worried about Robbin. If Thomas is found guilty, I don't know how she will take it."

"Robbin will be fine. I'm sure she has family and friends like you to offer her support if Thomas is found guilty."

"You said if. So there's a chance of him being found innocent?"

"That's for the court martial to decide."

Dominique dropped her head to hide her disappointment. "I guess that's it then. We're just waiting for the shoe to drop."

"I'm afraid so," Victor said, stepping closer toward her.

"Victor." He pulled Dominique into his arms and held her tight to his chest.

Dominique stiffened but made no attempt to pull away. She couldn't. She snuggled closer to him, drowning in the warm and masculine essence of him.

The contact sent shivers throughout her. Victor lowered his head to hers, and she closed her eyes as his lips brushed hers, lightly, Dominique couldn't help but respond. Victor deepened the kiss. His mouth moved slowly, sensually over hers, more deeply and hungrily. Dominique locked her arms around his neck. The response was his mouth became more demanding, causing a heat wave to wash over her. Victor locked his hips with hers. She could feel his arousal. She was lost. The kiss had her reeling. Then he froze in motion. If it weren't for the fact that she was panting heavily, she would have sworn that she imagined the kiss. She was still locked in the embrace.

Then Dominique heard it. The ringing of the cellular phone. *Not now,* she thought. *Ring. Ring.* She heard the sound again.

"I'm sorry," he whispered and reached inside his jacket pocket. "Hello, I mean, Colonel Sexton," Victor quickly corrected.

Dominique took the time to calm her racing heartbeat. "Outstanding, Benitez. I'll meet you there."

Dominique's head snapped up. The situation had changed immediately. One minute Victor was kissing Dominique passionately and then in the next he was making an arrest.

Before she could digest what was going on, Victor said. "I have to go."

"Is it Thomas?"

"Yes."

"I'm going with you," she demanded.

"What about what happened earlier between you and Robbin?" Victor asked.

"Robbin will need me," Dominique argued. "I want to be there for her."

"Fine. Meet us at CID," Victor said as they headed out the door.

Ω βσ

Robbin opened the door to Victor, Benitez, several civilian agents, and two uniform officers. Her heart dropped into her stomach at the site of them so soon again on her doorstep. She knew it wasn't good news.

"I'm sorry Robbin," Victor said softly.

"Who it is?" Thomas asked, coming from one of the rooms in the back. He stopped dead in his tracks when he saw them.

"Lieutenant Thomas Echols, I have a warrant for your arrest," Victor said.

"What?" Robbin gasped, looking frantically at Victor. "He didn't kill anyone."

"Listen to her!" Thomas exclaimed. "I didn't kill her!"

"We have evidence that says differently," Victor explained. "Positive identification by the resident manager puts you at the scene of the crime, along with your fingerprints."

Fear flashed in Thomas' eyes. "Sir, let me tell you—"

"Don't say another word without an attorney present," Victor instructed and handed Lieutenant Echols over to Agent Ross Tillman.

Robbin watched, desperately, as her husband was handcuffed and read his *Miranda* rights. "You have the right to remain silent. If you give up that right..."

"Victor," Robbin said with tears in her eyes. "You're making a big mistake."

Victor didn't have the words. He doubted anything he could say at the moment could offer Robbin comfort.

"Colonel?" Victor turned around to find Sergeant Juarez coming through the door. "Forensics is here."

"Great," Victor said and met the team at the door and began giving orders. "I want the entire placed checked for anything that will tie Lieutenant Echols to the murder. Check the closets, drawers, and cabinets. Leave nothing unchecked. You know what I want."

"Yes, sir."

While the agents were carrying out the instructions, Victor let Robbin know that Dominique was at CID waiting for her arrival. Robbin was visibly shaken. Victor didn't trust her to drive herself, and instructed one of the uniform officers to take her to the station.

Victor found Benitez and drew him aside. "I'm on my way to the station to see if Lieutenant Echols feels like talking."

Twenty minutes later, Victor entered CID and was met by Dominique and Robbin.

"Victor." Robbin sniffed. "I have something to tell you, something I remembered about the night Lieutenant Hill was murdered."

Robbin had Victors' undivided attention. When he questioned her earlier in the day and again in the evening, he sensed she knew more than what she was disclosing.

"We can talk in my office," he said. He looked at Dominique then led them down the hallway to his office.

Victor placed a chair for both women in front of his desk. "Ladies. Have a seat."

After both women were seated, he sat down behind his desk and made himself comfortable. "Robbin, you have something to tell me?"

Robbin glanced over at Dominique before she began. "On the night Lieutenant Hill was murdered, I saw a man standing outside the building across the street from her quarters."

Victor leaned forward. "You told me you were home with Lieutenant Echols on the night of the murder. Are you changing your story?"

Robbin sucked in her breath. She realized she just ruined Thomas' alibi. She nibbled on her lower lip, troubled eyes rested on Dominique and back to Victor. "Yes."

Victor gestured with his hand for her to continue. "Go ahead. You saw a man standing across the street from Lieutenant Hill's quarters." He opened a black notepad.

Robbin squeezed her eyes shut and gave a deep sigh before she continued. "After I left Cadence, I was on my way home when I spotted Thomas' car traveling in the opposite direction. I was angry he didn't show for my birthday party. I had my suspicion he was having an affair. I made a U-turn and followed him. I was careful not to let him know I was trailing him. Forty to forty-five minutes later he drove onto the post. He parked in front of the Officer's Quarters. I found an empty space a few feet from him."

"What happened next?" Victor said, encouraging Robbin to continue.

"Thomas got out the car and walked around to the passenger side and opened the car door." Robbin dropped her head. "That's when my suspicions were confirmed. Not only was he having an affair, but he was having it with Lieutenant Hill, my coworker." She shook her head in disbelief.

"You didn't know he was seeing Lieutenant Hill until that night?" Victor asked.

"No."

Dominique could only imagine what Robbin was going through. Working alongside the woman for the past several months only to find out about Lieutenant Hill the way she did. It had to be heartbreaking.

Victor nodded as he wrote. "What did you do after you found out about Lieutenant Hill?"

"After they went inside the building, I started to follow them. I was angry," Robbin emphasized. "My intentions were to confront them both."

Dominique opened her mouth to speak than thought better of it. Not sure she would not have reacted the same.

"As I was about to enter the building. It occurred to me that I didn't know what room they went inside." Robbin closed her eyes again.

Dominique glanced at Victor. His expression was unreadable. She couldn't tell what he was thinking.

"I decided to leave and approach Lieutenant Hill on Monday morning," Robbin said.

"So you left without speaking to your husband or Lieutenant Hill?" Victor asked.

"Yes. I left," Robbin said in a tone barely above a whisper.

"What time did you make it home?" Victor asked.

"Around 2:40 a.m."

Victor fired off the next questions. "Your husband?"

Robbin thought for a second. "Around three. He arrived about twenty minutes after I did."

"Which gives him an hour to commit the murder," Victor pointed out.

Robbin swallowed the truth then said, "Thomas didn't kill her. The man standing across the street could be the killer."

"This man. Can you describe him? Was he black? White? How tall would you say he was? What did he look like?"

"It was dark." Robbin wrapped her arms around herself. "I didn't get a good look at him. From what I could see, he was medium height, around five-ten, medium build, and the man was white."

Victor looked at Dominique then back at Robbin. The sketchy description Robbin gave him confirmed his suspicious. She would do or say anything to get her husband off the hook. It never failed. First it was the fake alibi that didn't pan out now it's a dreamed up suspect of another race. He looked at Robbin and sighed. It wasn't going to work. All the evidence he had pointed toward her husband.

Victor arched an inquisitive eyebrow. "You can't give me a better description?"

Robbin took a deep breath then said, "I didn't get a good look at him, but I'm positive about his race. It was strange, eerie. I turned around and there he was standing there. It was as if he was watching, waiting for someone. When I saw him, he stepped back behind the building."

"He saw you?" Dominique finally said out of concern.

Robbin frowned. "I parked under the light. He could have. I'm not sure."

Victor picked up the stack of papers on his desk, aware that both women were watching him closely. "Robbin why didn't you mention this man before?"

Robbin outstretched both hands in front of her. "I had forgotten about it. I mean, I've had a lot on my mind."

Victor swore quietly. He didn't want to hurt Robbin's feeling, but he had to be honest. "Robbin we don't have evidence pointing to anyone except your husband."

Robbin gave Victor a stormy expression. "You don't believe me?"

Victor zeroed in on the hard look Dominique was giving him. He gets the chance to work things out with Dominique after almost three years and this case was ruining it. "Without evidence to prove what you're saying, I can't do anything."

Without waiting to be dismissed, Robbin stood and walked out the door.

"What was that all about?" Dominique snapped. "Robbin is my friend and you had no right to treat her like that."

"How did I treat her?" Victor stood.

"Like you don't believe her."

Victor didn't like what he saw in her eyes but he had to be honest. "I don't believe her."

"Well I do." Dominique eyes locked with his.

"I'm not surprised."

"What if she's telling the truth?"

Dominique held up a hand to silence him. "Wait a second, Victor. Hear me out. What if there is another suspect. Robbin's life could be in danger. You heard what she said. He saw her."

"I don't believe there is another suspect. Robbin invented that story about another suspect to take suspicion off her husband, but I'm not buying it."

Dominique was doing her best to keep her composure. Beside her uncle, Victor Sexton was the most stubborn man she'd ever met. "So, you're not going to investigate?"

"Investigate what? There's nothing to investigate. Medium height, medium build, and Caucasian. The description is very sketchy and fits half of the Caucasian male population in the area. If I were to investigate, I would need more than that to go on."

Dominique knew he was right.

"Look, my agents questioned everyone in the quarters. No one saw a strange, Caucasian man hanging around the area on the night of the murder."

"Someone had to see him," Dominique pleaded.

"Not if he doesn't exist." Victor picked up some papers off his desk and walked over to the filing cabinet.

As far as he was concerned, there was nothing else to discuss on the case.

Dominique trailed Victor. "You know what I think?"

Victor opened the top drawer to the cabinet and gave Dominique his full attention. He could tell she was doing her best to be civil. In this situation he could understand her anger.

"I think you are in a rush to close this case before you retire."

Victor's eyes narrowed, not liking the comment she made. "I know you're angry so I'm going to pretend you didn't say that."

"Then why won't you look at the possibility that there may be another suspect?"

"Because there isn't evidence to indicate another suspect," Victor retorted. "What do you want me to do?"

"Follow up."

Victor shook his head in disbelief. He was not getting through to Dominique. "I know it's difficult for you to accept the truth, because you're close to Robbin," he emphasized.

Dominique gave him a hard look. Victor returned her look with a look of his own. "I followed the evidence. It led me to Lieutenant Echols. As far as I'm concerned, he's the killer."

Chapter Ten

DAY FIVE - TUESDAY

"*I* didn't kill her," Lieutenant Echols exclaimed. "How many times do I have to tell you that?" His face appeared tired and haggard after numerous hours of interrogation. "She was alive when I left."

"I'm not convinced," Victor replied. "Let me tell you what happened. Lieutenant Hill threatened to expose your affair."

"No!" Lieutenant Echols shouted.

"You couldn't let her do that." Victor paced casually behind Lieutenant Echols' seat. "Man who worked so hard to get where you are…"

Lieutenant Echols sighed, shaking his head in denial.

"You couldn't stand by and allow her to ruin your military career. You argued—"

"That's a lie." Lieutenant Echols voice rose again. He was shaking like a leaf on a tree.

"You strangled her. Isn't that what happened?"

"No it isn't!" Lieutenant Echols denied.

"Then what?" Benitez turned a chair backward, straddling it.

"I already told you what happened," Lieutenant Echols replied.

"Tell us again!" Victor snapped.

Lieutenant Echols leaned back in his chair. He wiped his hand over his face, trying to keep his eyes open. "I'm tired and sleepy. I need sleep!" he yelled.

"Tell us what happened that night?" Benitez quipped, ignoring Lieutenant Echols request.

Lieutenant Echols didn't speak for a long time. "We rented a hotel room for a couple of hours, had a romantic evening, then later, we went on a boat ride," Lieutenant Echols began in a groggy voice, "around the Baltimore Harbor."

"What's the name of the boat? What time did you leave? What time did you return?" Victor fired one question after the other.

Lieutenant Echols frowned. "I already told you I don't remember the name of the boat. We laughed. We talked, ate, and danced. The boat made it back to the dock around midnight. I escorted her home and then I left," he stated. "That's it."

Victor stared at Lieutenant Echols for a moment. "The photo we found of you and Lieutenant Hill together," he placed the picture on the table, "she wrote along the bottom: Tamara and Thomas Echols. Did you two ever discuss marriage?"

"I'm already married," Lieutenant Echols said through clenched teeth. "Regardless of what you think, I love my wife."

That's debatable, Victor thought. "So, you never discussed marriage?"

"I didn't. She did," Lieutenant Echols admitted. "I told Tamara I enjoyed being with her. She was a very beautiful woman." He looked from Victor to Benitez. "You saw her."

"Nice looking," Benitez said, glancing over at Victor. Echols was finally talking.

"Pretty," Victor admitted. "But..."

Lieutenant Echols ran his hand down his face. "I was never going to leave Robbin. I told her I was." He shrugged. "That's what she wanted to hear."

"You were stringing her along?" Victor asked.

"Yes. Tamara threatened to tell Robbin," Lieutenant Echols said softly. "So I told her that we had a future together."

"But you never had any intention of leaving your wife?" Benitez asked.

Lieutenant Echols nodded. "No. Never."

"And you expect us to believe that Lieutenant Hill didn't find out that you were stringing her along?" Victor leaned closer into Lieutenant Echols' face, his voice raised an octave. "You fought. Things got out of hand and you killed her. Maybe it was an accident and you didn't mean to kill her."

"No. No." Lieutenant Echols' slammed his hand on the table in protest. "You're not going to pin this on me."

"If you didn't kill her, who did?" Benitez threw in. "Help us out. Was she seeing anyone else?"

Lieutenant Echols' looked up into Benitez face. "I don't know. I never asked."

"What about enemies? Do you know anyone who would want to kill her?" Victor sarcastically asked. "Besides you."

"I have cooperated with you," Lieutenant Echols said in a firm tone. "I have told you everything that I know. But I'm not going to let you pin this murder on me. The next time you speak with me will be through my Attorney. Now take me back to my cell. I have nothing else to say."

ᘓ ᘔ

"I know what I saw." Robbin sat up against the headboard and accepted a cup of Hazelnut coffee from Dominique. "Why didn't Colonel Sexton believe me?" She closed her eyes a moment and dropped her head back, savoring the taste.

Dominique sat gently on the bed and helped herself to a cup of coffee from the bedside tray.

"Thank you, Dominique, for spending the night. You are a true friend." Robbin didn't bother to hide her depression.

Dominique reached out and covered one of Robbin's hands. "That's what friends are for. I know you would have done the same for me."

"Friends." Robbin managed a tight smile. "I didn't act like much of a friend last night when I allowed Thomas to ask you to leave."

Dominique offered a dry smile. "Don't worry about it. We have to concentrate on Thomas. Besides, I'm not so sure I wouldn't have done the same if I were in your shoes."

Robbin sat up straighter. "That's one of the things I like about you. You're always thinking about the other person. I haven't been able to think about anything else. I can't believe this is happening. It's like a nightmare. They wouldn't even let me talk to him last night."

Dominique took a sip of coffee to think about what Robbin disclosed last night in Victor's office. She admitted she was at Lieutenant Hill's quarters and she'd seen someone standing across the street. Victor was right, Robbin knew about the affair.

Dominique cleared her throat. "Robbin," she said and placed her cup and saucer on the tray. "What you told Victor last night about the stranger, was it true?" She wanted to know if Robbin was being truthful or was it a last desperate attempt to save Thomas. She scooted closer to Robbin. "Was it the truth? Did you really see someone?"

Robbin's hand stopped in mid-motion and she looked over the rim of the cup. "Of course it is."

"I know you want to help Thomas. That's why I have to know the truth."

Robbin looked Dominique in the face and caught her meaning. "I know I wasn't honest in the beginning and I understand your apprehension about me, but I saw him. You don't have to believe me." She placed the cup and saucer on the tray. Throwing the comforter back, Robbin got out of bed and strolled to her closet.

Dominique watched with confusion on her face. "Wait a minute, Robbin."

Robbin removed a pair of jeans and a Howard University sweatshirt. "First, Victor accused me of lying, now you." She laid the clothing on the bed and waltzed to the chest drawer, removing a pair of white underwear with matching bra. "I should have known you would take his side."

"I didn't say you were lying."

"Well, I'm going to go back and have another word with that *boyfriend* of yours." Robbin began dressing. "I'm going to find out what I have to do to convince him to look for the man I saw."

"You want me to go with you?" Dominique asked. "I'm worried about you."

"No. Don't worry about me. I'll be fine. You better hurry or you'll be late for work."

Dominique glanced at her watch. It was 6:30 a.m. She had thirty minutes before the shift began. She reached for the telephone on the table beside the bed and punched in some numbers. "Lieutenant Davies, this is Captain Frazier. I'm running late, but I should be there in an hour. Let everyone know. Also, Lieutenant Greene won't be in." She gave Robbin a concerned look. Instead of hanging up, she asked a few questions. "Is it busy?" She listened for a moment. "Doesn't sound as if it was too bad. Any of the other staff members call out?" She nodded then said, "Yes, I know about Latosha. She told me she had a doctor's appointment this morning. Anyone else?" She listened again. "Sounds good. I will see you later." She hung up and looked at Robbin. "I gave you the day off to take care of whatever you need."

"Thank you. I can't face anyone right now."

"I understand." Dominique gave Robbin a hug of encouragement.

Robbin forced a tight smile. "I'm sorry, Dominique. I didn't mean to blow up at you."

"I forgave you already. It's going to be okay." Dominique picked up her purse from the ottoman at the foot of Robbin's bed and placed it on her shoulder. "I'll call later to check on you."

ಇ ಇ

Dominique was running an hour and half late. Morning traffic on Georgia Avenue was bumper to bumper. She arrived home and made a beeline to the bathroom, showered, changed into her military uniform, and was out the door again.

As she sat in traffic, Dominique thoughts wondered to what had transpired in the last twenty-four hours. Everything was a mess. Not only the arrest of Lieutenant Echols, but also her relationship with Victor, if you can call it that. The arrest, Dominique can learn to handle. Her relationship with Victor, she wasn't so sure about. A shudder heated her body as she thought back to the kiss they shared last night. She could just imagine what could have happened if they weren't interrupted. As much as she was still attracted to Victor, she can't allow herself to get carried away, and believe things had changed between them. Victor was still the man who hurt her, and his rush to arrest Lieutenant Echols didn't help matters either. Any thought about reconciliation between them was a dream.

Dominique sighed. She better focus on something else, like Robbin. She was concerned about her and didn't want to leave her alone. She hoped Robbin would be able to get some rest. Maybe she could leave work early and swing by to check on her.

She drove up to the army gate, showed her military identification to the guard, and then drove into the underground garage. She managed to find an empty parking spot, but it was pure luck. Parking at Walter Reed was horrendous.

A few minutes later, Dominique walked through the doors of the hospital and headed in the direction of the emergency room. She stopped at the nurse's station before heading to her office.

"Finally made it." Charlene grinned as she hung up the phone.

"It was madness." Dominique plopped down in a chair next to Charlene's desk. "Driving along Georgia Avenue is just madness. Bumper to bumper."

"All the time," Charlene replied. "Regardless of the time you travel."

"Any messages?"

"A few," Charlene said, handing her several sheets of phone messages and the correspondence that had come in that morning.

"Thanks," Dominique said, absently, going through her messages. Nothing that couldn't wait. Several reporters had called. Her Aunt. Dr. Shell from Radiology. She would call back. "Let everyone know I'm here and I'll be out in a minute," she said over her shoulder on the way to her office. She tossed the messages from the reporters in the trashcan.

Dominique placed her purse in the bottom drawer of her desk and locked it. As she headed out the door she said a quick prayer. *Lord help me make it through the day.*

Around one o'clock the pace in the emergency room slowed enough for Dominique to make a trip to the hospital cafeteria to purchase lunch. She decided upon a salad with Italian dressing. She took a seat at the table in the employee lounge. It was the first time she had been off her feet in hours. She was greeted by Dr. Rice who talked nonstop about how much her and her husband enjoyed Robbin's birthday party. Several other employees trickled in taking late lunches. "Captain Frazier, have you spoken with Lieutenant Greene?" Charlene placed a Tupperware bowl in the microwave and set the timer. "How is she doing?"

"I spoke with her this morning," Dominique replied lightly. "She's holding up okay under the circumstances." Lieutenant Thomas Echols arrest was the buzz of the emergency room. It was the leading story on the local news and the morning paper.

"I still can't believe it." The timer on the microwave went off. Charlene removed the bowl and took the empty chair next to Dominique. "When CID was questioning me, I have never been so scared in my life. I never would have guessed Lieutenant Hill was seeing Lieutenant Greene's husband. I was blown away when I turned on the news and saw he'd been arrested for her murder." Charlene shook her head in disgust. "You never know people."

"You think Lieutenant Greene knew about the affair?" Dr. Rice asked, biting into a chicken salad sandwich.

"A woman always knows." Charlene shoveled a fork of spaghetti in her mouth then dabbed it with a napkin. "We have an instinct for that type of thing," she said, leaning closed to Dominique.

Dominique enjoyed working with Charlene. She was a beautiful person, very efficient at the registration desk, but she was nosy and was in everyone's business. She could just imagine what the environment would be like if Robbin was at work.

"Robbin didn't know about the affair," Dominique murmured in reply to Charlene's comment.

"What Lieutenant Hill did was scandalous," Latosha said, looking up from her Psychology book she'd been reading. Latosha Hunter was a nursing student in her second year of school at a local university. She was married to an army sergeant. "Sleeping with an employee husband... that's off limits."

"Would it had been better if Lieutenant Hill didn't work with her?" Dr. Rice asked.

"Of course not!" Latosha exclaimed. "I'm just saying, she was working with Lieutenant Greene every day, knowing she was sleeping with her husband." She waved her hand in mid-air. "Just lets you know how much character she had."

"None," Charlene chimed in.

"You can't just blame Lieutenant Hill," Dominique said softly. "Both were wrong."

"That true," Jacqueline Dupont, a civilian nurse said. "Let's not forget Lieutenant Hill is dead. It was a senseless death."

"You don't think Lieutenant Hill did anything to hasten her death?" Latosha chimed in.

"What does that have to do with anything?" Jacqueline argued. "He didn't have to kill her."

"He hasn't been found guilty of Lieutenant Hill's murder," Dominique said in Thomas' defense. "That's for the court martial to decide."

"He will be," Jacqueline said.

"I never noticed anything between them," Dr. Rice said. "Did you?" she asked, not addressing the question to anyone specific. "He would come to see Lieutenant Greene. They would go to lunch together. He seemed like a nice guy. I thought they made a nice looking couple."

"I noticed he wasn't at the birthday party." Latosha closed her Psychology book.

"Now we know why," Charlene said.

"That's because he was busy killing Lieutenant Hill," Jacqueline quipped.

Dominique shot her a look. Jacqueline has worked for Walter Reed over twenty years but Dominique had been working with her only a short time. Dominique noticed Jacqueline was a dedicated nurse who wasn't afraid to speak her mind. She has never been married, no children, and never had anything good to say about anyone or anything.

"I hope they give him the death penalty," Jacqueline said without feeling.

"They don't have the death sentence at Fort Leavenworth," Latosha argued.

Jacqueline rolled her eyes. "Yes they do."

"I feel sorry for Lieutenant Greene," Dr. Rice said, changing the subject "She is such a nice person and didn't deserve what happened to her. That's who we should be concentrating on."

"I agree," Dominique added.

"Let Lieutenant Greene know if she needs anything, anything at all," Dr. Rice said. "She can call me anytime. My door is always open."

They all nodded in unison.

"I wonder if CID will question us again." Charlene smiled.

"I hope not," Latosha replied, standing to her feet. She pushed her Psychology book into her book bag. "I never want to see them again."

"I would love to see Lieutenant Colonel Sexton again." Charlene fanned herself. "He's hot."

Dominique head swung around to look at Charlene.

"You mean Colonel Sexy," Latosha added.

Everyone laughed except Dominique.

"Colonel Sexy?" Dr. Rice's face beamed. "Aren't you married?"

"Married, not dead. That man is sexy." Latosha grinned.

"I didn't see a wedding ring," Charlene pointed out, waving her fork in mid-air.

"That doesn't mean anything today," Jacqueline said as Dominique was leaving the lounge. Though she and Victor were at odds, the last thing she wanted to hear was other women drooling over him.

ೠ ೞ

They had made an arrest in Lieutenant Hill's case, Victor thought as he entered CID. The first thing he'd done this morning was to stop by Military Community Lodging and paid respects to Lieutenant Tamara Hill's parents and son. They flew in from St. Louis to accompany their daughter's body home. He was proud to share the news that a suspect was in custody.

"Sir, General Goss phoned," Private Atkins said as Victor passed her desk. "He says to give him a call as soon as you get in."

Victor imagined the General would be on pins and needles until they had taken a suspect into custody. The arrest made the ten o'clock news last night. He'd followed orders, not giving demographics until counsel represented Lieutenant Echols.

"I'll give him a call," Victor said over his shoulder as he headed into his office.

There were several other messages on his desk. Victor settled himself in his chair behind the desk. He picked up the telephone and punched in the familiar numbers. On the third ring, General Goss's clear, authoritative voice answered. "General Goss, this line is secured. How may I help you, sir or ma'am?"

"Good morning, General Goss. This is Lieutenant Colonel Sexton."

"Colonel, congratulations on the arrest. Well done."

"Thank you, sir." Victor filled him in on what led up to the arrest of Lieutenant Thomas Echols.

ೠ ೞ

The killer stood staring at the Washington Post article on Lieutenant Tamara Hill's murder he'd cut out and tacked on the motel wall. He turned and walked over to the bed, kneeled, and removed the old battered brown accordion held with a rubber band. In the folder, he had memorabilia from his military career —

awards, medals, and photos he'd kept over the years. He pulled out pictures. The first, a company photo from basic training. He looked so young, proud, and eager to serve this country. Ready for whatever assignment that came his way.

He looked at the next photo taken five years later. His first special operation mission. The unit successfully apprehended a drug lord. Major Victor Sexton stood on the back row, his face unmoved. The rest of the men dressed in heavy camouflage, smiled, and acknowledged the camera lens. They were arrogant, cocky, and felt unstoppable. They were like family or so he thought. He stuffed the photos back in the folder.

Standing to his feet, he pulled the brown army tee shirt over his head. The clinking sound of his dog tags could be heard as he strolled over and stood in front of the mirror, admiring his muscular physique. He was always in good shape, but stronger now. He lifted weights daily. What else could he do in prison?

He flexed his left biceps, then the right. "Lieutenant Hill never stood a chance," he boasted aloud. He massaged the scratch on his right hand. She had dug her nails in his hand as he pulled the stocking tight. Her fingernail had broken the skin.

He resumed posing again, going through various poses. A moment later, he assumed the front leaning rest position and began during pushups. Soon the colonel would hear from him again.

He will never catch me. The colonel isn't smart enough. He even arrested the wrong man, he thought as he completed the first ten repetitions.

The woman had seen him...11, 12, 13, 14. He was pumped up and looking forward to snapping her neck as well.

erald Sexton looked up from his paperwork when Victor walked into the Office at the club. Victor looked fatigued. He'd been working nonstop since the murder of Lieutenant Hill.

"I heard on the radio you made an arrest in the Hill murder," Gerald said.

Victor made a beeline for the sofa. He stretched his long body out, crossing his legs at the ankles. "Yeah, I got him."

"You don't sound too enthusiastic about it."

Victor ran his hand over his baldhead in frustration. The gesture did little to erase the scene that played between him and Dominique in his office this morning. Her accusation about him rushing to make an arrest troubled him. "It's not that."

"What is it?" Gerald asked, not looking up while he continued to write.

"It's Dominique."

"I thought you two were getting along."

"I thought we were too."

"What happened?"

"The suspect I arrested is Robbin Greene's husband."

Gerald's head popped up. "What?" He came from around the desk, dragging a chair behind him. He planted himself in front of the sofa. "Did he do it?"

"Everything points to him." Victor closed his eyes. His long fingers massaged his forehead as if he were in deep thought.

"How's Dominique involved?"

"She believes I rushed to make an arrest in the case because I'm retiring in a couple of days." Victor didn't want to elaborate more on the situation at the moment.

Gerald straightened. "If he's guilty, how can she believe that?"

Victor swung his legs around and stood to his feet. He walked over to the personal refrigerator and helped himself to a bottle of water. "She believes he's innocent."

"Dominique and Robbin are close. Naturally she believes he's innocent." Gerald watched Victor grab an extra bottle.

"I wish it had turned out differently. Lieutenant Echols was having an affair with Lieutenant Hill," Victor explained, as he walked over to Gerald and handed him the bottle. He recaptured his seat.

"You're kidding," Gerald said drawn into the story. He'd wanted to know the circumstances surrounding the case.

Victor twisted off the cap, shaking his head from side-to-side. "He'd been seeing her for the past couple of months. Matter-of-fact, they were together the night of Robbin's birthday party," he explained, then took several gulps of the liquid. It disappeared in a matter of seconds.

"That's why he never showed up at the party," Gerald replied.

"True. I believe Lieutenant Hill threatened to make the relationship public if he didn't leave Robbin. If she did, he can be court martialed for adultery and conduct unbecoming of an officer."

Gerald arched an eyebrow. "But wouldn't she also be in trouble?"

"Big trouble."

Gerald shrugged. "Putting both of their careers in jeopardy."

"I have been there before. A woman scorned is capable of just about anything," Victor said emphatically.

Gerald knew he was referring to Dominique. "I wouldn't worry about Dominique. She's upset about Thomas. In time, she will see that you were just doing your job."

"Yeah, maybe." Victor's mind drifted to how she felt in his arms last night, the soft and warmth of her lips on his. Victor felt a jolt of heat push through him.

Gerald smiled at Victor's blank expression. "What happened between you two?"

Victor sighed. He placed the empty container on the end table next to the sofa. He'd never discussed what happened between him and Dominique with anyone. Victor and his brother were always close and he could speak to Gerald about anything and vice versa.

"Like I told you, we met in Germany three years ago. The first time I laid eyes on her, I thought she was the most beautiful, vibrant woman that I'd ever met." Victor grinned, thinking about the day he ran into Dominique in the military cafeteria. "I was suppose to be in Germany for two weeks. We began seeing each other. Getting along very well. I'd met the woman of my dreams. But during the second week of my assignment, I was called away on another assignment. A mission." Victor leaned back into the sofa. "I had to leave right away."

Gerald knew in his brother's former line of work that they could call him away, any minute, and any time. They never knew where he was going or how long he'd be away. Upon his return he never spoke about the assignments, and they never asked. "You didn't tell her you were leaving."

"No," Victor said in a low tone. "I didn't get the chance."

"You didn't see her again until your blind date?"

"Affirmative."

"No wonder she was angry."

"I deserve it."

"You think she is the woman of your dreams."

"She is." Victor leaned forward. "I'm doing everything I can to make it right. It's not working."

Gerald stood to his feet and laughed.

"Things were already difficult," Victor continued. "With the arrest of Lieutenant Echols, I don't know."

"She will make you suffer until it hurts."

Victor looked confused. "Gerald, what are you talking about?"

"That's what women do. You know that. They know when a man is really interested in them." Gerald grinned at Victor.

"Where do you come up with this stuff?"

Gerald considered himself a ladies' man and believed he knew any and everything about women. He placed his hand to his chest. "I've been through it. I know what I'm talking about."

Victor dropped his head and grinned. "Right."

"What's so funny?"

"Nothing."

"Hold on a moment. I'm going to give you the benefit of my expertise."

Victor rose from the sofa. "Never mind. I'll get through it on my own."

"Victor," Gerald said in a serious tone. "If you really want to make it work, don't give up on her."

Victor rolled his eyes and issued an exasperated sigh. "Have you been listening to me? She's mad at me."

"Aren't you the one who always told me that nothing in life ever comes easy?"

"Words I live by."

"Then you know what you have to do."

ভ ৪৩

The killer watched from across the street at PJ's Sandwich Shop as Victor exited Cadence and headed to his truck. After giving his contact the license plate number of the woman who'd seen him outside Lieutenant Hill's quarter, he'd gotten Victor's home address along with the supper club.

He watched as Victor pulled out into the busy afternoon traffic and passed him sitting at the outdoor cafe. Their eyes met and locked.

CB ⁊

"Was he released from prison?" Victor said to himself as he circled the block, or was his mind playing a trick on him.

He slowed the truck, looking over at where the man was seated. The chair was empty. A waiter was seating a couple. The vehicles behind him began honking their horns in frustration. One driver shouted obscenities at him as he drove around him.

Victor sped up and drove around the block again, bringing the vehicle to a halt inside Cadence's parking lot. Dodging traffic, he jogged to the other side of the street. He entered through the doors of the shop. The place was full, bustling with activity. He glanced around without luck. The man was long gone.

Victor climbed back into the cabinet of the truck and dialed the unit. "CID, Private Atkins, How—" the efficient soldier began to say, but Victor cut her off.

"Atkins, patch me through to Benitez."

"Yes, sir. One moment." She quickly transferred him.

"Captain Benitez," he said upon answering the phone.

"Benitez, I have something I need checked out."

"Go ahead, sir."

"Place a phone call for me to Fort Leavenworth and find out if they have released a prisoner by the name of Scott Chapman."

"Scott Chapman."

"Yes. I'll fill you in later."

"Yes, sir."

"Benitez, I need it yesterday."

During the ride, Victor couldn't get the fellow teammate out of his head. He remembered Staff Sergeant Scott Chapman as a dedicated, noncommissioned officer who lived and breathed the army. He was an exemplary soldier, until he went before a General court martial. They sentenced him to seven years for sexual assault on a female soldier while stationed at Fort Bragg, North Carolina.

The victim, Sergeant Letia Coles, testified she'd gone out on a date with Sergeant Chapman. She stated he'd been a perfect gentleman until he escorted her home. After saying good night, Chapman was upset about not being invited into her apartment. She testified she managed to physically usher him out of the door, but after going to bed that night, she'd wakened to find Chapman in her bedroom. He sexually assaulted her and afterward tried to strangle her, but somehow during the struggle she managed to break free and run next door for help.

Even though she showered, changed clothing, and didn't report the incident until the following day, they still indicted Chapman. They reduced him in rank to Private, forfeit all of his pay, and he got a dishonorable discharge.

As they were handcuffing him, Chapman turned to Victor, who was seated in the front row, and said through clenched teeth that he'd never forget what happened.

೦೩ ೮೦

What a day? Robbin thought as she put the shopping bags away. After Dominique left, she phoned Victor and got permission to visit Thomas in the military stockade. Afterwards she spent the afternoon shopping for personal items. She glanced at her watch. If she hurried, she could take a hot, long bath and dress before she dropped off the items to Thomas at the stockade.

Robbin padded off into the bedroom, pulling her shirt over her head. She rushed into the bathroom, turning the water on in the tub. She reached down underneath the sink, grabbing a box of bath crystals. She removed the rest of her clothing and stepped down in the inviting steam. The water removed the tension and stress of the days event. She laid her head back on the ledge and closed her eyes, allowing her mind to become blank. Not wanting to think about how her life had changed in the last couple of months.

Twenty-five minutes later, Robbin took the elevator to the buildings underground parking garage. It was practically empty. She rarely used the facility, but, since there wasn't any designated parking spaces, the upper level was filled. Gripping her bags in her left hand, she positioned her keys in her right hand. She picked up the pace, listening for sounds other than the click of her heels on the concrete. She spotted her car on the back row. A burned out light made the garage darker. The light had been burned out since last Friday. The building manager had been advised of the problem. It wasn't safe to be walking through the parking garage without adequate lighting.

Robbin approached her car with caution. She opened the door and was preparing to put her bags inside, when a strong embrace tightened around her neck. She could barely breathe. The bags hit the concrete, scattering about. Robbin twisted and turned, trying to break loose. It was useless.

He pulled the stocking tighter. Finally, she took her last breath.

೦೩ ೮೦

Dominique made arrangements to leave work early. When she informed Lieutenant Davies the reason for her early departure he was more than willing to cover the rest of her shift. As she was preparing to leave, Robbin phoned to say she wouldn't be home until later in the evening.

"I'm picking up personal items for Thomas. I don't know how long I will be. I will phone when I return."

With extra time on her hand Dominique found herself headed in the direction of her uncles' senate office. Upon her arrival, his Administrative Assistant, Bradford Farrell, greeted her and escorted her immediately into the senator's office. Two other men, Travis Warren, undersecretary of defense and Agent Milton Rae were in the office. Senator Upton dismissed them, came around the desk, and gave Dominique a hug.

"Hello, Princess," Senator Upton said, smiling. "To what do I owe the pleasure of this visit?"

"Do I need a reason to visit?" Dominique asked.

"Of course not," he said, dragging a chair next to his desk for Dominique. "I didn't think I would see you until the fundraiser."

Dominique sat in the chair. "A lot has been going on the last couple of days. Especially, the last twenty-four hours."

Senator Upton sat behind the desk. Whenever his schedule allowed he did his best to spend time with her. She could always talk to him about anything. Dominique had a happy childhood. The only unhappy time she could remember was when she was eight-years–old and discovered she was adopted. It took several years to get used to the fact that the two people she loved in this world were not her biological parents.

Dominique filled Senator Upton in on what transpired over the last day and her disagreement with Victor.

"He refused to investigate," Dominique said to Senator Upton. "Robbin told him she saw someone standing across the street on the night of the murder. He didn't believe her."

"I'm sorry about Lieutenant Hill. It's a tragedy, but you were wrong to suggest that Victor rushed to make an arrest. He's a very efficient agent."

Dominique looked at her uncle. "Whose side are you on?"

Senator Upton shook his head. "I'm not on anyone's side. I'm just saying that he did his job."

"In your eyes, Colonel Sexton can do no wrong."

Senator Upton threw his head back and laughed. "I wouldn't go that far."

Dominique walked over and stared out the window. The Capitol building could be seen clearly in the distance. "Three lives ruined."

Senator Upton swiveled his chair around watching Dominique. "I don't want to come off insensitive, but from what you told me, Lieutenant Echols caused what happened to him. You live by the sword, you die by it. Can't blame Victor for that."

Dominique moved from the window and propped a hip on the edge of the desk. "I know. I'm just so angry." She picked up a glass bald eagle figurine she'd given him on his 50th birthday.

"If you're going to be angry at anyone, focus on Lieutenant Echols." Senator Upton crossed his legs.

"I'm mad at him too. Can you believe Robbin gave him an alibi after she found out he was having an affair with Lieutenant Hill?"

"I'm not surprised. Women do it all the time."

Dominique frowned. "That doesn't make it right."

"No, it doesn't. I'm just saying that Robbin is not the first woman to stand by her husband. She won't be the last. Marriage vows say for better or for worse."

"The bible also says that thou shall not commit adultery." Dominique stood to her feet.

"It boils down to how much the other person involved is willing to accept. Some marriages can survive adultery. Some marriages can't. I've managed to stay married to Rosetta because I love and respect her. Not to mention she would kill me."

Dominique laughed. "You're right about that." She placed the figurine back on the desktop.

"Are you ready for Friday night?" Dominique had to change the subject. Talking about the Hill's drained her.

"I am ready. I think it's going to be a profitable night. I hope everyone digs deep in their pockets."

"I wouldn't worry," Dominique assured him.

"I'm trying not to, but according to the recent released poll, Robert Baines is now leading George Guliano by six percentage points."

Robert Baines, a two-term former Republican Virginia Senator had originally planned to run for governor, but decided to run a third term as a Democrat Senator. At his fundraiser last week, he raised $5 million. Senator Upton hoped to surpass that figure with ease.

"Uncle Harold, your constituents know you. You are on some great committees, have written some important legislation the general assembly has passed, and continues to make certain that citizens are heard and their needs met. They are not going to forget that."

Senator Upton managed a smile. "You're right. I should hire you to become my campaign manager."

Dominique returned his smile. "For the moment, I'm where I want to be."

"First Victor refused to work for me, and now my own niece."

Senator Upton had Dominique's full attention. She was unaware that he'd offered Victor a position. She could only imagine the situation if he were around on a daily basis. The thought of the kiss they shared last night caused her to shudder. "You offered Victor a job?"

"As one of my assistants. He turned me down, but I'm still working on him. He'd rather be a restaurant owner."

"There's nothing wrong with running a restaurant. Cadence is a very successful supper club."

"Now whose taking sides?" Senator Upton teased.

"I'm just saying, I've been to the club several times and he's happy about becoming part-owner."

Senator Upton cast Dominique a narrow look. "You've been to the club since Rosetta set you up with Victor?"

"Yes, for Robbin's birthday party and Victor invited me to dinner last night."

"I see," Senator Upton replied, amused.

"What's wrong with two friends having dinner?"

"Friends? Victor told me you didn't hit it off. Have things changed?"

"Things have not changed. We had dinner to discuss the case."

"He could have done that over the telephone."

Dominique was speechless. "True," she finally said. "Since I am Lieutenant Hill's commanding officer, I had some questions I wanted to ask him."

"Still could have been done over the telephone," he repeated, amused.

Dominique rolled her eyes upward. "He thought it would be better face to face." If Senator Upton raised this much fuss over them having dinner, she could just imagine what her aunt and uncles' reaction would be if they found out about her past relationship with Victor.

"Did you have a good time?" Senator Upton inquired.

Dominique pointed at him. "You're just as bad as Aunt Rosetta. I wasn't there to have a good time. I was there to find out about the case."

Senator Upton raised his hand in a surrendering gesture. "Okay. Okay. I'll stay out of it."

Dominique smiled and gave her uncle an affectionate stare. "Hmmm."

"Don't you think you should apologize?"

Dominique thought a moment. She had to admit her behavior

this morning was out of line. She hit a nerve with her accusation. "I will apologize, but only for the remark I made. Not about Robbin."

"That's fair." Senator Upton stepped forward, enclosed Dominique in his arms, then kissed her affectionately atop the forehead.

“”

The killer had gotten away with it a second time. Like Lieutenant Tamara Hill, Lieutenant Robbin Greene never saw it coming. He picked up the receiver of the phone in the motel room and punched in the numbers to his employer. "It's done," he said. "But we may have a problem."

"What problem?"

"Sexton saw me." He held back a laugh as he looked at the photo of Victor on the wall. The plan had worked out better than he hoped. He was to stake out Cadence to become familiar with his coming and going. Victor spotting him was an extra bonus. Deep down he was glad Victor knew he was released from prison. It will make the chase more competitive and finally put to rest who was the better man.

The voice on the other end was silent a moment then exploded. "You idiot. I thought I was hiring an expert."

"Who do you think you're talking too?" the killer hissed back.

The person on the other end took a deep breath and sighed, not wanting to get him worked up. "All I'm saying is this is getting out of hand. The situation was under control. Lieutenant Echols is under arrest for Lieutenant Hill's murder. There was no reason to kill his wife."

"She saw me. What was I supposed to do?"

"Nothing," the person shouted. "You were supposed to do nothing."

"I saw a situation that needed to be taken care of. I took care of it. That's what you paid me for."

"I paid for you to find the video tape, which you did not do. What you have done is made matters worse. Colonel Sexton saw you, which means he knows you've been released, which may lead back to me," the voice rose. "Which I don't want."

"Leave Colonel Sexton to me," the killer quipped. "I will locate the tape and deal with him."

"You better." the voice snapped and the line went dead.

Chapter Twelve

Victor opened the file, looking at the photo of Scott Chapman. Prison didn't age him much after seven years. He still looked the same. He flipped the page. He was released eight months ago on good behavior. Since his release, he hadn't held down a job for a significant length of time. He worked as a locksmith, janitor, construction worker, dishwasher, and now nothing.

According to the report, after he got out of prison he went back home to Mobile, Alabama and lived with his mother. Because he was unable to keep a job, she threw him out. Then he stayed in a run-down motel in the city until a couple of weeks ago. His parole officer stated that he stopped reporting in to him. Victor tossed the report on his desk. Now he was in DC. Victor rubbed underneath his chin. What was he doing in the area? A coincidence? With the training Chapman received he could commit this type of crime with ease. Victor trained him and other men like him to carry out their tasks with precision. The killer was definitely clever. Victor frowned. Maybe Robbin was telling the truth. Seeing Chapman today, he couldn't rule her theory out that there may be another suspect. But why? What would be his motive?

He looked up to see Benitez enter the office. "Care to fill me in?" He closed the door behind him.

Victor sighed. "I'm not sure what I have."

Benitez nodded. "Talk to me anyway."

Victor filled Benitez in on his past relationship with Scott Chapman, including the incident from this afternoon.

Benitez scowled. "He was just sitting there?"

Victor knew what he was thinking, because the same thought crossed his mind. Chapman wanted to be seen. "Having lunch. Across the street from Cadence and in plain view. Taunting me."

"You think he knew you were at Cadence?"

Victor sighed. "It's possible. Then again, he could have been a customer sitting out in this beautiful weather, enjoying lunch."

Benitez nodded. "Maybe. What do you want to do?"

Victor shook his head. "Legally, there's nothing I can do. He hasn't broken any laws that I know of." Then changing the subject, he said. "We went over Lieutenant Hill's quarters with a fine tooth comb."

"Yes, sir. The only fingerprints were the victim and Echols. We're still waiting on results from Lieutenant Echols' place."

"Is Lieutenant Greene still visiting her husband?"

"No, sir. She left several hours ago. Said something about picking up some personal items and returning later."

Victor picked up the computer printout on his desk. He found Robbin's home telephone number and punched in the number. It ranged five times before the answering machine clicked on. He left a message instructing her to phone him as soon as she received his message. "No one's home. In the meantime, let's go take another look at the crime scene."

"You think there may be some truth to the man Lieutenant Greene saw?"

"Chapman has a vendetta against me. There may not be a connection between him and Lieutenant Hill, but I don't want to leave anything to chance." Victor grabbed his jacket from the back of his chair. "Let's flash Chapman's photo around the quarters," he said just as someone knocked on the door. "Come in," Victor called out, putting his arms in the jacket.

Private First Class Bone poked his head through the doorway. "Colonel, you have a visitor," he announced.

Victor raised an eyebrow. He wasn't expecting anyone. "Show them in."

Bone disappeared and a moment later, Dominique walked in his office. Victor stood up straighter. She was the last person he expected to see since their disagreement this morning, but he was pleased.

"I'll pass the orders to the agents and wait for you outside," Benitez said. "Captain Frazier," he spoke on the way out the door, "it's good to see you again."

"Same here, Captain Benitez."

"I'll only be a moment," Victor said as the door closed.

"I'm sorry. I didn't know you were on your way out."

"Going to check something out."

"I will only be a minute," Dominique said, trying to pretend his heated gaze did not affect her. "I came by to apologize for my behavior this morning. I was out of line."

While she spoke, Victor was completely focused on her. He always loved the way she pursed her lips when she was nervous. "Don't worry your pretty little head about it. There may be something to Robbin's story."

Dominique looked surprised. "Really? What happened?" She fired questions at him. "Did you find the man Robbin saw?"

Victor threw his hands up. "Whoa. Hold up. I said maybe. I'm on my way out to Lieutenant Hills' quarters to take another look around and see if anyone saw this man lurking around." He reached inside his jacket and showed her a photo of Scott Chapman.

"This is the man Robbin may have seen?"

"His name is Scott Chapman. I figure we show the photo around the quarters and see if anyone saw him hanging around."

Dominique smiled with satisfaction. "Robbin will be glad to know the man she saw may not be all in her head. There may be another suspect."

Victor was having a hard time concentrating on what Dominique was saying; watching her soft lips move while she was speaking was turning him on. Her tongue ran across her bottom lips. It was meant to calm her nerves, but to him it was exotic. All he wanted to do was place his lips to hers, to feel her tongue mating with his mouth again. He gave himself a mental shake. This wasn't the time or place.

"Keep in mind this is just a lead. It may or may not pan out."

Dominique returned the photo. "I know." She pushed back a wayward strand of hair that had fallen in her face. "It's just good to know that you're following up."

"Just trying to do my job," Victor said.

"Should we get going?"

Victor's eyes narrowed. "What do you mean we? You're not going."

"Yes, I am." She knew he would try to protest, she quickly added, "If you don't let me come along, I'll just follow you."

"I will have you removed from the premises," Victor replied. "As the man in charge, I can do that, Captain."

Dominique swallowed the lump in her throat. "I will take my chances, Colonel."

Victor sighed. He knew she would and he didn't know if Chapman was involved. At least this way he could keep an eye on her. Not to mention they would spend time together.

A few minutes later, with Dominique with him, Victor pulled his vehicle out of the parking lot and headed in the direction of the Officer's Quarters. As he drove, Dominique's vision kept drifting over in his direction. His eyes remained on the road in front of him as his hands maneuvered the steering wheel. *Those hands,* Dominique thought, *definitely knew how to operate.* She felt heated when she remembered how they had worked on her. She had to think of something else.

"So, you were engaged?" Dominique inquired softly to break the silence.

Victor looked over at her in surprise. He let out a rough sigh and wished she didn't know about that part of his life. "Yes I was."

"I can't believe you were engaged." Dominique looked over at him. She wrapped her arms around herself, leaning back in the seat of the truck. She was doing her best not to be jealous.

The tone in her voice caught Victor off guard. "You want me to believe you waited around for me almost three years."

Dominique looked at him as if he'd lost his mind. "Were you engaged when we were together?"

Victor didn't answer for what seemed like eternity. "It was a year after we were together." Even though they were over when he met Felicia, guilt nudged him. "Her name was Felicia Connors."

"What happened?"

"She couldn't handle my job as a special operations officer. The long separations, secrecy, and last minutes deployment became too much for her. She called off the engagement a week before the wedding."

"I'm sorry," Dominique found herself saying.

"Don't be. It just wasn't meant to be," Victor said, returning his gaze on the road.

"Did you love her?"

Dominique was never a woman afraid to ask questions. Whenever she wanted information, she was direct and to the point.

Victor could easily choose not to answer the questions to protect her feeling. He didn't owe Dominique any explanations. What they shared was in the past, but he wanted her to know the truth. Looking over at Dominique, he said, "I thought I did." He shrugged. "I believe I did."

She winced, and it hurt her to know he could have loved Felicia. "Is that the reason you left special operations? Because of Felicia?"

"No," he said, giving her a quick glance. "I left because I wanted a career that was less dramatic."

"CID is less dramatic than Special Operations?"

Victor's straight, white teeth flashed against his brown skin. "It's a cakewalk compared to Special Ops."

"You're just like my uncle. The type of man who likes to live life dangerous, adventurous, and on the edge."

He shrugged. "Guilty as charged. I love this kind of work just as you love being a nurse."

She leaned back against the seat. "But won't you miss it when you retire? Running a club is not the same as running after the bad guys."

"You sound like the senator. Did he tell you he offered me a job?"

"He mentioned it."

Victor nodded when he brought the truck to a stop at a traffic light. "I admire the senator, but I'm not interested in working for him. I'll adjust to running the club."

"He's determined to have you on his staff."

"You're supposed to help me change my mind?"

Dominique chuckled. "No. No one can talk you into anything you don't want to do."

"I don't know. You're welcome to try," Victor said as he moved the truck forward again when the traffic light turned green. He made a left turn. "Are you ever going to tell them that we were," he cleared his throat, 'lovers'?"

"No," Dominique said hastily.

Victor glanced over at her then refocused his attention back on the road. "Why did you answer like that?"

She chuckled again. "I'm sorry. I didn't mean too. I can just hear them now, saying how we could work things out between us."

The right side of Victor's mouth curled up into a half-smile. He glanced over at Dominique but didn't respond.

"You should have heard the rave reviews you got when Aunt Rosetta was telling me about my blind date." Dominique arched a perfect eyebrow. "I thought next she was going to tell me that you walked on water, healed the sick, and made the lame walk."

He let out a loud laugh. She smiled over at him. How she missed hearing the sound of his laughter.

As if reading her mind, Victor said, "You could always make me laugh. I miss that."

A moment later the vehicle came to a stop in front of the Officer's Quarters. When they climbed out of the truck, the other agents, uniform officers, and Mrs. Cunningham met them. Victor gave instruction for Benitez to take a group of officers to go over the area across the street where Robbin said she spotted the stranger. He sent another group of agents door-to-door, showing Scott Chapman's photo.

Victor showed the picture of Chapman to Mrs. Cunningham, but she didn't recognize him. A moment later, she led Victor and Dominique up the walkway. She took the key from her sundress pocket, opened the front door, and stepped aside to let them enter.

"Thanks," Victor said. "We'll lock up when we leave."

Mrs. Cunningham nodded, then scurried away. They stepped inside the quarters. Dominique followed him inside the small living room and glanced around.

"What are we looking for?" Dominique asked, watching Victor as he prowled the room.

"We are not looking for anything," Victor said, pushing his large hands inside a pair of latex gloves. "I agreed to let you come along, but that was all I agreed too." He lifted a lamp, peeked inside the shade, and checked underneath. "Don't touch anything."

Dominique pushed out her lower bottom lip in protest.

"Fine. I won't." She glanced around the small living room. Even though the furniture was plain, brown military issue, Lieutenant Hill had done a nice job decorating it. The atmosphere was peaceful. It was hard to believe that such a tragedy had occurred here.

Victor kneeled on the floor, looking underneath a throw rug, then a large floor speaker. "I'm searching for anything we might have overlooked."

"I thought you went over this place from top to bottom," Dominique pointed out as she leaned over to take a closer look at an African piece of sculpture.

"We did, but that was before Chapman showed up. His appearance may put a new perspective on things. We may have overlooked an important piece of evidence."

Dominique removed the thin black strap off her shoulder, and placed the purse on the sofa. "Tell me about Chapman."

"He was one of my best men," Victor answered, picking up a bundle of mail from the dining room table. "A good soldier. A team player. He lived and breathed special operations. I remember when he first joined the team. He said he wanted to join the army since he was a little boy. It's a shame what happened to him."

"What happened?"

"He was court martialed for sexual assault. Sentenced to seven years, reduced in rank, forfeited of all pay, and a dishonorable discharge." Victor placed the mail back on the table.

Dominique shrugged. "If he's in jail, how is he involved?"

"He was released eight months ago. I've seen him in the area. I don't have any evidence at the moment, but I have a feeling he is involved."

"You've seen him?"

"Earlier today. Spotted him sitting outside PJ's Sandwich Shop, across from Cadence. I got the impression he wanted me to see him."

Dominique looked confused. "What do you have to do with this?"

"I testified against him at the court martial. Another female soldier filed similar charges against him months earlier, but she later dropped the charges."

"You think he threatened her?"

"I'm sure he did. She never elaborated on it. A couple of months later, she left the army. Anyway, the day he was sentenced, he threatened me. Said he would never forget that I testified against him."

"Why did he kill Lieutenant Hill?"

"That's the million dollar question."

"If he *is* the killer, murder is a huge step up from sexual assault."

"Yes it is and he can commit this type of crime."

"How do you know?"

"I taught him everything he knows," Victor said dryly.

All the talk about murder caused Dominique to shudder. She wrapped her arms around herself, then glanced around the room, running her arms up and down to head off the chill. "Looking for a clue you overlooked?"

"I'm not infallible. You know that better than anybody." Victor locked gazes with Dominique, causing his heart rate to speed up.

Dominique cleared her throat to break the sexual tension between them. "Neither am I," she said, going over to look at the huge CD collection. She needed to put some distance between them.

A music lover herself, Dominique looked farther down and found the Rhythm and Blues section. Next to it, she noticed a tab that read '*Love Music*.' She smiled and ran her finger along the section. Brian McKnight, Anita Baker, Sade, and Luther Vandross.

"I'm going to search the bedroom," Victor announced.

"I'll be here if you need me."

Victor had to concentrate on the situation at hand, he thought when he entered the room in search of clues they may have overlooked. He lifted the mattress; nothing was there. He moved over to the dresser. The top was filled with perfume, cosmetics, and toiletries. He opened the top drawer. It was filled with lingerie. He glanced towards the living room and imagined Dominique in the barely clad items. He quickly pushed the thought aside and pulled out the second drawer. Inside were military brown tee shirts, black sweaters, neatly rolled socks, and underwear. Nothing unusual. The next drawer was filled with wool sweaters and silk scarves.

Victor stepped over to the small closet, opening the doors. It was filled with military uniforms, shoes, hats, purses, more sweaters, and civilian clothing. On the top shelf were two romance novels, a shoebox, and a stack of magazines excluded from the previous search.

He stood with his hands on his hips, surveying the items. His staff had turned this place upside down. They found nothing to explain why Lieutenant Hill was killed. He sighed and thumbed through the novels. He replaced them and picked up the shoebox. Instead of shoes it was filled with family photos and a couple of personal letters. Putting the shoebox back, he picked up the magazines. She had a taste in various reading material, *Glamour*, *Army Times*, *Ebony*, and *Times*. Nothing of interest, he thought, leafing through the pages of *Time*. He paused when he came across a letter with a name on it: Senator Harold Upton. He raised the stationery up to the light, looking at the watermarks. It appeared to be authentic. It was dated December 2, 2003. The letter stated the arrangement had been taken care of. It wasn't signed. Victor frowned. A contribution to the senator? A tax write-off? He'd check it out, he thought and put the letter in his pocket.

Victor spent several more minutes checking out the bedroom, then moved onto the bathroom, but didn't find anything. As he headed back into the living room to Dominique, he decided not to share the discovery of the letter. It didn't say anything specific and could be from anyone in the senator's office. He walked in the room and found her looking at a CD. He shook his head. He told her not to touch anything.

"Dominique," Victor said over her shoulder. "I thought I told you not to touch anything."

Dominique swirled around wondering how long he had been standing there.

"Sorry, I was just looking at her music."

Victor tilted his head to one side, peeking at the CD she was holding. "What do you have in your hand?"

Dominique wished she never picked up the CD. He removed it from her hand. "She has a huge collection. I was wondering if we share the same taste in music." She could tell he didn't believe her by the smile on his face.

"The Best of Luther Vandross," Victor read aloud, and then looked Dominique seductively up and down. She was embarrassed and knew it showed on her face. "I know you have this one in your collection. We spent many romantic evening listening to this CD." His voice dropped an octave.

"Give me that." Dominique snatched the CD from his hand. Her hands trembling, she used the end of her shirt, carefully wiped it down, and placed it back in the rack. She turned to find Victor giving her a questionable look. She shrugged her shoulders. "I watch CSI."

Victor laughed. "Dominique, you are something else," he said, escorting her toward the door.

"Did you find anything?" Dominique asked.

"I'm not sure," Victor answered.

◌8 ◌9

Victor flipped the light switch on in Dominique's apartment.

"Come on in, make yourself at home. I'll be back in a moment." She disappeared in one of the back rooms.

Victor took the opportunity to look around this time. His eyes took in the elegance of the living room. The carpet was seashell, a warm cherry color split rattan table set surrounded a soft cream floral cotton sofa. A huge marble fireplace faced him as he sat on the sofa. The mantle was crowded with family portraits, military photos, and candleholders. On the glass-top table in front of him was a copy of the Stripes.

When Dominique returned to the living room, Victor had stepped into the den admiring the numerous certificates and awards on the wall. She joined him there.

Her gaze rested on his handsome physique as he read the military orders.

"Excuse the mess in here," Dominique said as she looked at the boxes still waiting for her to unpack. "I just haven't had time to finish unpacking."

Victor's gaze crept in Dominique's direction. "That's okay, I understand." He pointed at the awards on the wall. "I see you've been busy."

"Just a few." She smiled. "Not as impressive as your personnel file. Two Purple Hearts and a host of other awards."

"The senator told you?"

"You know he did."

Victor nodded as he continued staring at her.

Dominique cleared her throat, trying again to break the sexual tension between them. "Can I offer you something to drink? Eat?" she asked, heading into the kitchen. The further apart she was from him the better.

"No, thank you," he answered, following her into the kitchen. His long legs straddled a stool at the counter.

Dominique opened the refrigerator, leaning inside. "You sure? I have Apple Juice? Orange Juice? Day old meatloaf?" Not getting a response from Victor, she peeped around the door to find him pulling out his cellular phone. "Victor?"

"Yes," he answered.

"Did you hear the choices?" She grabbed a bottle of Apple Juice.

"Yes, I did. I'm fine, Dominique." He changed the subject. "Have you spoken to Robbin recently?"

"Not since this afternoon." Dominique took a sip, placing the bottle of juice on the counter. "She was going to purchase some items for Thomas and drop them off to him. She was supposed to phone me when she got in. I haven't heard from her yet."

Victor flipped his cellular phone open. He dialed Robbin's number. It ranged several times before the answering machine clicked on. He left another message for her to phone him as soon as she returned. "Still no answer. I'm sure she wants to know what's going on."

"I know she does. Thomas may be released."

"Even if he's cleared of murder. He's not off the hook. They can still get him for adultery."

"It's a lot better than murder."

"Why don't we talk about something else?" Victor asked, coming around the counter, standing in front of her.

Dominique looked up at him, taking in his powerful presence. Her heart was thumping loudly in her chest. She was sure he could hear it. "Like what?"

"You, for instance," he said, smiling down at her. "I enjoyed the conversation we began in the truck the other day. It gave us a chance to talk about something else beside the case."

"The case is important."

"So are we." Victor's facial expression became serious. "Are you still angry at me?" he quickly added. "About what happened in Germany."

"I was at first," Dominique finally said.

"And now?" Victor covered the small distance between them. "How do you feel now?"

"I'm not as angry," Dominique said, trying to pretend she was unaffected by the raw passion in his brown eyes.

Victor wanted Dominique to know how much he cared about her. "I've thought about nothing else since you came back into my life. Have you thought about me?"

"Maybe," she said, being vague.

"Why can't you give me a straight answer?"

"You're the CID agent. You tell me."

He grinned. "I want a yes or no answer. Is that so difficult?"

Dominique felt like a giddy schoolgirl on her first date. She didn't know why, Victor wasn't a stranger. "It's not difficult. You know how I feel about you, Victor."

Victor reached up and removed a tendril of hair from her face. "One day I want to hear you say how you feel about me."

Dominique blushed.

"Earlier when you picked up the Luther Vandross CD, what were you thinking about?"

He heard Dominique gasp. "What kind of questions is that?" She giggled. "You are so bad."

"Am I?" Victor pulled her into his strong arms. "I thought that was one of the things you like about me."

"It is." Dominique heard him take a deep breath, then gently pressed his lips to hers. She placed her arms around his neck, accepting the probing of his tongue inside her mouth as he was seeking more access.

"I missed you," Victor said, sucking on her bottom lips.

Dominique felt like she was standing before a hot furnace. "I missed you too," she whispered, returning the kiss.

Victor planted kisses along the nape of her neck. He closed his eyes and listened to the sounds of the intimate kisses, moans.

Dominique closed her eyes, her mouth was over his deeply, tasting his, feeding on his. It was as if she was trying to make up for times, when the ringing of his cellular phone echoed in the room. Neither acknowledged the interruption as Victor deepened the kiss. It continued ringing.

"Nique," Victor said, breathing hard. "I have to get that."

"No," Dominique groaned, recapturing his mouth again. "Do you have too?"

"I wish I didn't," he said and flipped the phone open. "Colonel Sexton," Victor said and listened tentatively a moment. "I'll be right there." He refolded the phone and met Dominique's sad eyes.

"I know you have to go," she said disappointed.

"There's been another murder."

Chapter Thirteen

Victor bought the truck to a sudden halt behind the civilian cruiser. There was also an ambulance and paramedic unit on the scene. He exited the vehicle and was met by Benitez. A crowd had gathered. Civilian uniformed officers had put up barricades to keep the curious onlookers at bay.

"I know you were trying to get some rest," Benitez said, crossing the barricade to meet Victor.

Victor smiled. "Not exactly. I left a very beautiful woman."

Benitez chuckled. "Tell me about it. Looks like we have another strangled victim, found dead in the garage about thirty minutes ago. That's all I know at the moment."

"Colonel Sexton, I'm Detective West with the Montgomery County Police Department," said the Caucasian, middle-aged man walking toward him.

Victor nodded and extended a hand. "This is Captain Juan Benitez. What do you have?"

"Thought CID would want to be in on this one. Looks like the same motive as the killing you had in the Officer's Quarters. We have a black female, early thirties. A pedestrian discovered her on her way to her vehicle." Detective West paused then added, "The witness was pretty hysterical when my partner and I arrived. My partner is with her now, sitting in the cruiser. I informed the witness you would like to speak with her. The Coroner is on the way, along with Forensics."

"Have you identified the victim?" Victor headed toward the covered body.

Detective West opened his notepad. "Victims' name is Lieutenant Robbin Greene."

Victor stopped in mid-stride. He felt like he'd been kicked in the chest, and he couldn't move for what seemed like eternity. "What?" He didn't believe he spoke until Detective West said, "That's the name on the military identification that we found in her purse." He handed Victor the military card.

Victor and Benitez stepped closer and surveyed the scene. The garage was dimly lit from several bulbs out. Victor didn't notice any visible video cameras. A heavy, iron green door was ajar close to where Robbin's body was found. The personal items were scattered next to the car.

"There is a hidden camera." Detective West pointed toward the corner above Robbin's vehicle. "It's broken. The manager said they put a work order into the security company and they were supposed to come out today to repair it but they never got around to it."

"What's their excuse for the blown out bulbs?" Benitez shook his head in aggravation. "Even if the camera was operational we may have been unable to see anything. The bulb outage makes it darker than usual."

"I thought about that," Victor answered and turned back to Detective West. "What about security guards?"

Detective West flipped the page in his notebook. "We questioned Bernie Mullens. He makes the round through here every thirty minutes, but he said he hadn't seen anyone or anything unusual. I told him to stand by, CID may want to have a talk with him."

"I definitely want to question him," Victor said.

Victor walked over and kneeled down next to Robbin's body. He inhaled a slight breath then lifted the blanket. If it weren't for the black stocking still around her neck, Victor would have thought she was in a peaceful sleep, but from the impression on her neck she had been strangled, just like Lieutenant Hill. "Damn." He dropped his head and recovered her. Benitez slapped him on the back.

Victor stood up to find Detective West staring at him. "You know the victim?"

Victor nodded his head. "Yeah," he said softly.

"I'm sorry," Detective West said.

"Not as sorry as I am."

"Colonel, her body is still warm," said Benitez from his crouch position. "My guess is she hasn't been dead long."

"It looks as if she was on her way to her car when she was attacked," Detective West explained. "Robbery doesn't seem to be the motive. Cash and credit cards are still in the wallet."

"I'm not surprised," Victor replied. He walked over to where the door was ajar. It led out to one flight of stairs and into a side street. A perfect escape route. In and out without being seen.

DAY SIX - WEDNESDAY

After Victor left, Dominique had a difficult time going to sleep. She could still feel the intimacy of his kisses on her lips, and she could still smell the male essence of him. She finally drifted off, but her dreams had been full of him. A warm feeling rushed to her face, then settled between her thighs. The man still had the same effect on her.

The ringing of the doorbell jolted her out of her thoughts and brought her back to reality. She looked over at the clock. It was 3:10 in the morning. Maybe it was Victor. He'd said he'd try to stop back by if he could. She pushed the covers aside and grabbed the robe off the ottoman at the foot of the bed. She padded to the door and peeped through the viewer. It was Victor. She smiled and quickly unlocked the door. Her smile vanished when she opened the door and saw the look of sadness on his face. Something was wrong.

Victor stepped forward. Dominique took a step backward. An eerie feeling came over her and she crossed her arms over her chest to head off the shivering. "Victor?" she said softly.

It was the hardest thing he ever had to do, but he wanted to tell her about Robbin's death before the news media telecast it. "I'm sorry, Dominique," he said in a broken voice. His eyes misted. "It's Robbin. She's—"

"No!" Dominique let out a loud scream and bolted from the room. She rushed into the bathroom and slammed the door.

Victor followed behind her. He turned the knob. It was locked. He knocked on the door. "Dominique," he called to her. Through the door, he could hear her sobbing. The image of her in tears touched him. "Nique, please open the door."

"Go away, Victor. Just go away," she cried out.

"I'm not leaving until you come out."

Minutes passed before the lock clicked and the door opened. She flew into his arms, her body shaking.

"Let it out," he cooed, hugging her tightly against him and stroking her hair.

"Victor," she said, clinging to his reassuring presence. "People are dying around me. What if he comes after me next?"

"No. No. That's not going to happen. I'm not going to let anyone hurt you."

Dominique trembled and he tightened his hold on her.

"I'm going to protect you," Victor promised.

Dominique looked up at him. What she saw was sincerity, warmth, and protection. Her eyes filled with tears. "I don't know what I would do if anything happened to you," Victor said.

Victor looked lovingly in her eyes. He reached one hand up and gently stroked the right side of her cheek. He was so in love with the woman he wrapped tighter into his arms. He would do anything to protect her. "I'm sorry about Robbin. If I would have—"

She silenced his words, putting a finger to his lips.

He sighed, dropped his head, and closed his eyes to compose himself. "Why don't you try and get some sleep," he said in a somber tone. "I'm going to—"

Dominique's eyes widened in fear as she cut him off. "You're not leaving, are you?" She held on to him tighter. She was afraid and didn't want to be left alone.

Looking in her eyes, he saw fear. "No. I'm not leaving." Victor took her by the hand and led her into the bedroom. He pulled the covers back, allowing her to slide between the cool sheets.

"I'm not able to sleep."

"Try," Victor commanded. He held her in his arms, speaking quietly to her until she fell asleep. After she drifted off, he went into the bathroom and took a shower. Maybe the water could wash away the guilt he was feeling, but he knew it wouldn't.

Ë ©

Time was running out, Victor thought to himself when he entered the main area of CID. It was busy with agents and uniformed officers. He stopped in the break room to pour himself a cup of coffee. He couldn't help thinking about Dominique. She took Robbin's death very hard. He didn't want to leave her this morning, but she assured him she would be okay. Taking a cup of coffee, he strolled down the hall to Benitez's office. Major Ito, a short, thin, Asian man, sporting Clark Kent glasses was in Benitez office. He'd personally hand carried Lieutenant Hill's autopsy reports.

"How's Captain Frazier?" Benitez asked upon Victor's entrance in his office.

"Not good."

"I'm sorry," Benitez said, closing a file on his desk.

"So give me some good news."

Victor was surer than ever that Chapman was responsible for both killing, but he had nothing but his instinct to connect him to both women's death. He'd hoped the security guard may have seen or heard something, but after questioning him it was obvious he knew nothing.

At Lieutenant's Hill quarters the agents had knocked on doors, showed Chapman's picture, and combed the area across the street. They came up empty. The killer was very careful. He managed to slip in and out undetected.

Major Ito spoke with perfect English. "I brought it over as soon as it was finished. The cause of death was asphyxia. A thick

113

impression was seen on the victims' neck. The killer applied enough pressure to obstruct the air passage and blood vessels to cause death. Fibers collected from the black stocking found around the neck was the weapon used," he explained. " But you already knew that."

"That was an obvious clue," Victor admitted.

Major Ito took a seat next to Victor, taking off his glasses. He reached inside his front fatigue pocket, retrieved a white handkerchief, and began cleaning his spectacle. "Pubic hair samples found on Lieutenant Hill were black," Major Ito continued. "Her pubic hair was brown. Also, DNA from the blood and semen collected from Lieutenant Hill suggests two different types. Lieutenant Hill and another person. If I had to guess, I would say Lieutenant Echols."

Victor nodded in agreement and leaned forward in his chair. "She had sexual relation before she was killed?"

"It was consensual. There wasn't any sign of bruising," Major Ito added.

"We know from the abrasion and defensive wounds on Lieutenant Hill that she fought for her life. I collected a flaky residue packed under the right thumb. It turned out to be dried human blood." Major Ito handed Victor the file.

Victor read down the sheet. "Lieutenant Hill scratched the killer?" he said more to himself, and then read aloud, "The dermis is consistent with Caucasian. This is the break we have been looking for," he said with a lopsided smile on his face.

"Looks like you may be right about your man, Chapman," Benitez threw in.

"Let's get a copy of his fingerprints and DNA from the military database. Also, get records of all phone calls coming in and out of Lieutenant Hill's quarters for the past month," Victor instructed.

"I'm way ahead of you, Colonel. Sergeant Juarez is already working on the phone calls. Just waiting for them to come in."

"Outstanding," he said, taking a sip of coffee. "There is a connection here. We just have to put all of the pieces together."

"And quick," Benitez said dryly. "What do you want to do about Lieutenant Echols?"

"He's free to go," Victor said flatly. Lieutenant Echols had been through enough. He was distraught over the death of Robbin.

"I have to run fellas." Major Ito came to his feet. "I'll be in touch," he said on the way out the door.

Victor reached in his jacket pocket. "I found this letter in Lieutenant Hill's quarters stuck between the pages of a *Time* magazine in her closet." Victor handed it to Benitez for inspection. "I can't see how Lieutenant Hill would be connected to Senator Upton."

Benitez quickly skimmed the letter. He shrugged. "A contribution to his campaign."

"Lots of people contribute to politician's campaigns."

A knock interrupted them then followed by Sergeant Juarez coming through the door. "Lieutenant Hill's phone records came over the fax." He handed the sheets of paper to Victor. "Calls were made within the last thirty days to Lieutenant Echols, her parents in St. Louis, the emergency room where she worked, Federal Credit Union, and Senator Upton's office on the day she was killed. I called the number to Senator Upton's office and got the secretary."

"Good job, Juarez." Victor browsed through the sheet of the numbers. Calls going through the secretary could not be traced. A dead end. No way to tell who the calls were forwarded to. He handed the pages to Benitez.

Victor picked up the phone. "I'm going to pay the senator a visit." He dialed Senator Upton's number. "Hello, this is Colonel Sexton of CID. Is Senator Upton in?" Victor said to Senator Upton's secretary. He listened for a moment. The senator was working from home this morning. "Can you transfer me to his home? Thank you." He waited for the connection. "Hello, Senator. How are you? I'm fine. I need to meet with you." He was silent. "I have something I need to discuss with you. I'll see you in about an hour." He placed the phone back in the cradle. "That's done."

"How do you want to handle the press?" Benitez asked.

On the way into work that morning there had been a few reporters on hand. "I know we're going to have to deal with them eventually," Victor said with sarcasm. "But for the moment the reply is 'no comment.'"

Benitez chuckled. "Yes, sir."

Victor glanced at his watch. "I better get going. I want to be notified of those results as soon as they come in," he said over his shoulder on the way out the door. "You can reach me on my cellular phone."

"Colonel," Sergeant Juarez said, running into Victor in the hallway. "General Goss wants to see you in his office as soon as possible."

Victor ran his hand along the back of his neck. He knew sooner or later he'd have to inform him of the direction the case has taken. He just needed more time. "Call him and let him know that I'm on my way."

ॐ ॐ

"What the hell is going on?" General Goss asked in a firm tone.

Victor stood, remained silent, and looked straight ahead as the assault began.

"The last time we spoke, you informed me that an arrest had been made in this case. This morning, I wake up to find out that another female officer has been strangled." His voice climbed. "How did that happen?"

Victor glanced at the General, waiting permission to speak.

"Well?" the general prompted.

"We made an arrest in the case, but we have discovered new evidence that Lieutenant Echols isn't the killer."

General Goss shook his head from side to side in disbelief. He strolled over to the window and looked out a moment, then looked back at Victor. "First, he is and now he isn't."

Reluctantly, Victor answered, "Yes, sir."

General Goss refocused his attention back out the window. Victor took the opportunity to look around his bosses' office. Each piece of furniture was too big or too dark in color. General Goss was a former pilot who served during the Vietnam War. On the wall were military photos from different assignments of his thirty plus years of a lustrous career. Pictures of him with powerful political figures: former Presidents Ronald Reagan, George W. Bush, and William Clinton; Secretary of Defense, William Cohen; and Secretary of State, Colin Powell. Next to the photographs were diplomas from West Point and Harvard University. Arranged on his desktop were family photos of his wife, Margie, there three adult children, and seven grandchildren.

"Then who is the killer?" General Goss turned to face Victor again.

"I'm following a few leads. One is a former soldier, Scott Chapman." Victor filled the General in on what his office uncovered on the case, including the letter found from the Senator's office.

"Senator Harold Upton?" he repeated and narrowed his eyes at Victor. "Isn't he seeking reelection?"

"Yes, sir. At the moment what we have is circumstantial. Nothing concrete. I'm on my way to see the senator."

"You two know each other?" General Goss went around the desk and sat in the Black, oversized chair. He clasped his aging hands together.

"Yes, sir. I had the honor of serving under him in the Persian Gulf and Haiti campaigns."

"You don't think this is a conflict of interest?" he asked in a calmer tone.

"No, sir, I don't," Victor answered in a voice that came from deep down inside. He wasn't sure where. He thought about what he would do or how he would react if the senator were involved. Could he arrest him? How would Dominique accept it?

General Goss stared at him for a moment. Not sure he believed him. "Okay, Colonel," he finally answered. "Just keep me posted."

"Yes, sir. Thank you, sir." Victor offered a snap salute that the general returned. He did an about face and let himself out.

Chapter Fourteen

*V*ictor strolled through the door of the Federal Credit Union. The bank was located inside the army medical center. Victor was the center of attention as both women and men employees looked upon his commanding presence.

He strolled confidently toward the customer service desk and flashed his badge. "I'm Lieutenant Colonel Sexton, CID. I would like to speak to someone in charge about getting a copy of one of your customer's bank records."

The Asian woman looked taken aback. "Uh...just a moment, sir." She picked up the telephone and relayed the nature of his visit. A moment later, she said, "Mr. Stanley, the bank manager will be right with you."

"Thank you," Victor said and took a seat in a chair across from the customer service desk.

A minute later, a short, balding, black man approached him. He looked closely at Victor over the rim of his spectacles. "Colonel Sexton?" he asked and extended a hand. "I'm Alphonso Stanley, the bank manager. How may I help you," he said, gesturing for Victor to follow. He led him into his spacious office and closed the door.

Victor took a seat across from his desk and removed his shades, crossing his long legs. "Mr. Stanley, I'm from CID, and I'm looking into the death of one of your customer, Lieutenant Tamara Hill. I need to get copies of her bank records. I would also like to know if she had a safe deposit box."

Mr. Stanley appeared hesitant. "Where are you from again?"

"CID. The Criminal Investigation Division," Victor repeated.

"I can't let you see those records without a court order," Mr. Stanley said, proudly.

"Not a problem." Victor removed the paperwork from inside his jacket and flashed his badge again for good measure.

Mr. Stanley read over the document then reluctantly took a seat behind his computer screen. "How far back would you like us to go?"

"I want to see monthly statements from the day she opened an account with your bank," Victor explained.

"What are you looking for?"

"Any unusual large deposits," Victor answered.

"Do you have an account number? Social Security Number?"

Victor opened his notebook and gave Mr. Stanley Lieutenant Hill's social security number. He typed through the appropriate screens and whistled aloud, glancing over at Victor.

"What did you find?" Victor came to his feet and walked around Mr. Stanley's desk to look over his shoulder at the computer screen.

"For a soldier, she was very well off." He positioned the computer monitor for Victor to take a closer look. "Unless the army pays better now than when I retired a couple of years ago."

"Not a chance," Victor joked.

Lieutenant Hill had been receiving an additional twenty-five thousand dollars a month for the past six months electronically into her savings account. At the time of her death she had a total of one-hundred-fifty thousand dollars.

"Can you tell me where the electronic payments are coming from?" Victor asked.

"All you have to do is ask." He typed into another screen. "The name of the payer is," he used a short stubby finger to find the name, "Devereaux & Associates. The payment came in on the first of each month for the past six months."

A few minutes later, Victor walked out of Mr. Stanley's office with copies of Lieutenant Hill's bank records. She also purchased a safe deposit box. Inside he only found a copy of her will leaving everything to her son.

An hour later, Victor waited in the spacious foyer of the senator's house as Caesar, the butler, announced his arrival. A moment later, he returned and ushered Victor directly into the study. Victor loved the room filled with commissioned art, expensive but tasteful furnishings, and brass pieces.

"Good morning, Victor," Rosetta said with a wide grin.

"Hello, Rosetta." Victor leaned down and kissed her on both cheeks.

"I'm sorry to drop in on such short notice."

"Don't be ridiculous." Rosetta placed her arm within Victor's. "You're welcome here any time. Come on in and make yourself at home. Harold will be down in a moment. He's on the phone again." She led him into the living room and sat down.

"I know he's busy taking care of details for the fundraiser." Victor took the seat next to Rosetta. "I just need a couple of minutes."

"We both have been so busy. I've barely seen Harold this week." Rosetta crossed her legs properly at the ankles. "Can I have Caesar bring you something?"

"No thank you, Rosetta," Victor answered.

"I guess you have been busy yourself, with the two murders. Poor Dominique. She is beside herself."

"She took Robbin's death very hard," Victor added.

"Thank you for being there for her. Harold and I appreciate that. First, it was Lieutenant Hill," she shook her head in disbelief, "now Robbin. I don't know how much more Dominique can take."

"I'm just glad I could be there for her," Victor admitted.

"I saw on the news you released Lieutenant Thomas Echols, Robbin's husband. Do you have another suspect?"

"I can't say anything about the case."

"I understand. You can't talk about it while the investigation is still going on." Rosetta changed the subject. "Let's talk about something pleasant." A smile appeared on her face. "Harold tells me you and Dominique had dinner the other night."

"Yes, we did. We had a wonderful time."

Rosetta's face lit up. "That's what I want to hear. You may be my son-in-law."

"Colonel." Senator Upton voice boomed into the room.

Victor came to his feet to show Senator Upton respect. The senator leaned down to kiss Rosetta on the cheek. "Sweetheart."

Senator Upton turned to address Victor. "Sorry to keep you waiting." He extended a hand then gave him a slap on the back.

"I didn't give you much notice."

"What do you want to talk to me about? It sounded pretty serious on the phone."

Victor glanced over to Rosetta. "Can we speak in private?"

"Sure we can. We can talk in the library," Senator Upton said.

Rosetta came to her feet. "You don't have to do that. I have some things to check on." She turned to Victor and said, "We will talk later."

"Of course, Rosetta." Victor waited until Rosetta disappeared before he removed the letter from his front shirt pocket. "I found this letter at Lieutenant Hill quarters. It's on your office letterhead."

Senator Upton put on a pair of expensive glasses before reading the letter. "What arrangements?" He flipped the letter over.

"I don't know, sir. That's why I'm here," Victor reluctantly said. "I thought you could tell me."

Senator Upton removed his glasses and handed the letter back to Victor. "I don't have any idea."

"It may be connected to the murders."

"It looks authentic," Senator Upton admitted. "It's not signed," he pointed out. "It can be from anyone and about anything."

Victor sighed. "I know. I would like to speak with your staff."

Senator Upton looked at Victor in disbelief. "You can't be serious. I'm in the middle of reelection. My fundraiser is day after tomorrow and all you have is a letter that may not mean anything."

"And it may mean something."

"I can't risk it."

"I apologize about the timing. There's nothing I can do about that."

"That's it?" Senator Upton said in desperation. "That's all you have to say? Do you know what the media will do to me once they get wind of this? You questioning my staff about those murders." He ran his hand down his face in frustration. "I can't afford this type of negative publicity. Not now."

"Two female officers are dead," Victor explained. "Robbin was a close friend of Dominique's. I thought you would want to do everything you can to help in the investigation."

Senator Upton's face went blank. "Victor, don't paint me out to be insensitive. My heart goes out to their families. But I have to look at the big picture. They are dead. I can't afford to have my name mixed up in this case." He shook his head. "No. I can't allow you to question my staff."

Victor straightened. At the moment he wished he were any place than where he was. He sympathized with the senator and he understood the negative publicity it would put on his campaign.

"I could always get a court order."

"I didn't say you couldn't question my staff. But it will have to be after the fundraiser."

"That's not how it works, and you know it. We can find a way to do this in secret. Get a gag order."

"I can't risk it. After all we've been through together you can't put this off until after the fundraiser."

Victor can see the despair in Senator Upton's eyes. "You know I can't."

"You mean you won't. What difference can a day or two make?"

"It makes a lot of difference," Victor replied.

"Dominique told me you want to close this case before you retire."

Victor caught Senator Upton's meaning. "You know me better than that, Senator. I'm following up on a lead."

"When Dominique told me of your reluctance to follow up when Lieutenant Greene's claim that she saw another suspect, I defended you. I said ,'Victor is only doing his job. He's following the evidence. He knows what he's doing.' Well, Lieutenant Greene is dead. I'm not about to let you kill my chances for reelection."

Victor felt like someone kicked him in the chest. Senator Upton was blaming him for Robbin's death. He felt bad enough without him rubbing salt into the wound.

"I can't believe you're blaming me for Lieutenant Greene's murder. I came here as a friend not an agent. I could have come to your office and started questioning your staff."

"You could have. What about you, Victor? Are you treating me as a friend?" Senator Upton stressed the word 'friend'. "I asked you to do me a favor. To put the questioning off a day or two. You refused. Just like you did when Dominique begged you to follow up on Lieutenant Greene's story."

Victor couldn't believe that Senator Upton was using the death of Lieutenant Greene to push his own political agenda gain. He didn't care about the murders. Victor closed the small gap between them. The two men eyed each other up and down like two soldiers preparing to do battle.

"Yes, I refused," Victor replied, breaking the tension between them. "I will have to live with that. But right now my job is to find out who killed them. With your hesitation I'm beginning to think there is a reason you're trying to divert attention from your office."

Victor saw the twitch in Senator Upton's jaw. He was doing his best to remain calm. "I'm going to pretend like I didn't hear that."

"Don't," Victor snapped. "I meant it."

"Be careful, Colonel," Senator Upton threatened. "Remember who you're talking to."

Victor didn't back down. "I know exactly who I'm talking to, *Senator*."

Senator Upton's shoulder sagged. "I guess we're at an impasse."

"I guess we are." Victor turned and began to walk away.

"I'm telling you to reconsider."

Victor turned back around. "I'm no longer under your command. You don't give the orders." Victor headed toward the door again. When he entered the foyer. He ran into Dominique standing at the foot of the stairwell talking with Rosetta. He wondered if they overheard the conversation.

"Let's talk about this," Senator Upton said, following Victor.

Victor's gaze went from Dominique to Rosetta noting the look of confusion on their faces.

"Victor, what's going on?" Dominique asked.

"It may be better if you spoke with the senator," Victor said, touching her on the arm.

"Go ahead and tell her," Senator Upton challenged. He was still fuming. "Tell Dominique you believe someone from my office may have killed Robbin and Lieutenant Hill."

Dominique and Rosetta gasped. Both women looked at each other.

Dominique turned back to Victor. "Victor, is this true?"

"I only want to question the staff," Victor said, answering Dominique question but looking at Senator Upton. Rosetta was trying to calm him down as they headed up the stairs.

"Why?" Dominique asked. "What makes you think someone from Uncle Harold office is involved?"

"I found a letter from the senator's office when we went back out to Lieutenant Hill's quarters," Victor carefully explained. "Lieutenant Hill made and received numerous phone calls from the senator's office. The last one made on the day she was killed."

Dominique's eyes locked with Victor. "You found a letter and you didn't tell me?"

Victor hated her voice was laced with pain almost as much as he hated for her to find out the way she did. "I didn't want to say anything until I found out what the letter meant. I still don't know what it means."

Dominique crossed the room before turning back to look at Victor. Her arms wrapped around her middle as if trying to hold herself together. She was hurt.

Victor attempted to walk toward Dominique. She took a step backward. "Listen, Dominique." He glanced up at the senator who was standing at the top of the stairs. He seemed to be enjoying the scene.

"You knew you were going to question my uncle. You never said a word."

"Dominique, can't you just trust me?"

"Why should I?" she fired at him. "You always manage to hurt me."

Victor reached for her and held her upper arm in a tight grip. "I'm not trying to hurt you. I'm just trying to find out who killed Lieutenant Hill and Robbin." Before she had a chance to answer, Rosetta ran down the stairs and grabbed her niece by the elbow.

"Lets go dear." She turned toward Victor. "And you ought to be ashamed of yourself. How can you possibly think my husband or his staff could have anything to do with those awful murders?"

Before Victor can answer they left him standing alone in the foyer.

A moment later he slid behind the wheel of his truck and turned the key in the ignition. Less than twenty-four hours to solve the case. But along the way Victor was losing all the people in his life he cared about.

𝒞𝒮 ℰ𝒪

Victor went back to CID. Reporters descended upon the truck like a swarm of bees. Cameras flashed, mini-cams rolled, and microphones pounced in his face. Victor exited the vehicles and questions flew.

"Colonel Sexton, another female officer has been strangled. Do you think it may be a serial killer?"

"Lieutenant Echols has been released. Do you have another suspect?" another reporter asked.

The questions came fast and furious. Victor moved quickly toward the door. "No comment," he shouted. "No comment."

As he was about to enter the door of CID, a man stepped in front of him, blocking his path. He looked to be in his late thirties, slim build, blonde hair, wide smile, and light eyes. He recognized him as Richard Forte, a reporter for CNN news. Victor groaned. He was the last person he wanted to see. If there's a story, he'd find it. He tried to sidestep him, but he stuck a microphone in his face.

"Colonel Sexton, sources say that you visited Senator Upton earlier today. Would you care to comment on the nature of your visit? Was it in connection to the murders? Is he a suspect?"

Victor looked surprised. How did he know about his visit to Senator Upton? "No comment," he said, sidestepping Richard Forte. Up ahead, Benitez opened the double doors for him.

"How did the reporter Richard Forte know about my visit to Senator Upton?"

"Good question. I don't believe it was anyone from this office."

"I hope not." Victor led Benitez into his office. He removed his jacket, placing it on the back of the chair.

Benitez took a seat across from Victor's desk.

Victor then spent a few minutes filling him in on what transpired. When finished, Benitez nodded. "Do you think the senator is involved?"

Victor ran a hand over his face. "Right now, I don't know what to think."

𝒞𝒮 ℰ𝒪

Dominique paced the length of her Aunt Rosetta and Uncle Harold's study, her mind running to and fro. It was no wonder with the news she'd learned today. On top of the death of Robbin, she felt like she was having a nervous breakdown. Maybe she should be out jogging to get rid of the tension, but she didn't have the energy. She couldn't believe the scene that played out between Victor and Uncle Harold. Was there a connection between the murders and Uncle Harold's office? Dominique's insides trembled as she thought about it. If someone from her uncle's office was involved, there will be a scandal. Something her Uncle Harold did not want. No matter, there was an investigation going on. Dominique had to be honest with herself. Victor would never deliberately hurt Uncle Harold's chances for reelection, she was sure of that. Though Victor purposely kept the letter from Dominique when she was beginning to trust him again, she had to see the bigger picture. As he'd calmly informed her, he may not be involved.

Dominique headed into the kitchen. She reached up into the oak cupboard, grabbed a cup, filled it with water, and placed it into the microwave. Her mind couldn't help but wander to the kiss they shared together. She crumbled, folded like a deck of cards under his touch. She retrieved her cup from the microwave. She was angry at herself.

Chemistry was never a problem between them. Timing was the issue. Dominique reached for the Herbal tea packet and dumped the bag into the mug of steaming water. Each time he said the name of the woman he almost married, her heart dropped. She knew she shouldn't be jealous, but Victor left her in Europe without a goodbye and later he was engaged. Dominique leaned against the counter with cup in hand. She forced herself to concentrate on something else. Was Uncle Harold's office involved in the murders?

radford Farrell worked his way up the political ladder. It had been a long, hard road, but he'd done it. Born into a poor family, he loved the idea of coming from nothing to achieve the success that he had. He had a high income, a wonderful wife, and a large, Victorian house in the Virginia countryside. He was surrounded by some of the most influential men in the world. Not bad for the scrawny kid from Forrest City, Arkansas, that was laughed at and picked on in elementary school. The people in his community and those on Capitol Hill knew about him. He liked feeling important.

He never knew his father who left home when Bradford was an infant. His mother had never gotten over his father. At the age of ten, he found himself in foster care after his mother died from drinking herself to death. Foster care moved him from home to home. Stepfamilies taking him in to receive a check. He was locked in closets, beaten, and sometimes fed enough to keep him alive. Despite all that, he managed to get good grades in high school and secured a full scholarship to Georgetown University. Once he earned a Political Science degree, he never looked back.

Bradford worked as Senator Harold Upton administrative assistant and problem solver. He listened to the complaints of disgruntled congressman and constituents. The ringing of the telephone interrupted his thoughts. He answered on the second ring.

"Senator Upton's office, Bradford Farrell speaking. How may I help you?" He leaned back in his black, leather chair.

"A letter was found in Lieutenant Hill's quarters," Senator Upton said on the other end.

Bradford sat straighter in his chair. The Senator was rattled. He didn't sound like his normal poised self. A situation of this magnitude could spiral out of control and cost Senator Upton the election. He couldn't allow that to happen. "Who has the letter?" Bradford asked.

"Victor Sexton, CID," Senator Upton replied. "Showed it to me personally."

Bradford had never met Victor Sexton personally, but he'd heard the senator speak highly about the fellow special operations officer on numerous occasions. The senator looked upon him as a son and Bradford knew the senator was hoping that Victor Sexton would join his staff. The senator had a past and if Victor Sexton began digging around, the information will surface and possibly cost him the election.

"What does he know?" Bradford asked calmly keeping the alarm out of his voice.

"Nothing so far," Senator Upton told him. "He wants to question the staff."

"Let him. The staff doesn't know anything."

"That's not the point, you idiot," Senator Upton replied. "We can't afford the publicity. If he begins to dig, sooner or later he's going to find out about Lieutenant Hill." That's not what Bradford wanted to hear. He bit back an expletive. "We don't need this right now."

A deep sigh came through the phone. "Tell me about it. You told me not to worry. You were going to handle this." Senator Upton voice rose. "I can't believe you left a paper trail. Which has led to me. Now I want you to fix this."

Bradford was usually on top of the situation. He was a genius at handling crisis — a great assess to his staff — but was lacking in common sense. Bradford leaving a paper trail was a prime example of that fact. "Right away. I'm sorry. I'll make a phone call."

"How long will this take?" Senator Upton asked. He'd run out of patience. He shouldn't be having this conversation with Bradford.

"I don't know, sir."

Senator Upton jumped to his feet. "What do you mean, you don't know?" he barked into the phone. "We went through a lot to keep this thing with Lieutenant Hill under control. This thing could blow up in our faces."

"I know that sir—" Bradford began to say as another tirade began.

"Where is the tape?"

"I don't know, Senator."

"Find it!" Senator Upton roared.

"I need more time," Bradford said.

"You have run out of time. Victor refused to delay the questioning and probably get a court order to pay us a visit. I don't have to tell you what that means if the media get wind of this. If I go down then so will you." The line went dead.

Bradford slowly hung up the phone. He knew the letter was a

mistake and tried to retrieve it, along with the tape. Chapman found neither. Bradford needed to calm down. Lieutenant Hill had been taken care of. Lieutenant Greene's murder was unfortunate. The letter was not signed and it cannot be linked to anyone in the office. The tape has to be found. He just had to make sure he got to it before Colonel Sexton.

ɢʀ

Dominique silently stood in the doorway of the library. She was reeling over what she'd just heard. Uncle Harold was involved in Lieutenant Hill's murder. Victor was on to something. She had to tell him what she heard. She quietly backed out of the doorway.

ɢʀ

Senator Upton hung up the phone, catching a glimpse of someone at the door. He hurried over to the door but no one was there. He rushed down the stairway and out the front door. He got there in time to see Dominique rushing to get in her car. She glanced back at him. He wondered how much of the telephone conversation she'd overheard.

ɢʀ

Dominique made the turn onto Interstate 395, dashing around a slow-moving Volkswagen. Not sure what she overheard, she had to put her personal feelings aside and think straight. That's what she needed to do.

As she drove along the stretch of highway heading for downtown D.C., she realized that part of her anxiety had to do with the fact that she told her uncle about what Robbin saw the night Lieutenant Hill was killed. Did her uncle hire Scott Chapman to kill both women? If so, why? Dominique rambled around in her purse until she found her cellular phone. She tried to keep her eyes on the road as she quickly dialed Victor's office.

"Let me speak to Colonel Sexton," Dominique said to Private Atkins. She listened as she was transferred to his office. He answered on the second ring.

"Colonel Sexton."

Dominique breathed a sigh of relief. "Victor, I'm glad I caught you. We have to talk. It's important."

Dominique didn't sound like her normal self. Something was wrong. "What is it?"

"I overheard a conversation between Uncle Harold and Bradford Farrell. You may be on to something."

"Come into the office." Until he knew how involved the senator was, Victor wanted Dominique close by his side. Dominique thought back to when she met Robbin there the night Lieutenant Echols was arrested. It was the first time she'd ever been in a station. She felt uneasy.

"Can you meet me at Cadence? I'm on the interstate. I can meet you there in about thirty minutes."

"Go straight to the club, Dominique," Victor commanded.

⅛ ⅚

Chapman entered through the Mahogany doors of Cadence. He glanced around the elegant, plush club. It was lunchtime and the place was full. There were even a few Caucasian customers. He didn't feel out of place. A tall, thin, well-dressed African- American man greeted him at the door. One glance and Chapman knew he was related to Victor Sexton. He mentioned he had a younger brother and sister.

"Good afternoon, welcome to Cadence." The gentleman extended a hand. "I'm Gerald Sexton, owner. I've never seen you here before. First time?"

"Yes it is," Chapman replied. "I'm new to the D.C. area. Your establishment came highly recommended," he explained, accepting Gerald Sexton's hand.

"I'm glad to hear that, Mr..." Gerald prompted, letting the man know he didn't catch his name.

"Davis. Roger Davis," Chapman answered. He'd heard the name on a television sitcom and decided to use it when he phoned to make his reservation. He'd been scouting the club for the past couple of days. He knew Victor wouldn't be at the club this late in the afternoon. Chapman smiled to himself. Victor was looking for him and he was having lunch at his club!

"Enjoy your lunch, Mr. Davis," Gerald said and gestured for Mya.

The hostess directed Chapman to a table in the back. It had an obstructed view, no window, and close to the emergency exit, just in case he had to make a hasty departure. He sat down and Mya handed him a menu. She took his order and then disappeared.

Chapman looked over at the woman already seated at the table next to him. The young, plain blonde stared. His eyes took in the clinging halter top she was wearing. Any other time he would approach her, take her home, and give her what she desired — him. At the moment he had business to take care of. Bradford phoned to tell him Victor discovered the letter he'd been searching for at Lieutenant's Hill quarters. He didn't find the tape.

The senator was furious, afraid the investigation will surface what's on the tape. If Victor didn't mention the tape, he didn't find it. The only thing Chapman could think of was that Lieutenant Hill gave it to someone. Maybe Lieutenant Echols. If Lieutenant Echols knew what was on the tape, he hadn't talked. The plan was to retrieve the tape before Victor.

Chapman's plan was to go further. He was just waiting for the right time. His time. He was sure Victor confirmed his release from prison. Chapman wanted Victor to know he'd been released and positioned himself outside of PJ's Sandwich Shop. The more Victor dug into the case, he could discover his involvement. That will lead Colonel Sexton straight to him.

08 80

"Hello, Gerald," Dominique said, stepping into the foyer. She glanced around looking for Victor. "Has Victor arrived?"

"No. I'm not expecting him," Gerald replied with an incredulous look on his face.

"He's supposed to meet me here." Dominique glanced at her watch. It was almost noon.

Gerald watched Dominique closely. She appeared shaken. "Are you all right?" He lightly touched her arm.

"I'm fine." Dominique slightly tilted her head to one side. "The past couple of days have been rough for me."

Gerald heard about the death of Robbin. His heart went out to her. "I'm sorry about Robbin."

Her head bobbed up and down. "Thank you, Gerald."

"Would you like to wait in my office until Victor arrives?" Gerald offered, leading the way. "I'm sure he will be here soon."

"Thank you," Dominique said, following him.

Ten minutes later, Victor entered through the doors of Cadence and headed to the bar.

"Afternoon, Colonel," Hunnicutt spoke as he replaced a shot glass on the counter. "Good to see you."

"Hunnicutt." Victor nodded. "How are you?"

"From what I've seen on television, a lot better than you." He raised an inquisitive eyebrow.

"Tell me about it," Victor replied.

"How are you holding up?"

"I'm hanging in there." Victor glanced around hoping to see

Dominique. She was nowhere to be found. Gerald would know if she'd arrived. "Where's Gerald?"

"He's in the office," Kim answered as she sauntered up to the bar. "He and Dominique Frazier went in together." She flashed Victor her best smile.

"Thanks, Kim." Victor pointed toward Hunnicutt. "We'll talk later."

"You got it, sir," Hunnicutt said to Victor's back as Victor hurried toward the office.

Hunnicutt couldn't help but notice Kim watching Victor until he was out of sight. She turned to Hunnicutt and grinned.

Victor opened Gerald's office door to find Dominique in the room alone. Upon his entry she rose from the sofa and forced a smile.

"I'm glad you could make it." Dominique cleared her throat, tucking a strand of hair behind her ear. "I didn't think you would see me after what happened this morning."

"You should know that I'm not easily offended."

Dominique nodded in agreement. "I should know that by now."

"You sounded urgent on the phone." Victor was looking her directly in the face. "What happened?"

Dominique nervously shifted from one foot to the other. Her heart turned over every time Victor looked at her. "I overheard a disturbing conversation between Uncle Harold and his assistant, Bradford Farrell."

Victor folded his arms across his chest. Dominique had his full attention.

"Uncle Harold was furious about you wanting to question the staff," she explained.

"I know." Victor shook his head, remembering the argument he and Senator Upton had several hours earlier. "We had it out this morning."

"I heard him tell Bradford to do everything he can to stop you from questioning them."

Victor wasn't surprised at the senator's move. He'd made it clear he would prevent the questioning from taking place. "That doesn't surprise me."

"You didn't hear him, Victor," Dominique replied, remembering the icy tone in her uncle's voice. "I've never seen him like that. He scared me." She dropped her head, wringing her hands together. "Uncle Harold knows more than you think."

Victor took a deep sigh. He'd gotten the same feeling. He didn't want to believe it. He wondered why Dominique was telling him what she overheard. She had to know the information could help bring down one of the most powerful men in the senate. The man who raised her.

"Why are you telling me? You could have kept this to yourself."

Dominique turned her back to Victor. She folded her arms around herself. Victor was correct. Her decision to repeat what she'd heard could land Uncle Harold in prison. "Robbin was my friend," she said, turning around to face him. "I want to know if he's responsible for her death."

"What if he's responsible?"

Dominique's mouth opened but nothing came out.

Victor touched her arm lightly. "You don't have to answer. How much of the conversation did you overhear?"

She ran her hand through her hair in thought. It was meant to be a sign of frustration, but Victor thought it was sexy.

"He's looking for a tape."

"A tape?" Victor asked anxious. The tape may be another piece of the puzzle. "What tape? What did he say?"

"I heard him say Bradford was responsible for getting it back from Lieutenant Hill."

Victor frowned. A tape could explain Senator Upton reluctant to cooperate. Where was the tape? What was on it? Was it what the killer was looking for?

"Does the senator know you overheard the conversation?"

"He saw me when I was leaving."

Victor sat down next to her on the sofa. "You may be in danger, Dominique."

"I don't think so." Dominique examined his expression, Victor looked worried. "He's my uncle," she finally said. "He would never do anything to harm me."

Victor placed her hands in his and squeezed. "We don't know that. This is serious business. A lot is at stake. Two people involved with this case have already been murdered."

"You think my uncle had them killed?" She removed her hand from his. "I admit what I heard doesn't look good for my uncle. He could be protecting his campaign for reelection. It doesn't mean he murdered anybody."

"That's true. I don't want to take any chances. I did once before and..." Victor's voice trailed off.

Dominique knew Victor was referring to Robbin. She looked at him. The fear in his gaze was undoing her.

"Until I know for sure who is involved, I want you close to me."

She understood Victor's concern. "That's not necessary. I can take care of myself." Dominique stood. "I don't need protection."

Victor got up off the sofa. "Where are you going?"

The expression in his gaze shook her. She struggled to come to terms with what she saw in his eyes. "I'm going home." After Robbin's death, she put in leave from her job for the next two weeks. She wanted to be in her own surrounding to put everything in perspective.

"Sweetheart, I don't want you to go home alone."

She breathe in a shaky breath and let it out slowly. "Victor, cut it out. You're scaring me."

He threw his hands up. "Good. I don't want anything to happens to you."

"Nothing is going to happen to me. I have the next two weeks off from work. I plan to use the time to finish decorating my place. That should keep my mind off this situation."

He glared down at her. "That's not going to make things go away."

"You have a better idea?"

"Come with me." Victor took her by the elbow and out the door.

"Where are we going?"

"Devereaux & Associates," Victor replied.

Dominique stopped in mid-stride and looked at Victor in surprise. Devereaux & Associates was the name of the accounting company that handled all of her uncle's business and personal finances. "You recognize the name?" Victor asked.

"Yes. They handle the family finances. Why?"

"According to bank records, for the past six months, Lieutenant Hill received an additional twenty-five thousand dollars electronically into her account. The payer is Devereaux & Associates."

CR ∞

Chapman finished his grilled chicken sandwich, French fries, and iced tea. He wiped his mouth with his napkin and then left a dollar tip on the table. As he made his way toward the entrance of Cadence, he noticed Victor and an attractive woman engrossed in a conversation with his brother, Gerald. He nonchalantly strolled to the bar, careful not to bring attention to himself, and took a seat on the stool.

Chapman swallowed and carefully turned his head to the side, giving Victor an icy stare. He had to stick to the plan which consisted of retrieving the tape and paying back the man who cost him seven years of his life.

"What will it be?" Hunnicutt asked him.

Ignoring his question, Chapman glanced back over his shoulder as

Victor and the woman were leaving. Chapman turned around to find Hunnicutt staring at him.

"Nothing for me," he answered and walked out behind Victor and Dominique.

ominique stood in the prestigious office of James Devereaux on wobbly legs. More damaging evidence surfaced connecting her uncle to the murders. She wanted answers.

"Dominique," Devereaux's handsome face beamed as he shook her hand, before bringing it to his lips. "It's good to see you again." He gave Victor a cursory glance before turning his attention back to Dominique. "It's been much too long."

He was ogling her, Victor thought. He didn't like it.

"I agree," Dominique said, returning his smile.

"How's the army treating you?" He moved in close, Dominique's hand still enclosed in his.

Victor had seen enough. He flashed his badge. "I'm Lieutenant Colonel Victor Sexton. I'm looking into the murders of Lieutenant Tamara Hill and Lieutenant Robbin Greene."

Dominique cut him a look.

"Yes. We spoke on the phone. Have a seat." James pointed to two chairs. "The two female officers that were strangled? I saw it on the news. Ugly business"

"Yes," Dominique answered. "Both women worked for me."

"I apologize for the short notice," Victor said after they were seated.

"It's no problem," Devereaux said, making himself comfortable behind the desk. "Anything I can do to help."

Victor nodded. "Thank you. I'm hoping you can answer some questions for us."

"If I can."

Dominique looked over at Victor signaling for her to take the lead.

Victor wasn't sure he was comfortable with the decision, not pleased with the way Devereaux was still looking at her.

Dominique handed James the printed copy of the electronic payments to Lieutenant Hill's bank account. "What can you tell us about this account?"Devereaux examined the statement. "What would you like to know?" He looked from Victor to Dominique.

"We want to know the name of the person sending the payments to Lieutenant Hill's account," Victor said.

Devereaux shrugged. "I can't give you that information."

"Can't or won't?" Dominique answered.

Devereaux sighed. "That's privileged information."

Dominique glanced over at Victor then back at Devereaux. "James, we're trying to solve two murders. We already know the payments are coming from my uncle's account. We just need a name."

Devereaux looked uncomfortable. "Does the senator know you're here?"

"Does it matter?" she said.

"Yes it does. As much as I want to help you, I can't let you see those records without proper authorization from your uncle."

"I'll come back with a search warrant," Victor added to the conversation. "I'll not only view the senator's account, but all of your accounts. I'm sure we'll find something."

Devereaux gave him a smug look. "You're CID, which means you don't have jurisdiction here. I don't take kindly to threats."

Victor didn't miss a beat. "It's no threat. I can easily contact the local authorities if that will make you feel better."

Devereaux stared at him, a muscle twitching at his lower jaw. "I have nothing else to say to either of you." He gave Dominique a hard look. "Any other questions should be directed to my attorney."

Victor looked at Dominique. Without a warrant there wasn't anything he could do about it. Reluctantly, Victor said, " I'll be back. I'll be sure to have a search warrant."

"I'll be here," Devereaux replied smugly.

The trail that began warm had gone cold. Dominique climbed into Victor's truck and closed the door.

Victor climbed in, sticking the key in the ignition. "I really need to take a look at those files."

"What are the odds the files will be there when you return with a search warrant?"

"Slim to none," Victor echoed. The ringing of his cellular phone interrupted them. "Colonel Sexton." He listened a second. "I'm on my way, General."

Dominique looked at him, curious. "The General?"

"A representative from the senator's staff is in his office. They are requesting my presence."

"Drop me off at the club. I'll pick up my car."

He frowned.

Dominique could see the worried expression on his handsome face.

"I don't think you should be alone," he replied.

"Victor, we already had this discussion. I will be fine," Dominique stressed. "Don't worry."

He turned toward her, took her by the shoulder, and stared into her eyes. "That's impossible. You know that."

"I know you have reason to worry. I promise I will be very careful. If anything looks or sound suspicious, you will be the first to know."

For a moment she thought he was going to argue with her then he issued a sigh and nodded. "You call me the moment you arrive home."

Victor turned the key, carefully maneuvering the vehicle out into traffic. As they drove the conversation flowed easily between them until he pulled alongside her car. He got out of the truck, came around to the passenger side, and opened her door.

Once in her car, she settled behind the steering wheel, making herself comfortable. "Let me know how the meeting goes."

"I will. Call me the moment you arrive home," he repeated.

"How long will you be?" Dominique found herself asking.

"A couple of hours." Victor stuck his head inside the window of the car and kissed her, opening her mouth, inviting the hot, sweet taste of his tongue.

Together their tongues took on a mating ritual. She heard herself purring softly as her hand gently touched the side of his face.

Victor pulled back, looking deep into her eyes. "I'll see and talk to you later."

After Victor drove off in the opposite direction, Dominique headed back to Devereaux & Associates. She parked across the street from the building and cut the engine. She sighed and tried not to think about Victor. He would never approve of what she was doing. She glanced at her watch. Victor was meeting with the General and a member of Uncle Harold's staff. Maybe she should have gone with him instead of pulling a foolish stunt like she was about to do. *What if you got caught?* an inner voice whispered. She leaned back against the headrest and closed her eyes, torn. Should she go through with it or should she leave? She could just imagine the headlines if something went wrong: *Niece of Senator Harold Upton arrested for breaking and entering.*

As she thought about the fallout from her actions, James Devereaux, accompanied by a woman, walked out of the building together arm-in-arm. Dominique's heart thumped wildly as she watched him open the Mercedes car door for his companion. She wondered what Mrs. Devereaux would think about this little scene.

As he strolled around the vehicle, Devereaux looked in her direction. She ducked down, hoping he hadn't seen her. When she looked up again, he was pulling out of the parking space and heading west.

ଓ ଓ

Victor couldn't help shake the feeling that something was wrong and it grew intense by the time he entered the General's office.

"Come in, Colonel Sexton," General Goss said as he flew around the desk to greet him. He had a nervous look fixed on his face. "I know you're busy. This will only take a minute."

"No problem, sir." Victor said, forcing his attention on the man sitting in the chair opposite from the desk, his legs crossed. He appeared to be examining Victor. He didn't speak. Victor felt the muscles in his jaw tightened as his eyes darted from the general to the stranger. Tension was thick in the room. Something wasn't right. Whatever it was, Victor had the feeling he wasn't going to like it.

"What's going on, sir?" Victor asked challengingly.

"Colonel Sexton, I'm Bradford Farrell, Senator Upton's Administrative Assistant."

Victor nodded as he acknowledged him. Bradford Farrell was the man Dominique said was given instructions to locate the tape. Now he's here in the General's office.

"This should be interesting," Victor thought.

"Let me start by saying it's a pleasure to finally meet you," Bradford said, flashing Victor a Colgate smile. "I've heard a lot about you from the senator. I feel like I know you, already."

Victor looked at Farrell through hooded eyes. He'd been around long enough to know when he was about to be snowed. "It's a pleasure to meet you. Dominique has told me about you."

Farrell smiled slipped instantly. "I'm sure she has."

"What can I do for you, Mr. Farrell?" Victor wasn't interested in the cat and mouse game the man was playing.

"Please call me, Bradford."

"I rather not," Victor said.

Bradford smirked. "That's fine. I'll get to the point. You paid a visit to Senator Upton this morning, questioning him about the murders of Lieutenant Hill and Greene."

"I didn't question the senator about the murders," Victor threw back. "I went to discuss a piece of evidence that was found at Lieutenant Hill's quarters."

"I'm well aware of the reason for your visit," Bradford admitted.

"Then tell me, why are you really here?"

Bradford took a seat in the chair and then crossed his right leg over the opposite knee. "The senator wanted you to put off the questioning until after the election, as a favor to him."

"I'm sure you know my reply to the senator."

"Colonel, that's the reason for Mr. Bradford's visit," General Goss threw in.

"Which is?"

Bradford reached inside his suit jacket, stood to his feet, and pulled out a white folded piece of paper. "It's a restraining order. You can't come anywhere near the senator, his office, or his staff."

Victor looked at General Goss then back to Farrell, who was pleased with himself. Victor grabbed the paper and followed with a silent expletive.

"I'm sorry we had to go this route, but like the senator explained to you the press and his opponents would have a field day with this," he said calmly. "We can't afford the publicity."

Victor skimmed the paper. "I see you covered all the bases."

Farrell smirked again. "We will be more than happy to work with the next commander of CID."

"I'm sure you will."

Farrell flushed.

Victor hit the paper with his hand. "Do you really think I will allow this restraining order to prevent me from investigating this case!" he snapped.

"Just stay away from the senator."

Victor pointed a finger in Farrell's face. "I'm going to solve this case with or without the senator's cooperation."

"At ease Colonel," General Goss commanded.

Victor ignored him. "You coming here today proves my theory. Senator Upton has something to hide or he wouldn't be going through all this trouble to keep me from investigating."

"What are you implying?" Farrell said with sarcasm. "Are you saying the senator had something to do with the murders?"

"That's not what Colonel Sexton is saying at all," General Goss said, clearly horrified at the suggestion. "I ordered him to be very careful in his approach to the senator."

"I was!" Victor said angrily. "I didn't ask one question about the murders."

"Now you can't." Bradford sneered.

On that note, Bradford picked his briefcase off the desk and headed toward the door. When he passed, Victor leaned over and whispered loud enough for only the administrative assistant to hear. "I know you're looking for a tape."

Bradford glared back at him and continued out the door.

Once the door closed, General Goss lit into Victor. "What the hell were you doing accusing the Senator of murder?"

"Sir, I didn't accuse the senator of anything."

Victor may as well have been talking to himself. The General was clearly agitated. "I have been getting phone calls all morning about this case. I told you not to speak to the press without clearing it with me first."

"Sir, no one in my office has spoken to the press."

"Stay away from the senator."

Victor shot the General a look as if he'd lost his mind. "Sir, he's the key to the murders."

General Goss dipped his head in frustration. "You don't know that for sure."

"Not yet but I'm close. When I do, this restraining order won't be worth the paper it's written on."

ის ფი

Victor was in a foul mood when he returned to CID. He didn't speak to anyone, heading straight into his office, slamming the door behind him. He paced up and down the length of the floor like a caged panther, trying to calm himself down. Victor made a fist, thrusting it in his other hand. He had to look at the senator's financial records to piece together the connection to Lieutenant Hill. The flush expression on Bradford's face confirmed there was a tape. He'd turned beet red when Victor mentioned he knew they were looking for it. There is a question of jurisdiction. He planned to contact Detective West to have a civilian judge order an arrest and search warrant, but he didn't have enough concrete evidence.

Benitez knocked then carefully stuck his head into Victor's office. "Is it safe to come in?"

Victor stopped in mid-stride. "Of course."

"You look like you're about to kill someone. No pun intended."

"I was close to punching Bradford Farrell face in."

"Senator's Upton's administrative assistant? What happened?"

Victor took a deep sigh. "Dominique phoned and said to meet her at Cadence." Benitez nodded.

Victor handed Benitez a copy of the restraining order, then filled him in on everything that transpired within the last couple of hours. When he finished Benitez had a bewildered look on his face.

"I don't care what restrictions are placed on me. Nothing is going to prevent me from solving this case." Victor began pacing again. "I'm close," he gestured with two fingers, "I can feel it. They know it."

"I'm behind you one hundred percent. You know that," Benitez said.

Victor looked at his executive officer. While he was retiring, Benitez had a little over ten years left before he can retire. Victor wasn't going to let Benitez ruin his military career because of his actions.

"I can't allow you to jeopardize your military career because of me."

Benitez closed the small gap between them. "I've only worked with you a short time. In that time you have never given me any indication that you would do anything out of line. From what you've told me and what I know about this case, Senator Upton is involved. If it costs my military career, well I can always sale oranges by the freeway." He chuckled.

"I don't think Maria will like that." Maria was Benitez's wife, a social worker. They had been married nine years and had two handsome boys, Miguel, age seven and Juan II, age five.

"Maria understands that I chose a career in law enforcement to make a difference. I'm not going to back down because someone is using their power and status to hinder this investigation."

"Don't say I didn't warn you," was Victor's response.

"Sir, I speak for the entire staff when I say we will back you however you choose to proceed. Not so much because you're the commander, but because we know you're fair and honest. Two officers are dead. We want to catch whoever is responsible. No matter where it leads."

"Thanks, Benitez. I appreciate that. I really do."

"How do you want to proceed? I don't have to tell you the clock is ticking."

Victor managed a small grin. "No. You don't."

Benitez was trying to lighten the intense situation. This had to be the worst time for Victor. Victor was a dedicated officer/agent and gave one hundred percent of himself to his job. He was an agent who never got emotionally involved in cases. This case was different; however, Colonel Sexton has managed to investigate with an open mind. A task Benitez knew couldn't be easy.

"I believe Lieutenant Hill wasn't taking any chances. She may have known her life was in danger and put the tape in a safe place."

"But where?" Benitez rubbed his chin. "We went over her quarters with a fine tooth comb."

"It wasn't in her safe deposit box," Victor added. "I'm thinking she could have given it to someone for safekeeping."

They looked at each other as if reading each other's minds.

"It had to be someone she trusted," Victor said.

"Like a lover," Benitez replied.

"Lieutenant Echols has to know or seen something. Lets go have another chat with our old pal."

ominique managed to slip into the building undetected. She'd watched and waited when a man dressed in a brown environmental uniform opened the side door and pushed a large, gray dumpster outside. That was her way in. When the man placed a doorstopper to keep the door open, she knew it was her lucky day. She'd given the man a few minutes, and then snuck inside the building. It had taken a moment for her to get her sense of direction. Glancing over her shoulder, she'd briskly walked over to the elevator. Devereaux & Associates were on the fourth floor.

The elevator came to a stop and opened silently. Dominique stepped off and moved cautiously through the abandon hallway. Though it appeared deserted, Dominique knew some members of the staff sometimes worked late. She had to be careful. A moment later, she heard the sound of someone whistling coming down the corridor. She looked to the right, spotting the janitor's door, and stepped inside. The room was filled with buckets, mops, brooms, and cleaning supplies. She hoped the person wasn't a member of the janitorial staff.

Dominique cracked the door and peeped her head outside the door. She breathed a sigh of relief when the security guard continued down the corridor and turned left. She'd have to hurry before the guard came back around.

She moved cautiously down the corridor, searching for James Devereaux's office.

His office was two doors from the receptionist desk. She pressed her ear to the door, listening for sounds or movements inside. Not hearing anything, she turned the knob. It was unlocked.

Carefully, Dominique entered the room, closing the door behind her. Her eyes scanned the room. It appeared that Devereaux may have stepped out and would return. She was racing against time. She noticed a file cabinet, a desk, and chair. On the desk sat a computer. Next to it was a stack of brown folders. She ran over to the desk looking through the folders, looking for anything connected to her uncle or the murders. There was nothing. She pulled out the drawers to the desk, thumbing through the folders. Again nothing. She hastily moved over to the cabinet, keeping a trained eyes and ear focused on the door. She leafed through the folders, finding the alphabet U. There wasn't a folder. Devereaux must have removed the folder after she and Victor asked about the account. She looked toward the door. She was about to leave when she glanced at the computer. She was knowledgeable in numerous types of software, but working against time. Taking a seat in the chair, her eyes fell to the bottom of the monitor.

Devereaux did not log off. She reopened the last document. It was filled with columns of numbers. She looked at the top of the page but didn't recognize the name of the clients. Devereaux could come in at any moment. Her heart pumping, she clicked on '*start*' and continued skimming to documents. There were many. She read the list, her eyes moving from the screen to the door. Near the bottom of the page, Tamara Hill's name appeared. Just what she needed. After opening the file, the text flashed on the screen. She located the financial records for the past several months and sent the document to the printer. She hurried over to the printer. When the final page printed, she stuffed the documents in her bag. Going back to the computer, she deleted the last command, all the time watching, listening for any movements at the door. She replaced the original file at the bottom of the screen as she'd found it.

Dominique's head popped up at the sound of movement outside the door. Her body was paralyzed in place. She watched as the doorknob turned. *Hide,* an inner voice screamed. She looked around frantically. She ran toward a door inside the office, closing it behind her. It was a small, dark closet. The only light was from underneath the door. She chewed on her bottom lip.

Dominique could hear someone moving in the office. Silently, she began saying Victor's name, wishing he were here. Suddenly the sounds of desk drawers were heard opening and closing, followed by the file cabinets. She frowned. Why would Devereaux be searching his own office? Using the strength of the adrenaline pumping through her veins, she slightly pushed the door ajar. Dominique froze in terror as she watched the back of a man searching through the cabinets. She pulled the door close, praying the man would not discover her.

She stood still, hoping the man could not hear her breathing. Her mind running to and fro. Was he looking for the financial records? Did her uncle send him? She gasped in silence. *Oh my God, what if the man is Scott Chapman.* What began as a great idea may cost her life. *Okay. Okay,* she chided to herself. *Just calm down. He doesn't know you're here, so just be quiet and you will make it out of this alive.*

A few minutes later, Dominique pressed her ear to the door. She didn't hear anything. Carefully, she pushed the door open, and stuck her head out. The room was empty. She made a dash to the door. Stepping out into the corridor, she looked up and down the hallway, wondering where the man was. She hoped he was long gone.

Dominique made her way down the hallway. She felt the eerie presence of someone and moved swiftly. She glanced over her shoulder but didn't see anyone. Taking the hallway to the left, she heard the sound of running footsteps behind her. Panic gripped her. With trembling fingers she frantically pushed the elevator button. It was on the eleventh floor. She couldn't wait. Looking around she spotted the exit sign to her right. She turned and ran toward the door. It led to a set of stairs. She moved quickly, praying she'd lost who was behind her. The thought was short lived when she heard the exit door open and the sounds of footsteps coming close behind her.

Dominique reached the bottom of the stairs, pushing the door open. She paused a second to get her sense of direction. She breathed a sigh of relief. She knew where she was. Taking the corridor to the right would lead her out the side door that she'd snuck in earlier. Once outside, she made a beeline to her car. As she fished around in her purse for her keys, it fell to her feet, its contents spilling on the pavement. "Oh my God," she cried, reaching down to retrieve her items.

ʘ Ɇ

"My wife is dead," Lieutenant Echols said. "Because of you. Now you're asking for my help."

Colonel Sexton and Benitez were standing inside Lieutenant Echol's apartment.

"I'm sorry about Robbin," Victor said sadly. "But we need your help in catching who did it."

Lieutenant Echols gave him a stern look. "You got a lot of nerves. You're the reason she's dead. She tried to tell you what she saw, but you wouldn't listen." He choked back a sob. "Now she's gone."

"I know." Victor shook his head slowly. "I know you're going through a lot right now. I sympathize with you. I can't imagine knowing what you're going through. But we believe the same person who killed Lieutenant Hill also killed your wife. So if you know anything," Victor pleaded, "anything Lieutenant Hill may have said, or done that was out of character before she died, tell us."

Lieutenant Echols was visibly shaken. For a long time he didn't say anything at all.

Victor had given up on Lieutenant Echols when he said, "Tamara was afraid for her life after the meeting." Victor glanced at Benitez.

"What meeting?" Victor asked.

"A week before she was murdered, she met with someone, a man, at the Mall in D.C. She didn't want to go alone, so I went with her. I kept out of sight."

Victor took out his notebook. "Did she say who she was meeting?"

"No," Lieutenant Echols said. "She didn't tell me. All she said was that he was powerful and well-connected."

"Did you get a good look at the man?" Benitez questioned.

"No. His back was to me."

"Did Lieutenant Hill ever mention what they discussed?" Benitez continued.

"No. She didn't."

"All the time you two spent together, you're trying to tell us you never discussed the nature of the meeting?" Victor asked in disbelief.

Lieutenant Echols sighed. "Like I told you before, we enjoyed each other's company. That was as far as the relationship went. She didn't tell me what they discussed. I didn't ask." He walked over to the coffee table and picked up a pack of cigarette. Removing one, he placed it in his mouth and lit it.

"Did she ever mention to you anything about a video tape?" Victor asked.

Lieutenant Echols blew a puff of smoke and frowned. "A tape?"

"We believe that's what the killer was looking for the night Lieutenant Hill was killed," Victor explained.

"She never mentioned anything to me about a tape!" Lieutenant Echols snapped. "Or anything else."

Victor had heard enough. It was obvious they weren't going to get anything out of Lieutenant Echols. "Thank you." Victor closed his notebook. "What you told us is very helpful."

"I just wish I could tell you more," Lieutenant Echols said in a soft tone. "Since Robbin's death I haven't been able to think straight. I even took up smoking again." He smashed the cigarette butt out in the ashtray.

Victor glanced over at Benitez. "We understand." He reached inside his shirt pocket. "If you think of anything else, give me a call." Victor handed him a card.

Lieutenant Echols accepted the card, placing it on the coffee table. "If I think of anything, you will be the first person that I'll call."

Victor and Benitez let themselves out.

"What do you think?" Benitez asked as they walked along the sidewalk toward the truck.

"I think he's lying," Victor replied, opening the door. "He knows a lot more than what he's telling us." He climbed behind the wheel. "What are the odds he didn't see the face of the man Lieutenant Hill met at the Mall? They never discussed the nature of the visit. No, I don't buy it. He knows whom she met and why they met. Get Agents Chin and Tillman over here. I want to know everywhere he goes."

"Colonel." Sergeant Juarez rushed to meet Victor and Benitez in the hallway of CID. "This just came in from Forensics. DNA from Chapman's military records matches what they took from underneath Lieutenant Hill's fingernails."

Victor's face beamed as he verified what Juarez revealed.

"Outstanding," he exclaimed, slapping the paper with one hand. Everything was falling into place. Benitez gave him a congratulatory slapped on the back. "I got him. This places him at the scene of Lieutenant Hill's murder. Now, we just have to tie together Chapman, the money, and the senator. I know there is a connection."

"How do you want us to play it?" Juarez inquired, basking in the news.

"Put an APB out on Chapman," Victor commanded. "The sooner we get him off the streets the better it is for everyone."

"I'm on it, sir," Juarez said.

"I need it yesterday," Victor said, heading into his office.

∞ ∞

Dominique sailed the car through the intersection to the sound of beeping horns as she flew around a corner and down a residential street before losing the vehicle following her.

Once home, she rushed inside, locking the door behind her. She fell against the door, shaking as the fearful images of the chase played in her mind. She clutched the financial information to her chest as she rushed to the phone, her head thumping as she punched the numbers to CID. She relayed it was an emergency and got Victor right away.

"Victor," she said still out of breath. "I got the financial records from Devereaux's."

"What?" Victor was in disbelief. "How did you..." he began to asked then decided to get the answers to his questions in person. "Don't move. We're on our way."

☙ ❧

"What you did was dangerous, reckless," Victor scolded. "Not to mention illegal. We won't be able to use this information because of the way it was obtained."

"What do you mean? You said you needed to look at the financial records. We know Devereaux was not going to turn them over to you. The records show Uncle Harold was paying Lieutenant Hill."

"That's what search warrants are for," Victor argued.

"There wasn't time to wait for a warrant. I got the information and made it out safe."

"Barely," Victor said, raising a finger to reiterate his point. "You never listen to me when I tell you something."

Dominique felt like a five-year-old being scold for disobedience. She hung her head. "It was the right thing to do," she mumbled.

"It took a lot of guts to do what you did." Victor reached out, grabbed her, and held her in his arms, grateful that she was all right. "I appreciate what you did. Just don't do it again. Understand?"

"Don't worry. I won't," she assured him. "From now on I'll leave playing detective to the professional."

The doorbell rang. Benitez opened the door and Detective West sauntered in. Victor phoned him on the way to Dominique's apartment and asked the Detective to meet him there. He wanted to fill the detective in on everything his department discovered on the case so far, the DNA linking Chapman to Lieutenant Hill's murder, and what Dominique gathered from Devereaux's office. With enough evidence, Victor was hoping Detective West could help him get a judge to issue a search warrant for Senator Upton's home and office.

"Thanks for stopping by," Victor said, leading Detective West into the living room. "Dominique, there is someone I want you to meet."

Detective West removed his black shades. At first glance there was something about him that Dominique saw in Victor. The serious face, the terse eyes yet, at the same time, they were pleasant to look into.

As he came closer, she realized they shared the same height. His hair was cut close to his head, dark in color. He appeared to be around 45-years-old and he possessed the same charismatic quality she'd first encountered in Victor. Dominique found her hand enveloped in a firm grip as she greeted him. Detective West smiled. "It's nice to meet you."

"I just wish it was under a different circumstance," Dominique said.

"We all do," Victor said, taking the seat next to Dominique on the sofa. He grabbed her hand, interlocking it with his own.

148

Detective West and Benitez sat in the chairs flanking them. Victor filled Detective West in on everything CID had on the case.

"That evidence from Devereaux's office isn't admissible," Detective West said. "Because of the way it was obtained."

Victor glanced at Dominique. "We're hoping to pick up Chapman soon. Maybe our surveillance of Lieutenant Echols will produce something." Detective West nodded and asked Victor, "You think it was Chapman at Devereaux's?"

"I don't know. Dominique didn't get a clear look at the man."

Detective West closed his notebook. "I'll go and take another look around at Devereaux's. The department is grateful CID is sharing everything that you have on this case. We didn't have anything solid. Forensics didn't find anything at Robbin Greene's murder scene or apartment."

Victor glanced over at Dominique. He saw the pain in her eyes when she met his gaze.

"I'm alright," she whispered, squeezing his hand.

"I know you have an APB out on Chapman," Detective West said. "I'll assign extra men to help cover the airports, train stations, and the bus terminals. Lock it up tight. He won't get out of town."

"No one has spotted him yet," Victor added. "With the extra man power it's only a matter of time."

"Lets hope so," Detective West said, standing. He headed toward the door. "I'll be in touch," he said over his shoulder as he let himself out.

Victor turned to Dominique. "Go and pack a bag," he commanded. "We're going to my place."

aesar escorted Bradford directly to the Senator's library. The senator was sitting at his desk scribbling on a document. He didn't bother to look up. "What do you have to tell me? It better be good news."

Bradford stepped forward to deliver the senator the latest information. "Colonel Sexton made a trip to the Federal Credit Union and then met Dominique at that club of his. A few minutes later, they left and went to Devereaux's financial services. Devereaux didn't tell them anything. I got your old friend Judge Tapp to issue a restraining order against the Colonel. He can't come no where near you or your office. I delivered it to him personally."

"A retraining order doesn't mean anything to a man like the Colonel. He will just keep coming. The man is relentless. I trained him that way. He's retiring tomorrow and then we will be home free."

"There's something we can do." Bradford's tone was dry.

The Senator's head snapped up. "Don't even think about it."

"I thought you wanted this thing solved. Stop him and this goes away."

"I do want this situation solved but the way this thing is going right now my money is on him. Do nothing. Lay low for a couple of days. Can you just do that?"

Bradford swallowed the lump in his throat. The statement was like a slap in the face. He was sick and tired of being put down and belittled by the senator. In his eyes he couldn't do anything right. All he ever heard lately was how great the Colonel was. Deep down he developed a hatred for him.

"Whatever you say, Senator. I have more news."

"What more can there be?"

"He knows we're looking for the tape."

"This is not what I expected to hear."

"Dominique must have told the Colonel what she overheard."

Senator Upton leaned back in his chair. He was speechless.

Bradford reluctantly added, "Dominique broke into Devereaux's."

Senator Upton leaned forward. "What do you mean she broke in?" He shook his head in disbelief. "What office? What did she take?"

"She broke into Devereaux's office. We don't know what she took," Bradford replied. Senator Upton stood and came from around the desk. His eyes stared into Bradford's. "It doesn't matter what she took. It's circumstantial. Lieutenant Echols was released from the stockade. I don't want any more surprises. Pay him a visit. Find out where the tape is. Do we understand each other?"

"Yes, sir." Bradford turned and walked out the library without a backward glance.

CB ED

Lieutenant Echols ejected a round in the chamber of his .22. He put the safety on and placed it in the small of his back. He knew what tape Colonel Sexton was referring to, what was on it, and who was looking for it.

The night Lieutenant Hill asked him to escort her to the Mall, he should have just said no. She was frightened and didn't want to go alone. He got a good look at the two men —the man she was meeting and another man standing nearby, which he remembered because, when the meeting was over, both men were engrossed in a heavy conversation. As he told Colonel Sexton, he did not hear what Lieutenant Hill and the man were saying, but he knew what was being discussed. Lieutenant Hill had told him everything during one night of pillow talk. She wanted money and lots of it. She was killed a week later and then his wife. Soon he could meet the same fate. For his own safety, he had to stay a step ahead of them.

He walked over to the phone, picked it up, and punched in a series of numbers. "I have what you're looking for. We need to talk."

CB ED

Dominique went into Victor's kitchen and turned the burner beneath the teakettle on. He'd given her a tour of his split-level house and requested that she make herself at home. Reaching into the cabinet, she removed a black army cup and a box of tea.

She heard Victor enter the room and could feel him watching her. She didn't want to talk about the case at the moment. She needed time to sort things out.

Victor turned her around to face him.

She tried to hide the inner misery from his probing stare.

"How are you doing?"

She felt him studying her profile as she stared at his face. "I'm okay, under the circumstances."

"I wish I had the words…" Victor began then fell speechless.

She sighed and then raised one shoulder. "The man I thought I knew, who raised me... I don't really know at all."

There was a tense silence.

"We still don't know all the facts," Victor replied, trying to lighten the situation. He reached out, putting his arm around her waist. "Let's just wait and see what unfolds."

She felt his arms tightened around her. No matter what happened she loved this man, nothing would ever change that.

The ringing of his cellular phone filled the air. "Excuse me." He answered the phone. "Colonel Sexton."

The teakettle whistled and Dominique removed it, pouring steaming water into the cup. She listened as he talked to the person on the line.

"Don't approach him. Just watch him. I'm on my way." He hung up and found Dominique staring at him.

"I had two of my men watching Lieutenant Echols. They followed him to a YMCA. He came out with a black gym bag. Twenty minutes later, he was spotted going into Senator Upton old office building in downtown, Washington, DC." Victor was moving toward the doorway.

"Why do you have men watching Lieutenant Echols? Didn't you release him?"

He turned back to find Dominique trailing him. "I did, but he knows more than what he's telling me."

"Then I'm going with you."

"No. You're not. No more adventures for you."

"Don't try to talk me out of it," Dominique argued.

"Forget it, Dominique. You're staying here. You promised to listen to me. I'll post one of my men outside," he said and gestured for Benitez, signaling the conversation was over.

୯୫ ୬୬

"Echols is still inside," Agent Chin said. "We haven't seen anyone else go in or come out."

"What could Echols be doing here?" Benitez asked, curiously looking around the old, abandoned building.

"Whatever it is, it can't be good." Victor's eyes scanned the building, spotting doors on the right and left side of the structure.

"We're going in for a closer look. Chin, you and Tillman cover the back. Benitez, take the left side and I'll take the right. Everyone be careful, watch your backs. We don't know what's going on inside. All right, Let's move."

The agents spread out, moving toward their assigned positions. Victor cautiously moved toward the right side of the building. Upon reaching the door, he fell flat against the doorframe. He slowly turned the knob. It opened. He moved inside what was once a general office area, illuminated by the bright streetlights outside. Victor moved from room to room, running into Benitez at the bottom of a small flight of stairs.

Victor tilted his head in a nod and they climbed the stairs. Reaching the second floor, Victor opened the door and they moved inside the second floor corridor. He pointed for Benitez to go to the right and he went left.

Victor moved along the hallway, stopping midway when he heard raised male voices coming from one of the offices. He strained to hear but couldn't make out what was being discussed. A moment later, a gunshot rang out, followed by a loud crash, and groans. He heard hurried footsteps and broke into a full gallop. Benitez was directly on his heels. Adrenaline pumping, Victor flattened himself outside the door to the office where he heard the men talking. Benitez was on the other side. Victor turned the knob and slowly entered the room in a half-crouch position, gun drawn, ready for fire. His eyes surveyed the surrounding. The shooter could still be in the room. Victor rushed over to an open window. He stuck his head outside. There were steps that led to a parking lot. He spotted Agents Chin and Tillman running around the corner of the building after someone. The sound of groaning from behind an old file cabinet broke the silence.

"Colonel," Benitez echoed, moving toward the sound.

Victor went over and knelt next to a body. He turned it over. It was Lieutenant Echols. He'd been shot in the chest.

Benitez pulled out his cellular phone and dialed 911.

"What happened Echols?" Victor asked. "Who shot you?"

Lieutenant Echols turned his head slightly and his mouth moved. At first Victor could not hear him.

"Key," he said in a voice barely above a whisper. He coughed.

Victor leaned closer. Echols moaned. He slightly raised his right hand but it fell back to his side.

"Just lie still," Victor ordered. "Help is on the way. Save your strength. Don't try to talk."

Lieutenant Echols grabbed Victor's arm, clutching him as he tried to rise. "Right," he whispered, "pocket." He coughed again and sputtered as he tried to sit up again. It was useless. He fell back gasping in pain.

Victor understood him and searched Lieutenant Echols' right pocket. He found a small, brown envelope and handed it to Benitez.

"Hold on Echols," Victor commanded. "Just hold on." He knew the attempt would be in vain. He'd been in enough combat to know the wound was fatal.

The sound of sirens flaring could be heard in the background. Echols's right hand slid down Victor's arm. "At the Y. Copy." It was as if he knew his time was near.

"Who did this to you?" Victor asked again.

Lieutenant Echols didn't answer. He couldn't. His body shuddered as he drew his last breath. Moments later, he was dead.

Victor dropped his head and then quickly turned away. He stood and looked at Benitez who was examining the contents of the envelope. He handed it to Victor. It was a key with the number 10 on it.

DAY SEVEN – THURSDAY, 12:09 a.m.

At CID Victor watched the videotape along with Detective West and Benitez. It was clear why the senator was anxious to get his hands on the tape. On it, Senator Upton was having sex with Lieutenant Hill. Once the media get a hold of the story, the senator's worst fears would come true. His chances for reelection would be ruined.

Inside the locker they also found a small, black notebook. Lieutenant Hill kept meticulous records of where she and the senator met, along with the dates. The information was damaging. They now had enough evidence to obtain a warrant to search the senator's home and office. With the search, Victor hoped to gather more information to connect Chapman to Senator Upton. He was sure the senator paid Chapman to retrieve the tape because Lieutenant Hill was blackmailing him. Robbin was killed because she saw Chapman.

"I'll see about getting a judge to issue search warrants." Detective West looked at his watch. It was after midnight. "I'll have to wake someone up, but with what we have uncovered, I don't think we'll have a problem getting them."

"That's fine," Victor said. "Give me a call when you get it. Anything on Chapman?"

"Nothing yet. We didn't find anything at Devereaux's either. It's like he's disappeared. If your men didn't get a description of the man fleeing Echols's murder scene, I would have sworn it was Chapman."

Victor scowled. "Something doesn't add up. If Chapman didn't kill Lieutenant Echols, who did?"

Agent Chin and Tillman chased the suspect but he got away. They managed to get a sketchy description. He was around 5'8", slim build, with blonde hair. He was wearing a blue sweatshirt and denim jeans. The man who killed Lieutenant Echols was shorter and thinner than Chapman. Forensics went over the murder scene. No fingerprints. Nothing. Victor wondered where the killer fit into the case.

"I figure Echols was at the building to sell the tape. Maybe take up where Lieutenant Hill left off," Benitez pointed out. "Blackmail?"

"Sounds like it. I'm glad Echols made a copy of the tape," Victor said.

Benitez took a sip of bottled water. "He knew the type of people he was dealing with. Why would he take a chance? Maybe Echol's killer and Chapman are partners. Maybe the senator thought Chapman couldn't get the tape, so he brought in someone who could."

Victor rubbed his forehead in frustration. "No, Chapman is more than qualified to get the job done. This is something else. I can't put my finger on it." He walked around the desk and took a seat. "Chin and Tillman still looking for witnesses?"

Benitez let out a deep sigh. "Yes, sir. Said they would check in as soon as they had something. It's getting late. Why don't we call it a night?"

Victor gave Benitez a weary look, "Yeah. You're right," He removed his gun holster from the back of the chair. "Lieutenant Echols' killer caught me off guard. Unless Chin comes up with a witness to his murder," his voice expressed frustration, "we have nothing."

 C<3 80

Dominique heard Victor knocking on the bedroom door. He'd left hours ago, and she wondered what he'd found out. She sat up straight in bed when she saw the look on his face. Something was wrong. She stood.

Victor loved this woman and didn't want to hurt her. With the evidence gathered against the senator, what he saw on the tape, there was no way to avoid that.

Dominique looked uncomfortable. She knew he was stalling. "Victor?" she prompted. "What did Lieutenant Echols say?"

"Lieutenant Echols is dead," he said honestly.

She slowly sank on the bed.

"There's more," Victor said, sitting in the chair next to the bed. "Before he died, he gave me a key. The key was to a locker at the YMCA. In the locker we found a tape and a notebook."

Dominique felt her insides become warm. She could sense where the conversation was going. "What was on the tape? In the notebook?"

Victor didn't answer. That only meant whatever was on the tape, he didn't want to tell her. She reached out, placing her hand over his. She looked in his eyes, telling him it was all right.

"Victor?" she prompted again. "Tell me."

She heard him take a deep breath. "Senator Upton having sex with Lieutenant Hill. She was blackmailing him with the information. She kept a record of all their meetings. It appears Lieutenant Echols tried to pick up where she left off and someone killed him."

For a moment, he thought she was going to say something when she opened her mouth to speak, but nothing came out. Her brown eyes misted. In response, Victor leaned over, enclosing her in his arms, simultaneously raising her to her feet. "I'm sorry."

She sniffed, releasing herself. "Who shot Echols?"

"We don't know. The killer got away."

"Chapman?" Dominique asked.

"It wasn't Chapman."

Dominique's eyes widened in surprise. "Then who?"

"We don't know."

"What about my uncle? Is he involved?"

"Detective West," he cleared his throat, "is in the process of obtaining search warrants for his home and office."

"Why?" She tried to control her emotions, but her feelings surfaced. "He had it all, power, money, a loving wife, a family that loves him. I don't understand why he would throw it away for a woman half his age. My age." She shook her head in disgust. "She worked with me every day. Sleeping with my uncle. Lieutenant Echols."

Victor listened intently, letting her get everything off her chest.

"I guess it's as you said," she continued. "People in desperate situations do desperate things. Lieutenant Hill, Robbin, and now Thomas. Such a waste of life."

Victor nodded in agreement. "We don't have anything that connects the senator to the murders."

"He's still responsible for three deaths. All because he tried to conceal his infidelity."

He dropped his head. "You're right. Look, why don't you try and get some rest? I'll check on you in the morning. If you need anything, I'm next door."

"Don't leave, Victor," she whispered. "I don't won't to be alone right now."

"You'll never be alone," he vowed. Climbing into bed. He enclosed her in his arms until she finally dropped off to sleep.

൫ ൯

Agent Bill Mallard was half asleep behind the wheel when Chapman tapped on the window of the vehicle. The tapping sound brought his head up and he tried to shake himself awake. Chapman stood on the street side of the vehicle. Agent Mallard rolled down the window and that's when he recognized him. It was too late; Chapman reached inside the window and with the quickness of a cat, snapped Mallard's neck. He slumped down in the driver's seat.

Chapter Nineteen

*V*ictor awoke and glanced over at the bedside clock and saw it was four-thirty in the morning. He'd only been asleep three hours. What had awakened him? He sat up and looked down at Dominique sleeping so peacefully. Careful not to awake her, he slid out of bed.

He quickly made his way downstairs. He checked the answering machine. There were no messages. Walking over to the window, he pushed the curtains back. The unmarked vehicle was still there. Everything appeared peaceful. Still he couldn't shake the feeling that something was wrong.

He turned and headed toward the kitchen when he looked toward the patio and saw a shadowy figure moving outside.

Victor grabbed his .38 from a drawer in a hallway table. He crouched slightly and carefully moved toward the patio.

Victor unlocked the patio door and slowly slid it open. He stepped outside, his weapon raised. No one was in sight. He carefully moved to the backyard. The only sound heard was the rustling of the leaves on the trees. He raced toward the front yard, but it was empty. The intruder had vanished. Where did they go so quickly?

He surveyed the yard, kneeling down to examine a fresh set of footprints. A moment later the sound of a car engine in the distance had him rushing into the street. He got there just in time to see a dark colored car racing toward him. Quick reflexes allowed him to move out of the way just in time. He landed in the front yard and rolled over in hopes of getting a license plate number. All he saw were the vehicle brake lights as it turned the corner.

"Damn!" he mouthed, getting to his feet. He ran to the unmarked car and slowed his pace when he saw Agent Mallard slumped in the seat. Reaching inside the window, he searched for a pulse, hoping he was still alive, but he didn't find one. His neck had been broken.

"Chapman," Victor said to himself.

‘’

"You think it was Chapman?" Benitez asked. Victor phoned him immediately after finding Agent Mallard. "It's suicide for him to show up here, knowing every Federal agency is looking for him."

Victor pulled a black shirt over his head. "I know it was him. Who else could it be? It's all part of a psychological game he's playing. Trying to prove he's the better man. What better way to do that than to kill one of my own men, right under my nose." Victor was beside himself. He had never lost an agent under his command.

Agent Mallard was a good man and agent. A friend. Married six years. His wife was expecting their first child.

"The man is out of his mind," Benitez said.

"When he was on my team, he made everything a competition between he and I. He always felt he was the better soldier."

"Why didn't you kick him off the team?" Dominique asked, moving into the living room. Luckily, she slept through the incident with Chapman.

"Regardless of his attitude, Chapman was a good soldier, but I was always better." Victor's eyes landed on Agent Chin coming through the door.

"We caught a big break on Lieutenant Echols murder." Agent Chin hurried into the room. "We found a witness, a Bridget Richter." He opened his notebook. "She got a good look at the man running from the murder scene. She saw him get into a black Mercedes and drive off. As he drove off, she wrote down the plate number. We ran the plates."

"Who is the car registered too?" Victor asked.

"Bradford Farrell, Senator Upton's Administrative Assistant."

‘’

Bradford entered his office on Capitol Hill. He was pleased with himself. He'd located the tape and destroyed it. He'd been assured that there were no other copies. No one will ever see it. No one else will ever know the senator's secret.

The Senator was on top of the world when Bradford phoned him last night and told him about the tape. He'd found it. Not that maniac he'd hired to find it. He paid Chapman extra money to keep quiet and insisted he leave the country. He was a wanted man. His face plastered all over the television. Everyone was looking for him.

Bradford was about to leave for a meeting when he looked up and saw Colonel Sexton and another man he didn't recognize enter the office. Several uniform officers followed them.

"Bradford Farrell?" Detective West asked.

Bradford could feel his body trembling as his eyes darted between the two men. He stood. "We have a restraining order against you. You're not supposed to be here. I'm calling the police."

"There's no need for that. I'm Detective West. I'm with the Police Department, Homicide." He flashed his badge and slapped the warrants into his hand. "You already know Colonel Sexton, CID."

Bradford didn't acknowledge Detective West or Victor. "Homicide? What do you want with me?"

"Let me answer that for you," Victor jumped in. "We're here to serve a search warrant and we want to talk to you about the murder of Lieutenant Thomas Echols."

The color drained from Bradford's face.

Victor reached into his jacket and handed Bradford the documents. How times had changed. It gave Victor satisfaction to perform the same action Bradford had done to him twenty-four hours ago.

"Murder? What are you talking about?" Bradford backed up, bumping into the chair behind him. "I don't know anything about a murder."

"A witness puts you at the scene of the crime where Lieutenant Echols was murdered, around 9:15 last night at the senator's old office building."

"I'm sure she won't have any problems picking you out of a line up," Detective West threatened.

Bradford attempted to speak.

"Before you deny it," Victor quickly added, "the witness wrote down your license plate number as you drove off."

"Bradford is this true?" Senator Upton asked, coming into the office. "You killed Lieutenant Echols?"

Bradford knew he was caught. "You told me to take care of the situation."

"I didn't mean murder!" Senator Upton snapped.

"Enough is enough," Bradford's face twisted with anger. "Lieutenant Echols wanted to pick up where that little bitch left off. I wasn't about to let you go through that again."

"Is that the reason you killed Lieutenant Hill?" Detective West asked.

"I didn't kill Lieutenant Hill," Bradford denied.

"You hired a man named Scott Chapman to do it," Victor said firmly.

Bradford rebuffed the idea. "I don't know anyone named Scott Chapman."

"Sure you don't," Victor said, his voice laced with sarcasm. "You hired him to get the video tape from Lieutenant Hill." He glanced at the senator. "The video tape, Lieutenant Hill was blackmailing the senator with." He turned back to Bradford. "The tape you killed Lieutenant Echols for. The tape he managed to lead us too before he died. The tape he made a copy of."

Senator Upton dropped his head, squeezing his eyes shut. He knew his world had just crashed down around him.

Bradford looked as if he would pass out. "I'm not saying another word without my attorney present."

"Smart choice." Detective West pulled out a pair of handcuffs and placed them on Bradford's wrist. "Bradford Farrell, you're under arrest for the murder of Lieutenant Thomas Echols." A uniformed officer led him away.

Detective West motioned for the officers to begin their search of the office.

Victor walked over and stood in front of the senator. He gave him a hard stare then nodded with his head. "Let's talk in your office." The expression on Senator's Upton face was grim as he led Victor down the corridor to his office.

Victor closed the door behind him. "Captain Benitez is on his way to search your home."

Senator Upton's eyes flew to Victor's face. Then he looked away. He turned his back to Victor, wringing his hands together. "How is Dominique?"

"She's devastated."

"Did she see—"

"The tape." Victor finished the sentence for him. "No. But she knows about it."

The senator bobbed his head up and down. "Thank you." He turned around to face Victor.

"I didn't do it for you!" Victor snapped.

"Thank you anyway," the Senator said, in a daze. "Who knows what she must think of me now," he said more to himself. "My wife. You. What do you think of me now?"

"It doesn't matter what I think. My concern is for Dominique and Rosetta. Because, if you arranged to have Lieutenant Hill and Greene killed, adultery is the least of your worries."

The senator's eyes stretched wide. "I never arranged to have anyone murdered." He walked over to his desk and sat in the chair with a thump. "I just wanted the tape. That's it! I never thought Bradford would go as far as he did," he lied.

"Did you know Bradford was meeting with Lieutenant Echols?"

"Yes. Bradford called me last night. Said he was meeting with Echols about the tape and that he'll destroyed it. That's all I know." He interlocked his fingers together. "I knew he'd do anything to protect the campaign. But murder..." He shook his head in disbelief. Rambling, "What am I going to tell my constituents?"

"Maybe you can use that fundraiser to come clean," Victor suggested. His cellular phone rang. He flipped it open. "Colonel Sexton."

"I have something to tell you." Gerald's voice came across the line as a photo of Chapman flashed across the television screen.

"Gerald, I can't talk at the moment. I'm right in the middle of something." He looked over at the senator who looked like a man defeated.

"This is important. It's about Scott Chapman."

Victor pepped up. What can Gerald know about Chapman? "What about him?"

"He was in Cadence yesterday. He introduced himself to me as Roger Davis."

"I'll see you in a few minutes." He glanced over at the senator. "I have to go."

"I'm really sorry about everything that has happened."

Victor nodded. He had mixed feelings. A part of him wanted to believe him. The other part felt the same as Dominique, that his obsession to conceal his infidelity had taken the lives of four people.

As he proceeded down the hallway, Dominique and Rosetta were headed toward him. A closer look at both women revealed they'd been crying. Victor hugged and kissed both women. He spoke with Dominique a few minutes, promising to call her later.

CR ဢ

Dominique and Rosetta entered the senator's office. In a sign of strength they were holding hands. Senator Upton slowly stood to his feet, the look of fear in his eyes. The women looked at each other. Dominique was the first to make a move. She went over to her uncle and threw her arms around his neck.

The senator patted her gently on her back. "I'm sorry," he whispered, and then looked over at his wife. Rosetta hadn't moved from the doorway. She just stood there, shoulders hunched under the expensive skirt suit she was wearing.

"Did you have them killed?" Dominique asked.

Senator Upton glanced briefly at Rosetta then back at Dominique. "No. I didn't." He placed his arm around Dominique's waist and stretched a hand toward his wife to join him on the sofa. At first, Rosetta still didn't move. A moment later, she placed her hand inside her husband's.

After they were seated, he patted Rosetta's hand in a loving manner. "I owe you and Dominique an explanation." He took a couple of deep breaths to compose himself. "I met Lieutenant Hill at a political function," he began. "We met a couple of times after that," he added suddenly.

Chapter Twenty

"That's him," Gerald said, looking at Chapman's photo. "The same man's face plastered all over the television. He walked right in yesterday around one. Said his name was Roger Davis and the restaurant had been recommended to him."

Hunnicutt removed the photo from Gerald. "I remember him," he added. "He stopped at the bar before he left."

Chapman was stalking him. Positioning himself outside of PJ's Sandwich Shop, showing up at Cadence, and last night at his home.

"Did Chapman arrive before or after me?" Victor asked Gerald.

"Before."

"Wait a minute," Hunnicutt explained. "That could explain why he was acting so strange."

"What do you mean?"

"You and Captain Frazier were standing in the doorway talking to Gerald. That's why he stopped at the bar. He couldn't leave without you seeing him."

"Do you remember who seated him?" Victor asked. "If he was driving?"

"Mya seated him," Gerald answered. "I don't remember if he was driving or not."

"Do you have her number? I may have to talk to her. Who was parking cars around that time?"

"Lonzo, Travis, Peter, and Marshall. They are all working except Peter. He won't be in," Gerald looked at his watch, "for another half-hour."

"All right. I'm going to have a talk with the valets. Maybe one of them will remember Chapman. Soon as Peter arrives, I need to talk to him."

"No problem," Gerald answered. "I'll call Mya. When Peter arrives, I'll send him to you."

"Thanks," Victor headed toward the front of the club. The three young men, all college students, were laughing and talking with each other when Victor walked up. Lonzo, the youngest in the group, saw him first and alerted the other's of Victor's approach.

They all became serious.

"Good afternoon, Colonel," Lonzo said. "How are you today, sir?"

"I'm fine, Lonzo. What about yourself?"

"I'm okay, sir. Just taking it one day at a time."

"I need to ask you guys a question."

They all looked at each other.

"Go ahead, sir," Travis said.

"Did one of you park a vehicle for this man yesterday around one o'clock?" Victor showed them the photo of Chapman.

Lonzo looked at the photo. He shook his head no, then handed it to Marshall and Travis. Victor got the same response.

Victor walked back into the club, frustrated. He went into Gerald's office and plopped down in the chair. He just sat there thinking. This was a case of teacher versus pupil. He was beginning to think he'd taught Chapman too well. He was like a ghost, drifting in and out without being seen. But like all criminals, sooner or later, he was going to make a mistake. He will catch him.

The cell phone rang, startling him. It was Benitez. "Colonel, just want to let you know we're finishing up here at Senator Upton's home. We didn't find anything."

"We didn't find anything at his office either. Send some agents out to Bradford's home." Victor rubbed his hand over his forehead.

"I'll get right on that, sir."

"I'm at the club. Chapman showed up here yesterday and introduced himself as Roger Davis. I questioned three of the Valets, hoping one of them remember him. So far, I've struck out. One more to talk to."

There was a knock on the door, followed by a young man sticking his head in the door. Victor waved him in. "He's here. I'll fill you in later."

"You wanted to see me, Colonel Sexton?" Peter Cobb asked. Peter stood 6'1" and weighed around 190 pounds. He was a sophomore, running back for Grambling State University and a straight 'A' student. He was majoring in Mathematics and headed for the NFL. Articulate and well mannered, he spent his summers working at Cadence.

"Yes. Come in and have a seat. How have you been?"

Peter took a chair across from the desk. "I've been doing okay."

"Good. I'll get right to the point. When you were parking cars yesterday around one o'clock, do you remember parking a car for this man?" Victor handed him the photo of Chapman.

Peter's forehead wrinkled a moment. Victor believed it was another dead end.

"Black 4-door, 95 Mazda with Alabama license plates," Peter recited. "License plate number ETL 749."

Victor couldn't believe his ears. He leaned forward to hear more. "You remember him?"

"Vividly." Peter shrugged, unaware that he may have just helped solve a murder case. "White male. 180 pounds. Dark hair, cut low to the head. He spoke with a southern accent. We don't get many male Caucasians in the club."

"What else can you tell me about the vehicle?"

"Like I said, it was black. Very clean inside. There was a pair of dog tags hanging from the rearview mirror. An army special operations sticker in the back rear window on the right side. A confederate flag sticker was on the left side."

"How do you remember so much detail?"

Peter smiled. "I have a photographic memory and I'm good with numbers. Why are you asking about this guy?"

"Haven't you been watching the news?"

Peter smiled slipped. "No, sir. I leave here and go to another job. What did he do?"

"Murder. Every law enforcement agency is looking for him. With the information you just provided us with, I believe we just caught him."

"Is there a reward?" Peter inquired.

"I'll see what I can do," Victor promised.

After Peter left, Victor phoned CID passing the information to other federal agencies to be on the lookout for Chapman's car. He was sure it was the same vehicle that almost ran him over in front of his house this morning.

Victor walked to the front of the club. He arrived at the bar to find Gerald, Hunnicutt, and several staff members watching the television positioned above the bar. CNN Reporter, Richard Forte and the rest of the news media were camped outside of Senator Upton's home.

"Bradford Farrell, administrative assistant to Senator Upton was arrested this morning for the murder of Lieutenant Thomas Echols," he was saying. Bradford's photo appeared on the screen. *"If you remember, the officer's wife was found strangled a couple of days ago in a parking garage at her apartment building. Lieutenant Echols was released from the army's stockade yesterday morning. He was a suspect in the murder of Lieutenant Tamara Hill. Well, you have to ask yourself, what is the connection to Bradford Farrell? Sources tell us that Bradford Farrell killed Lieutenant Echols to retrieve a video tape. A video tape of Senator Upton and Lieutenant Hill engaging in sexual intercourse."* A photo of the senator appeared alongside Bradford's. *"Lieutenant Tamara Hill was*

found strangled in her Officer's Quarters four days ago. Now, whether Bradford Farrell is involved with Lieutenant Hill or Robbin Greene's murder, the police is not saying. However, the police is looking for this man, Scott Chapman," A photo of Chapman replaced Bradford and the senator's, *"in connection with the murders. There is a $250,000 reward for information and capture of Chapman, who was last seen driving a black, 4-door, 95 Mazda. Alabama license plate number ETL 749. If you see Scott Chapman, don't approach him. He is considered armed and extremely dangerous. Call the local police or CID at (703) 555-2200."*

"I'm on my way to the office." Victor headed toward the door.

"The media circus is just beginning." Gerald fell in step with Victor. "How's Dominique?"

"I ran into her and Rosetta on my way over here. Both are taking it pretty hard."

"I can't imagine. Do you think Senator Upton is connected to the murders?"

"He says he isn't," Victor replied.

Gerald tilted his head. "What do you say?"

Victor sighed. "I don't know. I have nothing that connects him. Bradford isn't talking. I'll talk to you later." He headed out the double doors.

"Victor," Gerald called.

Victor turned back to face Gerald.

"Be careful," Gerald said. "I need you to help me run this place."

Victor managed a smile. "I will." He hurried to his truck.

C8 80

Victor settled behind the wheel of the truck. He was confident that Chapman would surface. He relayed his license plate number to every law enforcement agency in the country. With his face plastered on every front-page newspaper and television station, it was only a matter of time — time he didn't have much of. The ringing of his cellular phone broke into his thoughts.

"I think we got something, Colonel, that may be worth checking out," Benitez said.

"A woman, she wouldn't give her name, swears that Chapman is a guest at the Holiday Inn downtown Silver Spring on Georgia Avenue. We're on our way to check it out. How far away are you?"

"About ten minutes. I'll meet you there. Just in case, place a phone call to Detective West. Ask him to meet us there."

"Yes, sir."

Victor hung up, turned on the police lights, and floored the gas pedal. Vehicles began to part like the Red Sea. Though he believed it was a long shot, it wouldn't hurt to check it out.

Before he knew it, he was in front of the hotel. He jumped out of the vehicle and hurried inside the lobby.

A young, Indian woman was chatting on the telephone. She glanced up at him, then placed the phone in the cradle. "Good afternoon, sir."

"Afternoon." Victor reached into his jacket and flashed Chapman's photo and his badge. "I'm Lieutenant Colonel Sexton, CID. I'm looking for this man, Roger Davis. Can you tell me if you've seen him or if he's registered here?"

The woman carefully examined the photo. "I haven't seen him personally. Let me check to see if he's registered." She moved over to the computer. Her fingers began moving over the keyboard. "We have a Roger Davis in room 421."

"Thank you." Victor turned in time to see Benitez, Agents Chin, and Saunders come through the door and strolled toward them. "There's a Roger Davis registered in room 421. It may be Chapman."

"Detective West is a few minutes out," Benitez explained. "We have uniformed officers posted out front."

"Outstanding. We're not going to wait for Detective West." Victor turned to the hotel clerk. "Can I have the door key to room 421?"

The clerk paused a moment then surrendered the key.

Moving swiftly, the group of men entered the elevator, getting off on the fourth floor. Room 421 was down the hall and on the left.

"Be careful," Victor warned. "I don't have to tell you to keep your eyes and ears open. Chapman is dangerous. I want him alive if we take him."

The men nodded then took their position on each side of the door.

Victor knocked on the door with the butt of the weapon. No answer.

Victor knocked again. Still no answer. He looked at his men. They were ready for whatever was going to happen next. Victor inserted the hotel key in the door and unlocked it.

He cautiously entered the room, followed by the rest of the agents. It was empty. He looked around the room. It was occupied but was spotless. His eyes were instantly drawn to the news articles pinned on the wall above the desk. There were newspaper clippings on the murders of Lieutenants Hill and Greene. There was also an article on him. The photo showed him being interviewed by the media. Chapman had drawn a red x with a circle around his face. Victor smirked.

"No one's home," Benitez said, standing next to him.

"But we're at the right place," Victor answered, staring at the photo.

Next to the desk was a television. Across from it was a Queen sized bed and a place to hang clothes.

Victor pulled out desk drawers with extra force. He found a map of D.C., Maryland, and take out menus to local restaurants. He kept searching. Nothing to tie him to Bradford Farrell.

In frustration, Victor grabbed hold of the mattress and flipped it over. To his surprise a brown accordion folder was carefully hidden underneath the bed. Victor opened it and sifted through the contents. It was filled with military memorabilia from his old Special Forces unit. Looking at the pictures, he was reminded of happier times the team shared together. They ate, slept, and fought together. They were inseparable like brothers, looked out for each other, and were willing to die for one another. Now one member was tracking the other.

"Take this to the office as evidence," Victor said, handing the box to Agent Saunders.

Victor stepped out into the hallway to wait for Detective West. The ring of the elevator bell caught his attention. He looked towards the elevator and there stood Chapman, big as life.

"Chapman," Victor bellowed. Chapman's head popped up and he bolted for the exit door that led down a flight of stairs.

Victor bolted after him. The sound of moving footsteps echoed off the stairwell. He caught a glimpse of Chapman as he reached the first floor door, opened it, and fled through it.

The sounds of screams greeted Victor when he followed Chapman out the door.

Chapman had grabbed a woman and held a knife to her throat. Victor halted in his tracks and raised his weapon.

"Drop it, Colonel," Chapman ordered. "You may get me, but not before I slit her throat. You know I'm good at that."

Victor felt a cold shudder rush through him. He took a deep breath. He didn't want another dead body. "All right. I'm putting my gun away." Victor slowly placed the gun back in his holster. He raised his hands in a surrendering gesture. "I don't want anyone else to get hurt."

"Aren't you the righteous one all of a sudden, Colonel? I spent six years in Fort Leavenworth because of you!" Chapman yelled.

"Not because of me," Victor began to explain. "You—"

"Shut up!" Chapman cut him off. "It was because of you. You testified against me. My commander. I thought we were a team. A family. You betrayed me. Now you're paying for it."

"Then let her go," Victor pleaded. He placed a hand to his chest.

"Take me instead. I'm the one you want. Don't involve anyone else."

Chapman chuckled. "That was touching. 'Take me instead,'" he mimicked. "I will deal with you in due time. My time. I'll call you."

The woman squealed as Chapman dragged her backwards across the lobby and through the side exit door.

Victor dashed after them.

Once outside, Chapman shoved the woman aside and ran into the parking lot.

Victor yelled for Chapman to stop.

Chapman ran faster. An elderly man getting into a blue Cadillac was his next victim. Chapman pulled the man from the vehicle, hitting him with a martial arts blow. The man crumbled to the pavement. Chapman jumped inside the car and zoomed out of the parking lot.

Victor stopped running, raised his gun, and squeezed off five rounds. The bullets ricocheted off the back of the car, shattering the back window. He let out an expletive, turned, and ran back toward the truck. He placed the keys in the ignition. The passenger door opened. It was Benitez. They peeled away from the curb.

The truck gained enough ground to spot Chapman take a sharp right turn at a light. Benitez grabbed the radio, relayed the license plate number, make, and model of the car Chapman had commandeered.

Victor made the right turn and slammed his foot on the accelerator. The truck ate up highway in a hurry. They were inches away, but Chapman overtook another vehicle heading for the interstate. Victor followed. The vehicles weaved in and out of the lanes. Minutes later, Chapman exited the interstate and traveled down a one-way street.

Chapman sideswiped an oncoming vehicle but refused to slow down. He made a left turn into a residential district. With the high speed of the vehicles through the neighborhood, Victor was thankful no patrons were out and about.

Victor zeroed in on Chapman's car and rammed his rear bumper. Chapman tried to speed up. Victor stayed with him, ramming him again with extra force. The vehicle slammed into a parked car.

When Victor jumped out of the truck, Chapman was already out of the vehicle and on the move. He ran between two houses. Victor and Benitez were in hot pursuit. Chapman scaled a fence with ease.

"He went through the woods," a man yelled from the back porch.

Victor and Benitez sprinted through the trees. The opening led them to a shopping center. Victor frantically looked around and then threw his hands up in agitation.

Chapman was nowhere in sight.

ര ഇ

Chapman stood across the street from Dominique's apartment building. Time was running out for him. He knew it. Victor waiting for him at the hotel was a close call. But first he had unfinished business to take care of. He pulled the New York Yankees baseball cap further down over his head. He walked the short distance to the convenience store at the end of the street and used the pay phone. He dialed the number to CID.

"Colonel Victor Sexton," Chapman said.

"Colonel Sexton," Victor answered a moment later.

"I told you I'd call. Still looking for me?"

"Chapman?" Victor inquired. He was caught off guard. He stopped dead in his tracks. It was a bold move, calling him at the office. "Are you giving yourself up?"

Chapman chuckled. "That would take all of the fun out of our little chase." His voice became serious. "Didn't you have fun chasing me? I'm the better soldier. I've proven it. Three murders. One of your own men and right under your nose. The escape from the hotel. I could have taken you out any time."

"Then do it now!" Victor snapped. "No more games. You want me. Name the time and place."

"Temper. Temper, Colonel. My next victim is someone you care about. Come and stop me, if you can."

Click.

ര ഇ

Victor knew Chapman was referring to Dominique. He hurried out the door. Jumping into the truck, he turned on his lights, blowing his horn in frustration. He dialed Dominique's phone number but got her machine. He stomped down on the gas pedal, praying all the way to her house.

ര ഇ

Harold had an affair with Lieutenant Tamara Hill. It was the last thing Dominique wanted to hear. After Victor left, Harold had confessed everything to her and Rosetta.

He was full of apologies. He assured them the affair was over months ago and he had nothing to do with the murders. Tomorrow night at the fundraiser, he would pull out of the senate race to save the family more embarrassment. It did nothing to ease the pain and disappointment he'd caused and his marriage was in trouble.

Dominique's spirits were at an all time low by the time she left her aunt and uncle's home.

"I'll be all right," Rosetta whispered when Dominique was leaving. "We'll get through this."

Unable to sleep, Dominique walked into the living room and curled up on the sofa. Her mind wandered to Victor. There was no way she could rekindle her relationship with him now. Even if they did, the issue with her uncle would always be between them. Dominique shuddered and wrapped her arms around herself. She glanced at her clock. It was 11:30 p.m. After a few minutes of not finding anything interesting to watch, she turned the television off.

She headed into the kitchen for a glass of water. Instinctively, her hand flicked on the light. She walked over to the cabinet, opened the door, and removed a glass. She placed it on the counter then opened the refrigerator door. Suddenly, from behind her, she felt an eerie presence. Glancing out the corner of her eye, she caught the glimpse of a figure. *Chapman,* Dominique cried silently. Just as she was about to turn around, he grabbed her from behind, placing a hand over her mouth.

"Dominique!" he whispered in a harsh tone as he dragged her to the living room.

Dominique attempted to remove his hand but it was no use. He was too strong for her. Struggling, she breathed in shallow, quick gasps. Her chest felt as if it would burst.

"Stop moving!" Chapman hissed. "I'll let you go, but you have to promise not to scream. Deal?"

Dominique bobbed her head up and down in agreement. He removed his hand then pushed her forcefully onto the sofa. She landed with a loud thud. She got her first look at the man everyone in the county was looking for.

Chapman was average looking. Mid-thirties, blonde hair, blue eyes, clean cut with a medium build and height. He could easily pass for your next door neighbor. If you were to meet him on the street, you never would picture him as a killer. But those looks were deceiving. He was a cold-blooded killer.

"It's so nice to meet you."

Dominique rubbed her throat. "Chapman?"

"You know who I am." He boasted. "I'm sure the Colonel has told you all about me."

"He told me you're a rapist and a killer," she spat out.

He pulled a knife from his back pocket and casually strolled toward her "Then you better do everything that I say."

Dominique began to shake. She was sure she was about to be victim number four. "What do you want?"

"Not what," he ran the cold steel blade along the side of her face, "who. I've already called him. I'm sure he's on the way. So we will just wait."

"Victor isn't coming here."

"Don't test my intelligence. We both know you're special to him." Chapman's eyes took in the two piece, silk short set she was wearing.

She nervously wrapped her arms around her chest and crossed her legs. It was no use. She felt naked under his stare. Violated. "I can't blame him." He reached and touched one of her legs. She slapped his hand away. "You're a beautiful woman. He was always a lucky man. Even with the ladies."

"Don't touch me!"

"Don't worry sweetheart." He reached out, tightly gripping her face. "When I kill you, you won't feel a thing."

CB ED

Driven by fear, Victor raced with record speed to Dominique's front door. Once there, he rung the doorbell, calling her name. He got no answer.

He went to the back of her apartment unit. He tried the glass patio door. It slid open. *Lord, don't let me be too late.* He knew he wasn't when he heard Chapman's voice from the front of the apartment. He peeped around the wall to the living room. Dominique was seated on the sofa with Chapman pacing the floor behind her. She was safe. He drew his weapon, eased forward, slowly, trying not to be heard.

Chapman sensed his presence. "I knew you would come, Colonel," he said, running his hand through her hair. He forcefully grabbed her up by the arm, placing her between him and Victor with the knife at her throat.

Victor had to remain calm. He took a deep breath. What he did in the next few minutes could either save or end Dominique's life. He realized he was as close as he was going to get for the moment.

"Drop the knife, Chapman. Let her go."

"One step closer and I'll snap her neck." He tightened his grip around Dominique's neck. "You know I'm good at that."

For the first time Dominique looked into Victor's face. Fear glittered in her eyes. She had reason to be. Her eyes spoke to him. He nodded, signifying for her to trust him.

"Come on Colonel." He jerked her backward, purposely touching one of her breast. "Save her like you did her friend. She died quickly. She felt no pain. I'll make sure she does the same."

Dominique squealed.

Victor had to keep his head. He knew it was another one of Chapman's head games. "I don't think so, Chapman!" Victor shouted. "You're not getting out of here."

"Who's going to stop me? You?"

"Exactly. Now let her go," Victor yelled again. "She has nothing to do with this. This is between you and me. You said you're the better soldier. Prove it."

"Tough talk coming from a man with a weapon."

"Is that what's bothering you?" Victor lowered the weapon, never taking his eyes off Chapman. He slowly placed the gun on the floor. He spread his arms apart to show he had no other weapons. "Now it's between you and me."

Chapman laughed. "You're right. This is between you and me. But I plan to take care of her first." He jerked Dominique backwards once more. She squealed again. "Then I'll take care of you."

Across the room, Victor stood waiting for the right moment. It came when Dominique bit down on Chapman's arm and then stepped down on his left foot. Chapman let out an expletive. She quickly scurried to safety on the other side of the room.

That was all it took. Victor rushed toward Chapman with the speed of a defensive linebacker.

Chapman hit Victor in the back and stomach, knocking him to the floor.

Victor was up immediately, swinging.

Chapman managed to sidestep the blow.

Victor came back with a martial arts blow to the right side of the head.

Chapman was dazed but managed to stand. Victor followed with a series of blows to the face.

Chapman shook them off. He charged at Victor, sending him crashing against the wall.

Victor's body landed with a loud thump. The impact was so hard, Dominique's diplomas, pictures, and awards fell to the floor, glass shattering everywhere.

Chapman was like a man possessed. He landed flurries of kicks to Victor's chest and abdomen.

Victor slumped over to one side in pain.

Chapman smiled a sinister grin, proud of himself. He slowly and methodically grabbed Victor by the shirt collar, standing him to his feet. He hit Victor with a right blow to the side of the face, then a left. Blood appeared at the corner of Victor's mouth and he fell back against the wall.

"Say it, Colonel. I'm the better soldier. Your girlfriend knows it. Now you know it," he grunted. "When I finish with you, she's next."

Without thinking Dominique jumped onto Chapman's back. She hit him with a combination of fists alongside the head. She scratched at his eyes, anything to deter him from hurting Victor.

Chapman flipped her off his back like she was an annoying gnat. She landed hard on the floor, the wind knocked out of her.

Chapman casually strolled back over to Victor and tried to hit him again, but Victor blocked the blow, throwing a right hook that sent Chapman stumbling backward.

Victor followed with a left uppercut that dropped Chapman to his knees. That gave Victor the opportunity to put him in a headlock.

Faster than the blink of an eye, Victor snapped Chapman's neck. Chapman's body twitched. He gasped his last breath then his body went limp and slid to the floor. Victor stood a moment, dazed, looking down at his former comrade.

He shook the cobwebs loose and rushed over to Dominique.

"My head," she whined. Her head was throbbing.

"Are you all right?"

He took her in his arms and hugged her tight. "It's over," he said, closing his eyes in relief.

"Victor," she said, holding on to him for dear life.

He held her close, relieved that she was safe. He'd just about lost it when he saw her in Chapman's presence.

He helped her over to the sofa. She was sobbing softly. He sat next to her, then took her in his arms again. "I'm here," he said, pressing his lips to hers.

Her response was to cling to him tighter. "I felt a presence behind me. I turned around and there he was."

"You're safe now," Victor murmured.

"You're hurt." Dominique reached up, touching the bruises on his face.

"It's nothing a little tender loving care can't take care of." He kissed the back of her hand.

"I'll make sure you get that for the rest of your life."

Victor managed a smile. "I'm looking forward to that."

Minutes later, the ringing of the doorbell interrupted the moment. Victor walked over and opened the door. He came face to face with a worried looking Benitez, Detective West, and a number of uniformed officers.

"Is everything all right, sir?" Benitez looked around the damaged room. "Where's Chapman?"

Victor nodded towards Chapman's body lying in the middle of the living room floor. Benitez rushed over to check for a pulse. "He's dead. What happened?"

"I broke his neck," Victor said nonchalantly. He reached for Dominique's hand. "Let's go."

As they walked out the door, Victor heard Benitez say. "The time is 12:02 a.m." For Victor it was music to his ears. It was the end of the seventh day.

ʘβ

The retirement ceremony ended and the after party moved to Cadence. It was official. Victor was a full time civilian. He smiled. His eyes looked around as fellow soldier, family, and friends came to help him celebrate his new status. But Dominique standing next to him made the event more memorable. Engaged to be married, they looked forward to beginning their lives together. "I'm really going to miss you, Colonel," Benitez said. "CID isn't going to be the same without you. Are you sure you don't want to do the remaining four?"

Dominique looked up at Victor. She'd wondered the same thing. Victor only needed four years to retire at twenty years. When she questioned him about it, he simply said he'd had enough of the military lifestyle and wanted a change. "I'm positive." He enclosed Dominique in his arms. "Dominique will be the only military member in the family now."

A moment later, the doors open and General Goss came in. Victor and Dominique walked over to greet him.

"General Goss," Victor said, extending a hand. "I'm glad you could make it."

"I wouldn't miss it for the world," General Goss said. "It's only a small token of what I owe you. I'm sorry the investigation went the way it did. I'm just glad you didn't follow orders that time."

Victor had to laugh. "Me too."

General Goss focused on Dominique. "Captain Frazier, I'm sorry about Senator Upton."

Dominique looked at Victor. Her eyes misted. At the fundraiser, her uncle announced he was pulling out of the senatorial race. The publicity and scandal had taken its toll on the family. He and Rosetta left the country to escape the media frenzy that surrounded the case. "Thank you, sir."

General Goss straightened his shoulder then smiled. "What's this I hear about a wedding? You're going to marry this man?"

"As soon as I can," Dominique said.

Victor beamed. "That's right. I'll make sure you get an invitation."

"You better," General Goss said. "I'm going to miss you. You're one of the best commanders I've had the pleasure of working with. If you ever need anything, don't hesitate to call me, especially if you change your mind about coming out of retirement."

Victor chuckled. General Goss asked him to reconsider retiring, guaranteeing him he'd remain in the area the last four years and the rank of Colonel. "I'll remember that, sir."

General Goss strolled off to mingle with the other guests.

Victor embraced Dominique in his arms. "Let's sneak away to my office. I haven't kissed you in hours. Not to mentioned there's a sofa in there," he whispered, his breath hot against her ear.

The implication of them together sent waves of excitement through her. "We can't leave. It's your party." His tongue nibbled at her earlobe and she forgot what she was saying.

"They won't miss us." His lips left her ear to recapture her lips.

"Take it to the bedroom," Benitez teased. A moment later, his cellular phone rang. Victor stared at Benitez while he conversed with the party on the other end. From the look on his face and the conversation, Victor could tell something terrible had happened.

"I'm on my way," Benitez said. He looked around the room and found Agents Chin and Saunders. He waved them over. "I'm sorry, Colonel but we have to leave."

Victor frowned. "What happened?"

"Another body has been found," Benitez explained.

About The Author

$\mathcal{S}$ammie Ward is a Author/Writer/Publisher born and raised in North Little Rock, Arkansas and now living in Maryland home. She has written over forty-five short stories for Black Romance, Black Confessions, Black Secrets, Bronze Thrills, Jive, True Black Experience, and True Confessions Magazine. She's also the author of the novels, In The Name of Love, Love To Behold, 7 Days, and It's In The Rhythm. She was recognized as a Literary Diva in Heather Covington's *Literary Diva: The 100+ African-American Women in Literature.* She's also the CEO/Founder of Lady Leo Publishing. You can visit the website at: www.ladyleopublishing.org. She loves to hear from fans so drop her an email at: ladyleopublishing@comcast.net or by snail mail at P.O. Box 14283, Silver Spring, MD 20911.

LADY LEO PUBLISHING

Love With a
Younger Man
Candy Caine

In Rapid Succession
AngelFire

Bringing You The Best In Confessions, Short Stories &Novellas

Lady Leo Publishing
P.O. Box 14283
Silver Spring, MD 20911
Email: info@ladyleopublishing.org
Website: www.ladyleopublishing.org